EMMA DONOGHUE
SELECTED PLAYS

Emma Donoghue

SELECTED PLAYS

KISSING THE WITCH

TRESPASSES

I KNOW MY OWN HEART

LADIES AND GENTLEMEN

DON'T DIE WONDERING

OBERON BOOKS
LONDON

WWW.OBERONBOOKS.COM

Collection first published in 2015 by Oberon Books Ltd
521 Caledonian Road, London N7 9RH
Tel: +44 (0) 20 7607 3637 / Fax: +44 (0) 20 7607 3629
e-mail: info@oberonbooks.com
www.oberonbooks.com

CONTENTS

Introduction

Emma Donoghue was born in Dublin in 1969 into a middle-class background. She has lived and worked in Ireland and the United Kingdom and now lives in Canada with her lover and their son and daughter. She has been open about her sexuality in the context of an Ireland highly resistant to lesbian identity, despite significant changes in attitudes to homosexuality, marked by decriminalisation and antidiscrimination legislation in 1993.

She is an accomplished, successful and prolific writer of novels, short stories, biography and history. Since the publication of *Room* in 2010 she has become a leading figure in serious fiction and writes and lectures about her work internationally. Her film adaptation of *Room* is due for release in 2015. Donoghue's imaginatively wide and scholarly knowledge of and interest in lives in earlier centuries and in a variety of locations reveals how prominence in the contemporary Irish canon continues, however, largely to demand national navel gazing, as well as valuing the male gaze over the female. Her success internationally is recognised in her country of birth, but grows out of larger literary contexts.

With her first novels, *Stir Fry* (1994) and *Hood* (1995), Donoghue explored the love lives of young gay Irish women. Her academic research into women's friendships led to her *Passions Between Women: British Lesbian Culture 1668–1801* (1993), and her novels subsequently foreground the experience of women in different historical contexts and are often based on vivid re-imaginings of historical documentation.

Alongside her fiction output, Donoghue has continued to write intermittently for the stage, and for radio. In Ireland, her career as a playwright points towards a hugely vital and influential sphere of theatrical production by independent companies and festivals that is often under-recognised culturally and critically in favour of production in mainstream venues, most especially the dominant Abbey Theatre. Glasshouse Productions, the company responsible for two of Donoghue's successful Dublin productions, is a case in point. Glasshouse was set up in 1990 by four talented women to perform the work of Irish women playwrights. Among an impressive record of innovative and challenging productions, many of new writing, two of the most valuable shows they devised were entitled *There are No Irish Women Playwrights 1* and *2*. Ironically titled, the performances comprised excerpts from both contemporary plays (Part 1) and from the work of neglected and forgotten writers such as Teresa Deevy and Kate O'Brien (Part 2). Glasshouse premiered *I Know My Own Heart*, then, with financial support from the Arts Council of Ireland, Glasshouse commissioned Donoghue to write *Ladies and Gentlemen*, which they initially produced as a rehearsed reading (directed by Katy Hayes), and then as a full production (directed by David Byrne), both at Project Arts Centre.

Emma Donoghue occupies a contested and contesting space in Irish literature and theatre. As a gay woman, working across the genres of fiction, theatre and history, she is a writer challenging categories of gender and national identity interests, history and contemporary experience.

In this essay I will suggest some of the key themes and images arising from Donoghue's plays for theatre, focusing particularly on *I Know My Own Heart* (1993) and *Ladies and Gentlemen* (1996). As an Irish woman playwright Donoghue is one of a marginalised group. Her plays illustrate a feminist concern with women in history, the historicisation of lesbian identity, the recovery of the stories of remarkable women, and with ongoing aspects of patriarchal control across centuries. Women's access to subjectivity has not improved progressively, but is a continuing contest for expression and meaning, as the critic Catherine Belsey would describe it, advancing and receding through a combination of particular political, social and individual circumstances that offer a ground for subjectivity.[1] Donoghue chooses surprising and invigorating stories of women who found space to live as they wished and to fulfil their desires. Her dramas, both fictional and theatrical, relate to Adrienne Rich's concept of a 'lesbian continuum' in their representations of the many aspects of women's bonds, while in the plays examined here, women's sexual bonds are placed centre stage.

Donoghue has a strong sense of the complexity of interrelationship between the personal and the historical/political, and this allows her to explore gender as a key aspect of human identity, dramatising the struggle of individual characters bound by the limits of gender regulation. Basing much of her drama on real people's lives and historical events, Donoghue reveals the feminist investment in truths overlooked or discounted; the recovery of women's experience is a necessary counter to its hegemonic erasure. She also subverts expectations of gender and of lesbian identity, and our understanding of their historical contexts. In writing for theatre she exploits the unique opportunity offered by the stage to explore gender as performance and to destabilise essentialist notions of gender identity as a business of binaries: masculine versus feminine, women versus men.

The Irish context for women playwrights continues to marginalise their work. The context for women playwrights in the UK has developed differently, chiefly through the establishment in the 1970s and 1980s of feminist and left-wing theatre companies that prioritised new writing by women and valued the new dramaturgies they brought to performance. When Donoghue foregrounds remarkable women she takes a different approach, showing how women step outside the boundaries placed on heterosexual definitions of womanhood. Thus, it is in their lesbian content that the plays are truly radical.

As a gay playwright Donoghue's work counters the cultural invisibility of lesbian experience. The development of gay theatre, traced by Nicholas de Jongh in his history of stage representations in London and New York in the twentieth century, moves from virtual invisibility into codified representations of gay characters whose queerness remained invisible to straight audiences while being understood by those cognisant of the codes. De Jongh draws the reader's attention to the separate history of lesbian theatre, but many of the same issues of reticence, evasion and avoidance of censorship through coding apply to both homosexual and lesbian representations on stage. The relationship between the stage and the audience is definitive in recognising how discourses of gay identity are regarded. Until the gay liberation movement of the

1960s, audiences were straight-identified, so that gay meanings had to be disguised. In more recent decades, writers may assume gay identity as the premise of the play, and challenge straight audiences to acknowledge same-sex desire.

The requirement of codification in the style of Wilde and Coward lapsed with censorship, and it would seem obvious that Donoghue, writing from the 1990s onwards, should have no need of it. However, her plays are concerned with codification in two ways: first, historically, how gay women found ways of expressing their sexuality by inventing coded expressions in language, gesture and appearance; second, how the theatre both reflects and imposes an expectation of conventional feminine behaviours represented by performance codes that may be linked with genres such as vaudeville, comedy or melodrama. One example of this expectation is how female characters are acceptable as protagonists in comedy, while this is virtually unknown, and would be considered unseemly, in melodrama. Donoghue uses theatrical images of performativity to play with theatrical gender conventions and to reveal the material, historicised limits placed around femininity both onstage and in real life.

THE PLAYS

I Know My Own Heart (1993)

I Know My Own Heart: A Lesbian Regency Romance received its first professional production in April 1993 by Glasshouse Productions at Project Arts Centre in Dublin. For this lunchtime production Donoghue edited the original script so that it ran within the requisite sixty-minute limit of the lunchtime form. In the autumn of that year the full-length script, in two acts, was restored for evening performance in Dublin's Andrew's Lane Theatre. The director, Katy Hayes, has remarked that the subtitle of the play drew in audiences for whom the content was refreshingly novel.[2]

The play is based on the diaries of Anne Lister (1791–1849), who lived near Halifax in Yorkshire. During the period dramatised Lister was heiress-in-waiting of her uncle's estate; at the end of the play she finally comes into her inheritance and packs her bag for Paris. In fact, Lister travelled widely and died in Georgia. Lister, as Donoghue describes in her programme note for the production, 'broke all the rules of Regency ladyhood'. She was not interested in marriage but in geometry and Greek; she travelled alone, had a vigorous sexual appetite, and wrote intimate details of her 'romantic friendships' in her diary. Parts of her diary were, literally, coded. The hieroglyphic script, a combination of arithmetical symbols, numerals and Greek letters, was deciphered by historian Helena Whitbread, who published selections from the years 1817–24 with Virago Press in 1988 under the title *I Know My Own Heart*. Donoghue pointedly remarks that although she has taken liberties in shaping the diaries into dramatic form, the play and Lister's sexuality 'is no invention: it is grounded in the startling details she chose to record for posterity'.

The title *I Know My Own Heart* applies at a variety of levels in the play. It is ironic as it applies to the succession of Lister's lovers and to the confusing attractions to women of conventional wifehood and motherhood. Lister's sexual desires are active and changeable, yet the title also asserts across the action of the play Lister's determination to remain proud of her love for women. As the spotlight of her sexual needs falls on different women, Lister refuses the pressure to censor her actions, and (at least privately) to accept the silence surrounding her sexuality. Her social position is privileged, yet compromised by her lack of independent means while her uncle lives. Marianne and Nancy Brown are the daughters of a respectable local farmer, at a lower level in the social hierarchy, but not entirely out of bounds. Lister falls in love with Marianne, who then accepts a financially advantageous proposal of marriage, despite her reciprocal feelings for Lister. The affair between the two women continues under the pressure of separation, of the sexually transmitted infection originating from Marianne's profligate husband, and of Lister's promiscuity. Another exquisite irony is that Lister and Marianne's liaison is made possible by the latter's marriage, since they can now spend time together without giving rise to social censure.

In the meantime, Lister's friend Tibs shares her confidences and allows the playwright to make explicit the nature of the women's relationships. Dramatic irony comes into play as the audience realises Tibs's unrequited love for Lister, who is entirely careless of her friend's feelings. Tibs assuages her jealousy of Marianne by luring Lister into an affair with the younger sister Nancy, but the strategy is unsuccessful in unseating Marianne in Lister's heart. As Lister guiltily logs the conquest in her diary she remarks, 'Strictly speaking, I know the word "incest" is not appropriate, there being no link of marriage or blood' (p. 156), wryly pointing towards how lesbian identity subverts patriarchal regulation of sexuality and new paradigms are called for where none exists. A further amusing example of this arises when Anne questions whether Marianne considers herself, as a married woman, to be committing adultery when they have sex: 'You are, after all, another man's wife' (p. 141).

It is Marianne's pregnancy and her discovery of Anne's affair with her sister that precipitates the end of their relationship. This coincides in the play with Anne coming into her inheritance, whereupon she departs for Paris, taking with her Rousseau's *Confessions*, from which the title of the play is taken. In their last dialogue, Marianne asks Anne: 'Do you think we're being punished?' (p. 169), recalling the conservative theatrical convention whereby gay characters were penalised for their unorthodox sexuality, ending as exiles or suicides. But Donoghue refuses to punish her characters, and Lister leaves the audience in a mood of optimistic excitement as she sets out alone on a new adventure.

The form of the play is highly unusual; excerpts from Lister's diary, and from selected letters between the characters delivered to the audience, are written fluidly in one continuous sequence with scenes of dialogue between characters. Thus, the script indicates a shared space where the private discourse of diary witness is continuous with the public discourse of conversation at a variety of social levels. As Anne Ubersfeld writes, '[i]t is commonplace to demonstrate how spatial relations among characters [. . .] correspond to a material hierarchicisation'. In this case the borderless playing space works to destabilise social hierarchies. The borders between private and public, between the physical body and the body politic fail, and the pain of loss, silence and uncertainty marks each character's transgression of patriarchal definitions of femininity.

Although the divisiveness of social class challenges essentialist notions of allegiance between women in the play, it does not always win out over sexual desire. The space of the action is criss-crossed with tensions arising from Anne's own social snobbery, Marianne's and Nancy's social ambitions, and all characters' awareness of the expectations of their behaviour in public. Early on, Anne is dismayed by her attraction to Marianne, 'a girl completely outside my social sphere', and in the same conversation displays a hilarious snobbery about her suspicion that Marianne's mother drinks too much: 'Tipsiness is undesirable in any woman [. . .] but quite unacceptable in the mother of the girl I . . .' (p. 119). Donoghue's sensitivity to registers of language is evident in all of her work, and *I Know My Own Heart* achieves a seductive playfulness while it functions to define what is sayable and unsayable. In the first scene, sisters Marianne and Nancy remark the artificiality of expression required in phrasing a letter: 'it's merely a polite code' (p. 113) and prepare the audience for the masks that language affords and enforces in what follows. Elsewhere the codes required for use by women in describing their experience recur: 'a feminine complaint' [menstruation] (p. 116), 'interesting condition' [pregnancy] (p. 143), and most strikingly where Anne teases Marianne to specify where she wishes to be touched, a playful scene that suddenly turns angry:

ANNE: [. . .] What is the word you are looking for?
MARIANNE: There is no word for it. (p. 162)

Women's bodies, their specifically womanly experiences, are betrayed by the silences observed by society, and invention must fill the space. Thus, Nancy observes: 'People like you make their own rules' (p. 151). Marianne's Lacanian statement reflects how the body requires language to attain subjectivity, and recognition, to express desire.

Codified expressions for sexual activity include the word 'kisses' in both its usual meaning, and in its codified meaning as orgasms, an ambiguity that reflects the play's suggestion of a fluid continuity between stages of physical intimacy, and a challenge to singularly purposive phallic sexuality. Playfully, Donoghue draws the audience into exchanges that are discreet and yet entirely explicit, but also tantalises them with what remains to be revealed, for example when Anne whispers of her exploits into her lover's ear, leaving the audience to read its own meaning into Marianne's astonished reaction (p. 125).

The body is the terrain on which the conflicting forces of desire and social propriety are engaged, so that the performance challenges the audience to confront not only the language of lesbian desire, but its embodiment too. In a series of love scenes the intimacies that fuel the psychological and emotional drama are enacted, the actors' bodies showing what cannot be told in a powerful erotic subtext. The details of codification through gesture, appearance, physicality and costume have the potential to reshape conventional theatrical representations of woman, to confuse divisions between masculinity and femininity, and to interrogate the limits we place around gender identity. Decisions that reflect secure gender binaries, however, may work to reassure an audience's heterosexual expectations and reassert conventional masculine/feminine polarities. In the Glasshouse production of the play, the director Katy Hayes remembers how Donoghue, having seen a dress rehearsal, considered that the dress of the actor playing Anne should not be so pretty. Claire Dowling, however, who played the lead, felt it impossible to perform the role in the alternative, much plainer dress that was suggested. Paradoxically, she required the more 'feminine' costume in order to characterise Anne Lister's extraordinarily proactive desires, energy and hunger for experience.[4]

In the Regency period, the sartorial division between women and men was absolute, a difficult set of prohibitions for a contemporary audience to grasp. Marianne is appalled to think that Anne might actually appear in trousers, for example. When Anne says she may take to wearing frills and bonnets for the sake of more female company, Tibs reacts: 'How very unnatural that would be' (p. 144), and Anne secretly dreams of dressing completely in men's clothes, 'driving my own carriage, being my own master' (p. 142). Her gender identity, if not feminine, is deflected into masculinity as the only alternative. The question of what clothes are 'natural' is effectively historicised. As Marjorie

Garber has argued, clothes are an aspect of gendered discourse of power and are no more natural than any aspect of social control.[5]

A Brechtian sense of gesture as gender transgression appears textually in the play when Anne reflects on how taking Marianne's arm in public may lead to social ruin: 'a slight readjustment of the muscles, no more. Such a small gesture to bear so much weight' (p. 116); *I Know My Own Heart* in performance creates a daring and invigorating framework to bear the weight of our gender anxieties, to gaze into the almost lost life of Anne Lister, and through her, to reimagine womanhood.

Ladies and Gentlemen (1996)

In his book entitled *Camp: The Lie That Tells the Truth*, Philip Core explores the connection between camp and 'a secret within the personality which one ironically wishes to conceal and to exploit' (p. 9). *Ladies and Gentlemen* is set against a background of American vaudeville and features characters whose identity is expanded and made complex through the trope of performance. In the play, what is concealed and what is exploited or revealed on late-nineteenth century US popular stages is analogous to the social boundaries defining gender, and the two worlds of the stage and the real lives of the performers blur, often to liberating effect. The cross-dressing traditions of vaudeville, and centrally, female impersonations of the male made famous by performers such as Vesta Tilley, become in Donoghue's play a mode of communication, a way in which, as Core notes, 'homosexuals and other groups of people with double lives can find a *lingua franca*' (p. 9). Speech and song lyrics operating on several levels of meaning at once reflect this double vision, parallel meanings coexisting, destabilising orthodoxies.

Again Donoghue bases her narrative on real-life events and real persons. Annie Hindle worked as a vaudeville performer and was married twice, to a man and to a woman. The other performers' careers are archived in the New York Public Library, and the songs that run throughout the action are a combination of adaptations from Victorian originals and additional lyrics by Donoghue which in the first production were set to original music composed by Carole Nelson. The playwright introduces an Irish character in Annie Ryan, a poor immigrant woman who finds work as Annie's dresser.

At one level then, *Ladies and Gentlemen* recovers and explores a remarkable life or lives, but it is also a postmodern piece of theatre, deconstructing the fiction of gender binaries, dramatising the performativity of gender roles, playfully staging the linguistic and bodily texts of representation itself so as to interrogate their workings. Several key images of self-reflexivity and meta-theatricality punctuate the play, while the stage space floats between representation of a historical scene and being its Pirandellian self.

Annie Hindle is an English/American male impersonator at the centre of a group of vaudevillians: Gilbert Saroney (an American female impersonator), Ella Wesner (a dresser who launches a career as a performer), and Tony Pastor (an Italian/American vaudeville manager). Into this world of costumed identity and popular songs that veer from sentimentality into vulgar double entendre – 'Dirt's in the eye of the beholder' as Gilbert remarks (p. 255) – comes Annie Ryan, a young Irish orphan who has run away from the convent that paid her fare to the States. Two Annies in the dressing room (and in the cast) are soon distinguished by Annie Hindle when she rechristens her namesake Ryanny. The point of identification between the two is not lost, however, and lies waiting to be fulfilled in the narrative.

The play opens with Annie on the night of her comeback to the stage in 1891 and from this point the action is played in flashback as she remembers events over the past eleven years, including the failure of her abusive marriage, her first meeting with Ryanny, Ella's departure to make a career of her own, Annie's and Ryanny's falling in love and their happiness in marriage, and Ryanny's illness and untimely death. These scenes move year by year from 1880, while between each year we return to the 'end' of the story in 1891, emphasising Annie's memory as the framing device. The looped time structure of the play relates closely to the use of stage space, both aspects transforming on the instant in location and period through Annie's recollection.

The energising relationship in the play is that between

Annie and Ryanny, their falling in love, and their marriage. Helen Thompson, referring to aspects of Donoghue's novels, remarks that the writer's 'work is an alternative narrative to the marriage plot',[6] but in *Ladies and Gentlemen*, marriage between women is central to the play. Early on Ryanny states that she is determined to get married, and this creates narrative tension as the action proceeds and the audience speculates whom she will wed. The prolonged scene at the end of Act I leads up to the resolution of this.

Annie's first effort at proposal becomes an absurd performance. Lacking the courage to address Ryanny herself, she addresses instead the dressing room costume dummy, comically named Miss Dimity. To find the words for her feelings is a challenge to Annie; the songs she sings in her performances remind her constantly of normative values: '[h]omes, weddings and partings, that's what they're all about' she observes (p.214). When Ella recommends persuasion, Annie exclaims: 'How? [. . .] There aren't any songs about things like *this*' (p. 215).

Ryanny finally suggests that they marry 'for real' (p. 223), Annie taking the name Charles Hindle. Once they have agreed and are reeling with elation, Annie's cue is called. She sings 'Home' *'accompanied, with all the romance she can muster'*, while *'RYANNY watches* [. . .] *as if from the wings'* (p. 225). In this moment, the stage occupies two spaces: the fictional space of the play, the vaudeville stage on which Annie performs, and the actual space of the venue where the performance is taking place. In parallel, the audience occupies two identities: its members are the 1886 audience watching Annie Hindle, with Ryanny peeking from the sidelines, and they are the audience of *Ladies and Gentlemen*. Donoghue places us in a spatial 'not/but', the phrase Brecht used to express the double vision of theatre, its facility in accommodating conflicting images or realities without one eliding the other. The audience is not in 1886, but it is. Annie Hindle is not a man, but in performance she is.

When Gilbert finds a Unitarian minister who will perform the ceremony, the wedding proceeds. Annie asks Gilbert if he will prompt her if she dries during the service, pointing up the porous membrane separating a vow from a line in a theatre script, separating ritual from the ritual performed onstage; Gilbert replies: 'But if I whisper "I do" I'll end up married to Ryanny, and then you'll have to shoot me' (p. 229). The first act ends with an *'imaginary'* tableau of Annie and Ryanny in *'the formal pose of a Victorian husband-and-wife photograph; a flash goes off '* (p. 231). When Ryanny tosses her bouquet over her shoulder at the audience, the theatre space has become their imagined space.

In Act I the rhythm of movement between different times in Annie's life develops at a regular pace, settling with an extended scene at the end of the act. In contrast Act II switches into higher gear in a whirligig of reflection and enactment. The effect of this is to blur the historic moment onstage with the present moment of performance, releasing the audience into a pure space of performance. Annie's closing delivery of the song 'A Real Man' is the apotheosis of this effect.

Throughout Act I and in most of Act II the scene is set in a theatre dressing room, the only exception being the home scenes set in Annie's and Ryanny's New Jersey cottage. The dressing room, equipped with a skip full of costume items, a costume dummy, mirror and make-up box (p. 175), is a reinvented closet. This closet is not a place of hiding but a theatrical laboratory for gender identity. The show-business context of the play invites reflexive images of theatricality and self-consciousness, and objects onstage speak of pretence and transformation. Annie's 'letters box', in which she keeps correspondence from adoring female fans, attests to the effectiveness of her identity as a man on the vaudeville stage, while the company manager's 'show-book', recording his script as master of ceremonies and the order of acts in the show, brings the metatext of performance on stage.

Dressing and re-dressing themselves as women, as men, Annie and Gilbert reveal gender as gesture, rehearsed and perfected, appropriated and discarded. In Act I, Annie, preparing to take to the stage again, '*is remembering how to walk in trousers*' (p. 189). The image of Annie binding her breasts in preparation for her act becomes ironic and moving after Ryanny's death from breast cancer. Perhaps the relationship between clothes and behaviour is best expressed by Gilbert when he says, 'I can't sing in a suit' (p. 258).

Ladies and Gentlemen exploits the entertainment value of vaudeville performance, musical, comic, playful and fluidly structured in time and space. It tracks the growing censorship of performers in American vaudeville as the nineteenth century progressed and standards of respectability were increasingly demanded by bourgeois audiences. However, it also uses Annie Hindle's story to evidence, across history, a precedent for happy marriage between women. When Tony jeers at her relationship with Ryanny, Annie retorts 'We were a family' (p. 262). History for Donoghue is not 'fixed and defined', but is rather, as Steve Pile and Nigel Thrift describe it, like a map, 'detachable, reversible, susceptible to constant modification'.[7] The play recovers Annie Hindle's remarkable life, while it enacts real challenges to the limiting certainties enforced in gender regulation.

SUMMARY

Donoghue's work for theatre meets the feminist purpose of recovering women's experience in history, marking their struggles and their often extraordinary initiative in finding space to express their subjectivity, their sexuality and their love for one another. In *Ladies and Gentlemen*, Ryanny urges Annie not to forget their happy life together despite the lengthening shadow of her imminent death:

> ANNIE: What use is remembering?
> RYANNY: [. . .] You must. If you don't remember everything, it'll be like it never happened. Like I never got across the ocean, or we never met, or there was never this house at all, just the bare beach. That's what scares me most: being forgotten.

Critical commentary on Donoghue's plays is rare. Her profile as a novelist is more developed. As a lesbian playwright, her work may be doubly marginalised: first as women's work, and second as lesbian work. However, the success of Dublin productions of *I Know My Own Heart* and *Ladies and Gentlemen*, both in well-respected venues, proves that there is an audience for lesbian plays.

Theatre companies aiming to perform representations of gay and lesbian lives such as Muted Cupid (founded in Dublin in 1984) have made important contributions to Irish theatre, and have been largely written out of critical commentaries. A key change has been the development of the Dublin Gay Theatre festival which features an impressive programme of visiting and home-grown work for gay and straight audiences. *I Know My Own Heart* was revived as part of the festival in 2006. *Don't Die Wondering*, broadcast on BBC Radio four in 2000, was adapted for stage and produced by DAYMS at the Teachers' Club in May 2005 as part of the festival. This later play is set in contemporary Celtic Tiger Ireland, and deals with the return home of a young lesbian chef and her attempt to live 'out' in a small Irish community. It presents issues of discrimination against gay women at work and socially, in a convincing and engaging way, and declares its purpose frankly, using conventional form, but with wit and humour.

As a writer whose interests and subject matter reach way beyond Ireland, one might expect that Donoghue's work would be particularly relevant in studies of cultural interchange and trends of globalisation in Irish theatre. Patrick Lonergan's recent study, however, limits discussion of the 'queering' of Irish stages to male homosexuality, and confines detailed discussion to homosexuality on the Abbey Theatre stage.[8]

Emma Donoghue's work as a playwright points towards a growing counter-movement in Irish theatre, in its concern with diasporic Irishness, with life outside Ireland, with the history of lesbian sexuality and gender identity. Her dramaturgies are original in form and radical in content, but they have huge audience appeal through her foregrounding of the appeal of character, and wryly empathic concern for human fates.

Cathy Leeney

PRIMARY SOURCES

Works by Emma Donoghue

Don't Die Wondering: Radio Play, unpublished manuscript (2000).

I Know My Own Heart, in *Seen and Heard: Six New Plays by Irish Women*, Cathy Leeney (ed.) (Dublin: Carysfort Press, 2001), pp. 99–160.

Ladies and Gentlemen (Dublin: New Island Books, 1998).

SECONDARY SOURCES

Belsey, Catherine, *The Subject of Tragedy: Identity and Difference in Renaissance Drama* (London: Routledge, 1985).

Conrad, Kathryn, 'Occupied Country: The Negotiation of Lesbianism in Irish Feminist Narrative', *Eire-Ireland*, Vol. 36, Nos 1–2 (Spring/Summer 1996), pp. 123–36.

Core, Philip, *Camp: The Lie That Tells the Truth* (Louisville, KY: Plexus Publishing, 1984).

de Jongh, Nicholas, *Not in Front of the Audience: Homosexuality on Stage* (London: Routledge, 1992).

Dolan, Jill, 'Gender Impersonation Onstage: Destroying or Maintaining the Mirror of Gender Roles?', *Women and Performance*, Vol. 2, No. 2 (1985), pp. 5–11.

Garber, Marjorie, *Vested Interests: Cross-Dressing and Cultural Anxiety* (London: Routledge, 1992).

Hayes, Katy, telephone interview, Dublin, 3 July 2009.

Lonergan, Patrick, *Theatre and Globalization: Irish Drama in the Celtic Tiger Era* (Basingstoke: Palgrave Macmillan, 2009).

Morales Ladron, Marisol, 'The Representation of Motherhood in Emma Donoghue's *Slammerkin*', *Irish University Review*, Vol. 39, No. 1 (2009), pp. 107–21.

Peach, Linden, *The Contemporary Irish Novel: Critical Readings* (Basingstoke: Palgrave Macmillan, 2004), quoting Steve Pile and Nigel Thrift, *Mapping the Subject: Geographies of Cultural Transformation* (London: Routledge, 1995).

Rich, Adrienne, 'Compulsory Heterosexuality and Lesbian Existence', in Catharine R. Stimpson and Ethel Spector Person (eds), *Women, Sex, and Sexuality* (New York: William Morrow, 1980), pp. 62–91.

Sedgwick, Eve Kosofsky, *Tendencies* (Durham, NC: Duke UP, 1993).

Thompson, Helen, 'Emma Donoghue: Interview', in Caitriona Moloney and Helen Thompson (eds), *Irish Women Writers Speak Out: Voices from the Field* (Syracuse, NY: Syracuse UP, 2003), pp. 169–80.

Ubersfeld, Anne, *Reading Theatre*, trans. Frank Collins (Toronto, ON: University of Toronto Press, 1999).

Wandor, Michelene, *Carry On, Understudies: Theatre and Sexual Politics* (London: Routledge & Kegan Paul, 1986).

NOTES

1. Catherine Belsey, *The Subject of Tragedy*, pp. 1–10.

2. Katy Hayes, telephone interview, 2009.

3. Anne Ubersfeld, *Reading Theatre*, p. 104.

4. Hayes, op. cit.

5. Marjorie Garber, *Vested Interests*, pp. 1–20.

6. Helen Thompson, 'Emma Donoghue: Interview', p. 169.

7. Quoted in Linden Peach, *The Contemporary Irish Novel*, pp. 76–7.

8. Patrick Lonergan, *Theatre and Globalization*, pp. 145–52.

KISSING THE WITCH

Scenes

Act One

Act Two

Kissing the Witch

Adapted by Emma Donoghue from her book
Kissing the Witch (1997).

Kissing the Witch was commissioned and first produced by
the Magic Theatre, San Francisco, Artistic Director Larry
Eilenberg, directed by Kent Nicholson, 2-25 June 2000.

Dramatis Personae

FIRST woman, 20s.
SECOND woman, 30s/40s
THIRD woman, 50s
MAN

In **The Tale of the Rose**,
First plays Rose,
Second plays Beast,
Third plays Witch and Old Woman,
Man plays Father.

In **The Tale of the Skin**,
First plays Donkey,
Second plays Donkeyskin,
Third plays Queen and Spinster,
Man plays King and Prince.

In **The Tale of the Handkerchief**,
First plays Princess,
Second plays Queen,
Third plays Maid,
Man plays Bridegroom.

In **The Tale of the Voice**,
First plays Fishgirl,
Second plays Witch,
Third plays Fishwife and Lady,
Man plays Merchant.

In **The Tale of the Witch**
First plays Fishgirl,
Second plays Witch,
Third plays Dying Witch and Village Woman,
Man plays Boy and Village Man.

ACT ONE

FIRST, SECOND and THIRD come on as the Witch.

THIRD: Oh, I know what they say about me. The gulls bring me all the gossip.

FIRST/SECOND: Knowing what they say about you is the first step to power.

THIRD: I don't have a name.

SECOND: What would I do with a name?

FIRST/SECOND/THIRD: I'm the Witch.

FIRST: The one in your dreams.

SECOND: In your nightmares.

THIRD: I've spent half a lifetime in this cave, and my bones have grown as hard as iron.

SECOND: I sleep on stone, with my arms wrapped around me like snakes.

FIRST: Nothing touches me in the night except the occasional spider.

THIRD: Nothing disturbs me, except…people.

SECOND: Whining, needy people.

FIRST: What they bring me is always the same.

THIRD: Lies.

SECOND: Excuses.

FIRST: Evasions.

THIRD: But I can't help anyone unless they tell me their story.

SECOND: Terrible tales.

FIRST: Fabulous tales.

SECOND: Old tales in new skins.

THIRD: What people want of me is always the same thing.

FIRST/SECOND/THIRD: Transformation.

FIRST: 'I'm sad. Make me happy!'

SECOND: 'I'm a mess. Make me magnificent!'

THIRD: 'I'm limp. Make me a stallion!'

SECOND: If I ever told them the truth, I'd say, 'Patience. Wait long enough and time will change you so much you won't know yourself.'

FIRST: Poor hurrying fools, they think this short life is all there is and they've only got one story. They don't remember who they were before, and they have no idea who they'll be next time.

THIRD: In my dreams, I can see all the way back, to the life I lived before this one, and the life before that one, and the life before that.

FIRST/SECOND/THIRD: We're not separate. We live each other's lives over and over again like actors swapping parts on a stage.

THIRD: I'm sick of the whole business, personally. I've been through so many transformations, I'm worn out.

SECOND: I've worn crowns and rags, nuns' habits and bridal gowns.

FIRST: I've been every kind of girl, from the wisest to the most foolish.

SECOND: When a boy changes his life, it's called an adventure. When a girl does the same, it's only a fairy tale.

THIRD: I remember a story, a strange one.

FIRST/SECOND/THIRD: It's a tale of a rose.

THE TALE OF THE ROSE

THIRD plays the Witch.

THIRD: Once upon a time, there's a girl called Rose.

FIRST plays Rose.

FIRST: No!

THIRD: Trouble. That's how most stories start. That's what desperate girls do: they go to the Witch.

FIRST: The fishermen say she lives in a cave, high on the sea cliff. They tell terrible tales about her: her cave is lined with the bones of drowned sailors, with skeleton legs for a door, skeleton hands for bolts, and a full mouth of teeth for a lock.

THIRD lets out a long laugh, which makes FIRST spin around in panic.

FIRST: They say she's got a stoop, a stick, a wart on her nose and a whisker on her chin. They say her white hair has a trace of red in it like old blood on sheep's wool, and her nails curl like roots. One of the fishermen swears he saw her once, taking a bath in a little pool with her tentacles spilling over the rocks. With a single glance from her watery eye she can turn men to limp fish.

THIRD steps forward.

FIRST: Is it you? Are you the witch?

THIRD: Who's asking?

FIRST: Rose. This can't be happening to me.

THIRD: Tell me.

FIRST: I can't.

THIRD: How can I help you unless I know your story?

FIRST: I don't know where to begin. I'm Rose. I'm beautiful.

MAN plays her Father.

9

MAN: My beautiful, darling daughter.

FIRST: Or so my father tells me.

MAN: A pristine face. A smooth, blank page with nothing written on it. No wonder all the young men want to marry you.

FIRST: But I want none of them, Father. They're as dumbly besotted as dogs.

MAN: What do you want, if not a husband?

FIRST: I don't know. A bit of magic. Something as improbable and perfect as a red rose just opening.

   MAN laughs, then reads a letter.

MAN: Oh daughter, my poor daughter. All my ships have been lost at sea.

THIRD: So now you've come down in the world.

FIRST: I get used to being poor. I learn to scrub and sweep and scour. Every day I go down to the river and pound my father's shirts white on the black rocks. My hands grow numb, and my hair tangles.

MAN: Rose. Such news! One of my ships has come safe to shore at least.

FIRST: Magic!

MAN: I must set out in the morning. Tell me, daughter, what should I bring you back, now we're rich again. A silken dress? A fur-lined cloak, to keep the wind out?

FIRST: A rose, Father. A red rose just opening.

THIRD: So does he bring you what you ask for, your kind father? Does he?

FIRST: I know he loves me.

THIRD: I never said he didn't. Tell me.

FIRST: I can't.

THIRD: Then get out of my cave. You're wasting my time, little girl. I haven't got as many years left as you, remember?

FIRST: I'm sorry.

THIRD: I don't want sorry. I want your story.

FIRST: All right then. My father comes home through the snow. He's half frozen. He's holding the rose I asked for.

MAN staggers in, head down.

FIRST: Father!

He looks up at Rose in shock, then falls at her feet.

MAN: A blizzard…a castle.

FIRST: You're delirious.

MAN: A stolen rose…a hooded beast. Daughter, I've sold you.

FIRST: Sold me?

MAN: For a single red rose, and a box of gold, and my life. I promised the Beast the first thing I'd see when I reached home. I thought the first thing might be a cat. It could have been a bird.

FIRST: Oh, Father!

MAN: I gave my word.

She flees back to the Witch.

FIRST: What does it mean to give your word to a monster?

THIRD: You'll have to go, you know.

FIRST: I didn't come to hear this. I came for help.

THIRD: Well, the truth's all I've got for you today.

FIRST: Why should I deliver myself up to this Beast? *I* never made any stupid promise.

THIRD: You can wait, and do nothing.

FIRST: Yes.

THIRD: Tend your little garden, and scrub clothes on the rocks in the river. Wait till the night the Beast comes for your father.

FIRST: No!

THIRD: What kind of story do you think you're in, girl? What did you expect, a happy ending?

FIRST: I don't know. It's all happened so fast. Father never even saw the Beast's face.

THIRD: But the Beast saw your father's face. The Beast smelled your father's smell. What's to stop him tracking your father down?

FIRST: No!

THIRD: What's to stop him?

FIRST: Me.

She goes to the MAN.

FIRST: Father, I'm ready to go.

MAN: My Rose.

Distraught but relieved, he leads the way.

FIRST: By rights I should be feeling betrayed, but the curious thing is, I'm shaking with excitement. I go as a hostage, but it feels as if I'm marching into battle.

MAN: Old woman! Which way to the castle?

THIRD: *(As Old Woman.)* You don't want to go there.

FIRST: We must. *(Confused.)* Don't I know you?

THIRD: No one goes near that castle. No wedding or christening up there for as long as I can remember. The King died raving, a long time back. There was a young Queen, too, after him, but now there's only the Beast.

MAN: We know.

THIRD: At sunset you can glimpse him walking on the battlements, but none of us has ever seen his face. Folk say he exiled the Queen, or maybe locked her up in the dungeon, or some say ate her up.

FIRST: Folk say a lot of nonsense. I see a light, Father.

MAN: The gates are standing open. There. The Beast is waiting for us.

FIRST: The Beast is waiting for me.

SECOND comes on as the hooded, masked Beast and speaks hoarsely, as if unused to conversation.

SECOND: Welcome, Rose.

FIRST: God help me.

SECOND: Do you come consenting?

FIRST: I do.

MAN: Oh daughter, forgive me.

FIRST: The Beast seems like a man, except for his face. All swaddled in darkness. Could he be burnt, or deformed? Was he born with the features of a lion or a wolf?

SECOND: Welcome to your castle.

FIRST: Though I explore it from top to bottom, I can find no trace of the missing Queen. Instead there's a door with my name on it, and the walls of my room are white satin. A hundred dresses cut to my exact shape, and thousand books, and a magic mirror that shows me whatever I want to see. I have keys to every room in the castle except the one where the Beast sleeps. The first book I open says in gold letters –

SECOND: 'You are mistress there. Ask for anything you wish.'

FIRST: But I don't know what to ask for. I have a room of my own, and time, and treasures to explore. I sit in my white satin room reading tales of wonder. I have everything I could ask except my father. Except the key to the story. I am always alone apart from dinner, when the Beast likes to watch me eat.

SECOND: More wine, Rose?

FIRST: Thank you.

SECOND: You find the castle cold?

FIRST: A little.

SECOND: I will have more fires lit.

FIRST: The Beast is always courteous. I wonder what violence lies behind it.

SECOND: You like to read, Rose?

FIRST: Very much.

SECOND: Tales of magic?

FIRST: Those above all.

SECOND: You're beautiful. And yet you weep.

FIRST: I've never been so lonely.

SECOND: Ah. I've never been anything but lonely.

FIRST: I stand in my room before the magic mirror. I look deep into the pool of my own face and try to guess what the Beast might look like behind the mask. The more hideous my imaginings, the more my own face seems to glow. The Beast must be everything I'm not: dark to my light, rough to my smooth, hoarse to my sweet. That night at dinner, he says -

SECOND: You have never seen my face. Do you still picture me as a monster?

FIRST: You know I do.

SECOND: You have never felt my touch. Do you still shrink from it?

FIRST: How could I not?

SECOND: If I cut a slice of fruit, could you take it from my fingers?

FIRST: You know I couldn't.

SECOND: What if I let you go, Rose? What then? Is there any chance you might stay of your own free will?

FIRST shakes her head and goes.

FIRST: When I look in the great gold mirror, I think I can make out the shape of my father, lying with his feverish face turned to the wall.

She runs to the Beast.

FIRST: Beast! You said I was to ask for anything I wanted. My father's sick and I must go to him.

SECOND: Will you come back?

FIRST: I give you my word.

SECOND: When?

FIRST: On the eighth day. My word on it.

She sets off.

FIRST: The journey's long. The sky's as dark as ink by the time I reach the cottage.

She rushes to embrace her sick Father.

MAN: Rose?

FIRST: Who else?

MAN: How is it possible?

FIRST: Magic. By the third day, my father can sit up in my arms. By the fifth day, he's eating at table and patting my knee. On the seventh day, he starts to beg.

MAN: Stay, Rose. Stay.

FIRST: I gave my word.

MAN: What does it mean to give your word to a monster?

FIRST: I don't think the Beast is a monster.

MAN: What is he, then?

FIRST: My father's eyes follow me around the cottage. There's only one place to go for help. Witch!

THIRD: Who's that screeching in the middle of the night?

FIRST: It's Rose. I'm desperate.

THIRD: What do you want this time?

FIRST: My father needs me, but I think the Beast may need me even more. Tell me what I should do.

THIRD: If you don't know that by now, I can't help you.

FIRST: I think I know. But I'm not sure. And I'm afraid.

THIRD: That's called the human condition.

FIRST: Wait!

She grabs the Witch, who shakes her off.

THIRD: Nobody touches me.

FIRST: I'm sorry.

THIRD: What's your greatest fear?

FIRST: That if I go, I might never come home again.

THIRD: That's right. If you go to the Beast, you'll never come home again.

FIRST straightens, ready to go.

FIRST: It's sunset when I reach the castle, and the gates are hanging open, but no lamps are lit. I run through the grounds, searching behind every bush, every tree. Beast? Beast, where are you? At last I come to the rose garden, where the first buds are bunched against the night air. No!

SECOND lies crumpled. FIRST runs over and breathes her heat on the mask. She pulls it off, revealing SECOND's face, and recoils in shock.

FIRST: I see that the Beast is a woman. And that she's still breathing.

She kisses SECOND.

SECOND: Rose?

FIRST: This is strange magic.

SECOND: What other kind is there?

FIRST: Tell me. Tell me why you did it. The young Queen – was that you?

SECOND: For too many years I lived alone in this castle, refusing to do all the things queens are meant to do, setting all my suitors riddles they could make no sense of. Finally the day came when I knew no one who could see my true face.

FIRST: So you made a mask.

SECOND: And since that day I've shown my face to no one.

FIRST: Until now.

SECOND: Until you.

FIRST: Such a face to hide away.

She reaches to touch the face of SECOND, who flinches, then lets her.

SECOND: If you were to stay…

FIRST: Yes. I'll never go home again.

SECOND: The villagers will start telling travelers that this castle is inhabited by a beast and a beauty.

FIRST: Or two beauties.

SECOND: Or two beasts.

FIRST: Tell me your story. Who were you before you swapped your crown for a mask?

SECOND: Ah, that's a strange story. It's a tale of a skin.

THE TALE OF THE SKIN

SECOND plays Donkeyskin, the younger self of the Beast.

SECOND: Once upon a time there's a king.

MAN appears as King.

SECOND: Once upon a time there's a queen.

THIRD appears as Queen, and they embrace.

MAN: I have rich fertile lands, money-bags and jewel boxes.

THIRD: I have golden hair, lily cheeks, ruby lips.

MAN: We live in the castle surrounded by gardens where something is always in flower and something else in fruit.

THIRD: Beyond the gardens stands a huge bramble hedge, and beyond the hedge, an evergreen forest where the leaves never fall.

MAN: We have everything in the world we could possibly want –

THIRD: Except a child to inherit all this happiness.

MAN: My Queen becomes convinced she is barren. We swear complicated vows and swallow boiled frogs.

THIRD: At last, I grow big.

MAN: I order all the bells rung, and put a chicken in the pot of every family in the kingdom.

THIRD: The day our little princess is born, the midwife lifts her into her father's royal arms.

MAN: She has her mother's golden hair, her mother's lily cheeks, her mother's ruby lips.

THIRD: And the three of us live wrapped up in each other like a nut in its shell.

SECOND plays the young princess, Donkeyskin.

SECOND: From the first day of my life, I wear gold mesh gloves so that nothing will ever soil my fingers. For many years I don't even learn to walk because I'm carried everywhere by the most sure-footed servants. Every month, on the date of my birth, there are fireworks.

MAN: Dance for us, daughter.

THIRD: The only lesson you must study is the list of your own perfections.

MAN: Your face is the fairest.

THIRD: Your wit the sharpest.

MAN: Your dancing the most graceful.

THIRD: And your heart the kindest in the whole kingdom.

SECOND: I believe every word of it.

THIRD: Now, the one strange thing about the King my husband is that his favourite creature, out of all the splendid mounts that snort and stamp in his stables, is a donkey with lopsided ears.

FIRST plays Donkey.

SECOND: I am allowed to stroke Donkey's ears on feast days, but never to ride her. That's the only thing I'm forbidden.

MAN: Our darling daughter is never to be thwarted.

THIRD: No one must ever make our baby cry.

SECOND: But the years pass and I'm growing up. I'm getting restless. I swell in strange places: it's as if some unseen hand is magicking me into a shape that's not my own. Mother, I've been wondering, why is dinner always at four o'clock?

THIRD: Why, my dear, everything is done just as it's always been done in this castle for hundreds of years.

SECOND: Father, I've been wondering, why do we never go past the bramble hedge?

MAN: Why, no one goes past the hedge if they can help it. Haven't we everything we need right there?

SECOND: They're right, of course they're right. But poisonous feelings begin to creep through me. Greed – though there's nothing I lack. Anger – though I'm the luckiest girl in the world.

THIRD: How's my little darling this morning?

MAN: No smile for your father today?

SECOND: I have to get away from them. At the top of the castle is an old town that my mother says is empty, but I've heard sounds coming from there. So one afternoon I climb the stairs to the very top, and turn the handle.

She discovers THIRD as the Spinster, working at a spinning wheel.

SECOND: Who are you?

THIRD: What business is it of yours?

SECOND: I am the royal Princess.

THIRD: They call me Spinster.

SECOND: Whatever is that whirling thing?

THIRD: Haven't you ever seen a spinning wheel before? How do you suppose your dresses get made?

SECOND: I've never thought to wonder.

THIRD: Try it.

SECOND: Oh, I mustn't. I'm never to do any work.

THIRD: I'll tell you this much, Princess, life is long and you'll never get through it without dirtying your fingers.

Stung, SECOND sits down at the wheel and tries it. When the needle pricks her finger she cries out. THIRD laughs, and SECOND runs away.

She bumps into MAN.

SECOND: What is it, Father?

MAN: The Queen has fallen ill. Fetch the best physicians in the land!

SECOND: I don't understand. What does *ill* mean, Father?

MAN: No!

SECOND: My mother is dead. My father runs to the royal stables and weeps on his beloved Donkey till her hide is soaked. The next morning there's blood on my sheet. The maid tells me what this means. I have no mother anymore, and I must be a woman. Snow lies on our castle like a shroud, and in the spring the lilies stand tall on my mother's grave. My father stays locked up in his chambers with his Donkey, sleeping between her legs every night. Father?

No response from MAN.

SECOND: Royal father, your courtiers urge you to wash yourself and find a new wife. For the sake of your subjects. For the sake of me, your daughter.

MAN: No one could ever compare to my dead queen. Where in the world will I find such golden hair, such lily cheeks, such ruby lips?

His eyes fall on his daughter.

SECOND: Father?

MAN: Tell me, do you love me?

SECOND: Of course.

He kisses her.

She panics and flees.

MAN: My beauty. My darling come back. You'll be mine again and more than ever before.

SECOND flees to the Spinster.

SECOND: Spinster, help me. The courtiers say my father's mind is unhinged, so he takes me for my mother. They call it a natural mistake.

MAN: Beloved!

SECOND: They tell me he means no harm, and beg me not to shock him with the truth.

THIRD: You'll have to buy yourself some time.

She whispers instructions to SECOND, who goes to the MAN.

SECOND: Your Majesty.

MAN: You love me.

SECOND: Of course.

MAN: But if you love me, why won't you lie down beside me in my bed? Why won't you marry me?

SECOND: You've torn my dress. I need another before I can be married. Would you take me for a commoner? I will have a dress as gold as the sun.

MAN: You, Spinster. Make her what she asks.

SECOND: The days go by.

MAN: When will my new bride's golden dress be finished?

THIRD: When it's good and ready.

SECOND: But Spinster works so meticulously, so slowly, that a whole month passes and I'm still safe.

MAN: At last the day has come.

SECOND puts on the golden dress.

MAN: Dance for me on this our wedding day.

SECOND: I need another dress before I can be married. Would you take me for a vagabond? I will have a dress as silver as the moon.

MAN: You, Spinster. Make her what she asks.

SECOND: The days go by.

MAN: When will my little bride's silver dress be finished?

THIRD: When it's good and ready.

SECOND: But Spinster works with such tender care that another two months pass and I'm still safe.

MAN: At last the day has come.

SECOND puts on the silver dress.

MAN: Dance for me on this our wedding day.

SECOND: I need another dress.

MAN: No more dresses!

SECOND: Just one more, one last dress before I can be married. Would you take me for a beggar? I will have a dress as glittering as the stars.

MAN: You, Spinster. Make her this final thing she asks.

SECOND: The days go by.

MAN: When will my bride's glittering dress be finished?

THIRD: When it's good and ready.

SECOND: But Spinster works with such infinite slowness that another three months pass and I'm still safe.

MAN: At last the day has come.

SECOND puts on the glittering dress.

SECOND: Shall I dance for you?

MAN: Not today.

He seizes her.

SECOND: I have one final request.

MAN: No.

SECOND: The last thing I'll ever ask of you, I swear.

MAN: I've given you golden and silver and glittering dresses.

SECOND: I will have a cloak made of the hide of your favourite donkey.

MAN: Anything but that.

SECOND: Winter's coming. The wind whistles through this palace. Would you have me be colder than the dumb beasts? Am I not your daughter, and your bride?

MAN walks away, weeping.

SECOND: That night I weep too, into my pillow, from relief, because he will never kill his Donkey.

MAN embraces Donkey.

SECOND: I'm safe at last.

MAN cuts Donkey's throat and lifts off the skin. He throws it at SECOND's feet.

MAN: I've done all you asked. Tomorrow is our wedding day.

SECOND tries to calm herself.

SECOND: Worse things happen in stories, I suppose. He's not a goblin, or a bear, or a monster. He's only a madman. And my father. Spinster!

THIRD: Time to run, Princess.

SECOND: But he'll kill me. I belong to the King as surely as the beasts in the fields. He could skin me like he's skinned his beloved donkey, and who's to stop him?

THIRD: You'll go in disguise.

SECOND: Go where?

THIRD: Beyond the gardens, beyond the bramble hedge, beyond the evergreen forest, into the wide world. You'll travel to a distant land where no one knows your face or your name. No more golden hair, no more lily cheeks, no more ruby lips.

SECOND: What can I take with me?

THIRD: Only your three dresses, and your mother's wedding ring, and your donkeyskin.

SECOND: It smells of blood and shit, but it keeps me warm. I only hopes the wolves will take me for a rotten carcass. The stars look down on me and laugh. So this is the freedom I used to dream of, when I was a restless girl. As I trudge from one kingdom to the next, I shed every layer of pride. I forget I was ever a princess. I forget I ever had clean hands. I live on what I can beg or steal. I learn all the lessons of the donkey. Eat anything that doesn't move. Snatch any warmth going. Suffer and endure. Stinking Donkeyskin! That's what the children call me, throwing old boots at my head. I move on. I've never felt so ugly, or so faint, or so strong. I've lost count of the months by the time I come to a strange kingdom where the trees lose their leaves every year. It looks like the end of the world. I sleep on a pile of crackling red leaves. It comforts me that all things are sharing in my fall.

She flinches at the sound of horns and dogs.

SECOND: The hunt!

She hides.

MAN plays the young Prince.

MAN: Take it alive if you can!

SECOND: Call off your dogs. I'm not a beast.

MAN: What are you?

SECOND: Who wants to know?

MAN: Only the Prince of this kingdom.

SECOND: I'm a poor creature without father or mother.

MAN: What are you good for?

SECOND: Nothing, I suppose, but to have boots thrown at my head.

MAN: You may work in the royal kitchens.

SECOND: So I, who was born a princess, am now the least of turnip-peelers and ash-rakers. But I'm too busy to think about my mad father. It astonishes me to find that work can be like a rope on a ship in rough water: something to hold onto. And at least I'm let sleep by the dying fire every night, and I can dream about the face of the young prince who caught me in the woods, and took me in.

She sniffs the air.

SECOND: Spring! It's a feast day, and all the servants are let off their duties, even stinky old Donkeyskin. Down by the river I catch sight of my reflection.

She winces, and washes herself, swapping the donkeyskin for her glittering dress. Music starts up, and she dances for her reflection.

SECOND: A ball. Do I dare? No one challenges me when I walk into the great hall; the dress's magic opens every door. I remember just how a princess is meant to behave. I smile every so prettily and keep my belly pulled in. *(Making conversation.)* Indeed. Very true. Do you think so? Under the thousand crystal chandeliers I dance with a series of elderly gentlemen who have nothing to say but don't let that stop them. Indeed. Very true. Do you think so? And the eyes of the young Prince follow me around the ballroom.

MAN: May I have the honour of this dance? It seems to me as if we've met before.

SECOND: Indeed?

MAN: But I must confess, I don't know your name.

SECOND: Very true.

MAN: There's something so oddly familiar about you, and yet you're not like anyone else here. You're a swan among these common ducklings.

SECOND: Do you think so?

She laughs and evades him. Down by the river she puts her donkeyskin on again.

SECOND: In the kitchens, no one can talk of anything but the stranger: her golden hair, lily cheeks, ruby lips. They say the Prince is searching every inch of the castle for his missing beauty. They say he's mad with love. Inside my stinking donkeyskin I walk like the princess I am. I wait. I know exactly what's going to happen. It's how all the best stories end.

MAN: Come here, you. Who are you again?

SECOND: A poor creature you found in the woods.

MAN: What brought you to my father's kingdom?

SECOND: Fear and need.

He peers into her face.

SECOND: I smile, to make it easier for him. My features haven't changed since last night at the ball, if only he can see past the dirt. My voice is as sweet as ever, if only he'll let himself listen to it. Is the man drugged, that he can't hear my heart calling to him? Surely he'll know me, any minute now, and burst out laughing at the absurdity of all disguises?

MAN: She must be gone.

SECOND: I could cry out, but it's no use: either he knows me or he doesn't. I'll drop my mother's wedding ring in his soup bowl; that'll give him something to think about when I'm far away. I'll scatter the golden and silver and glittering dresses by the river. Let him think his lost beauty drowned.

MAN finds the dresses and gathers them up, heartbroken.

SECOND: Sicken for love, Prince. Suffer and work for it as I've suffered, as I've worked. Follow me over a mountain of iron and a lake of glass, and wear out three swords in my defense! But you won't follow me at all, will you? All you'll do is weep for a spotless fairytale princess who never was.

She wraps the donkeyskin around her and goes.

SECOND: After months of walking I reach the land of my birth, and I go straight to my mother's grave. Spinster! Where is my father?

THIRD: When you ran away, he turned his face to the wall and died. Your throne is waiting.

SECOND: I don't want it. I've changed. I haven't the heart to play at being a queen.

THIRD: It's your throne, all the same.

SECOND: You don't understand.

THIRD: Don't I? You wouldn't say that if you knew my story.

SECOND: Tell me, then. Who were you before you became the Spinster in the tower?

THIRD: Ah, that's a strange story. It's a tale of a handkerchief.

THE TALE OF THE HANDKERCHIEF

THIRD plays Maid, the younger self of Spinster.

THIRD: I was a queen too, in my day, but I began as a maid. Born with nothing, ended up with a crown. How did I manage that? Here's my secret: I wanted it badly enough. No money, no beauty, but that didn't stop me. What matters is the stuff you're made of. Strength will always bubble to the surface, like oil in the sauce.

She ties on an apron.

THIRD: If you're born a servingmaid, daughter to a servingmaid, who was daughter to a servingmaid in her turn, you know not to expect too much of life. My mother dies of tiredness. With her last breath she makes me promise to be a good and humble maid for the rest of my days. I promise, and I kiss her waxy forehead, but I know I'll break my word. I bide my time; I keep my apron clean and my head down. By the time I'm the age my mother was when she died, I'm a maid in a great Queen's palace.

SECOND plays the Queen. FIRST plays the Princess. They play with a jeweled ball.

THIRD: The Queen is a widow. All she loves in the world is her great white horse and her daughter.

SECOND: Throw it high, my darling.

FIRST throws the ball feebly.

SECOND: Never mind, dearest, never mind.

THIRD: The Princess is reckoned beautiful, but that's mostly because of the fine dresses I sew for her. The girl has no wit, no gumption, no taste for politics – not a single qualification for royalty. What she likes best is to walk in the palace gardens, up and down the shady paths. It's a perpetual mystery to me why some are born high and some are born low, and nobody gets what they deserve.

The Queen comes in with a miniature portrait.

SECOND: Daughter.

FIRST: Yes Mama.

SECOND: I have finally chosen you a husband from among your suitors – the young king of a land that lies just a day's ride away. What do you say to this face?

FIRST: As you wish, Mama.

SECOND: That's my good girl.

THIRD: She doesn't seem to have any opinion about the man she's about to marry. She stands very still as I try her trousseau on her for size. My hands look like hen's claws against the shining stuff.

SECOND: And daughter, you must never forget your royal blood.

FIRST: Yes – I mean no, Mama.

THIRD: I listen, my mouth full of pins. I deserve it, everything this twit of a girl is about to receive: the encrusted coronet, the velvet train of state. It should be mine: the Queen's bunch of a hundred tinkling keys. I want all the paraphernalia of power. But my blood is not royal. My blood is as common as piss.

SECOND: My dearest girl, I'm afraid I cannot accompany you to your wedding. The times are troubled, and I fear to leave my own kingdom unprotected.

FIRST: Oh, Mama!

SECOND: But my great white horse will carry you to meet your husband, and I've filled its panniers with gold and silver and jewels. And you shall have this maid to wait on you.

THIRD: That's the first I've heard of it.

The Queen takes out a dagger and a handkerchief. She presses the point into her finger and marks the cloth with her blood.

SECOND: Here are three drops of my own blood, spilt for your sake. Keep this handkerchief, my darling, and it will be a talisman to guard you from all harm.

THIRD: You see why I hate the girl?

The Queen kisses her daughter goodbye. The Princess and the Maid mount their horses.

THIRD: We ride along for some hours without speaking, the Princess lost in daydreams, mounted high on her mother's white horse, and me jolting along behind on the most decrepit nag they could find in the stables. The sun crawls up the sky. Suddenly there's a glint in the trees: a stream.

FIRST: Maid, please fill my golden cup with some cool water.

THIRD: If you want it so much, get it yourself.

She covers her mouth in shock at her own comment.

Equally astonished, FIRST climbs down and gets water from the stream.

THIRD: We ride on for hours until the sun begins to sink. We come to another river.

FIRST: Would you…if you please, Maid, could you fetch me some cool water in my golden cup?

THIRD: I do mean to say yes this time. I've already taught the girl a lesson. But when I open my mouth what comes out is: No! If you want to drink you have to stoop down for it.

FIRST climbs down and fills her cup again. The handkerchief falls in.

FIRST: My handkerchief!

THIRD: As if saying what it is will bring it back.

THIRD gets down, retrieves the handkerchief and offers it to FIRST.

FIRST: It's all muddy.

THIRD: Do you not even know how to wash a handkerchief? You scrub it on a rock like this, and scrub harder, and keep scrubbing until your fingers are numb. Look, the spots are coming out too. Your mother's royal blood is nearly gone. Now there are only three faint marks left. And then you find somewhere high off the ground and leave it to bleach in the sun.

THIRD throws the handkerchief high into a tree.

THIRD: Hers is the look of the rabbit, and it brings out all the snake in me. Take off your dress.

FIRST: I beg your pardon?

THIRD: Take off your dress, or I'll strip it from your body with my bare hands.

31

FIRST obeys. THIRD takes off her own plain smock.

THIRD: Look. Where's the difference between us now?

She gets herself a drink with the golden cup.

FIRST: I don't like this game.

THIRD splashes herself with water.

FIRST: I don't understand.

THIRD: You will.

THIRD puts on the Princess's dress.

THIRD: Go on. What are you waiting for?

FIRST puts on the Maid's smock. THIRD gives her a drink of water.

THIRD: Who do you think I am?

FIRST: I don't know anymore.

THIRD: I'm the Queen's daughter now. I'm the bride-to-be of the King whose court we're riding to. I'm the Princess, and –

FIRST: No!

THIRD: Say it. Say I'm the bride.

FIRST: But you're not.

THIRD: Say I'm the bride.

FIRST: If you really were, it would need no saying. You're a hideous old maid.

THIRD knocks the golden cup out of FIRST's hand.

THIRD: Say I'm the bride, or suffer for it. If you ever hint otherwise, from this day forth, I will rip your throat open with my fingernails.

FIRST looks at THIRD's hands.

THIRD: So what if my hands are red and calloused from half a lifetime spent scrubbing your linen? That's soon fixed.

She pulls on a pair of white gloves. She seizes FIRST by the hair.

THIRD: Say I'm the bride.

FIRST: I can't say what's not true.

THIRD: If you cross me in this, I'll take you into the forest, chop out your heart, and cook it for my dinner. Say it.

FIRST: You're the bride.

THIRD: And what are you?

FIRST: The Maid?

THIRD: That's right, you're my maid. Remember that. Now swear that you'll never tell anyone what has happened by this river.

FIRST: I swear.

THIRD: By the open sky.

FIRST: I swear by the open sky.

THIRD: On your mother's name.

FIRST: I swear on my mother's name.

THIRD mounts the white horse, and FIRST the nag.

THIRD: So we ride on. The dress is heavier than I imagined, but my bones feel as if they were made to bear it. It's dark by the time we reach the palace.

MAN plays the King, her bridegroom.

MAN: It is my bride?

THIRD: Who else?

MAN: Greetings, my lady.

THIRD: You find me older than my picture?

MAN: Just a little.

THIRD: As are you. One should never trust a picture.

They share a laugh. He leads her towards the palace, but glances back at FIRST.

MAN: Your maid?

THIRD: Oh yes, I almost forgot her. Come along, bring the bags.

FIRST climbs down and obeys.

THIRD: My back prickles as I entered the palace. If the girl is going to denounce me, this will be the moment. But she doesn't say a word.

FIRST starts scrubbing the floor.

THIRD: When is our wedding day to be?

MAN: Not for a few weeks yet, I'm sorry to say.

THIRD: No need to be sorry. The slow-cooked stew is the richest.

THIRD charms the whole court.

THIRD: I know just how to behave as a princess, from my lifetime of watching and waiting. I sweep through the long corridors, taking delight in every pane of glass I'll never have to wash.

MAN follows her around, fascinated.

THIRD: Confess it, you'd prefer a younger bride. Small peas are sweetest.

MAN: But fine wines ripen with age.

She grants him a kiss.

THIRD: At times I almost forget that I'm acting, because I know who I am: I look down and recognize my true costume. This is what I was born for. But always at my back, I can feel the girl watching me. See to my hair!

FIRST: Yes, your Highness.

THIRD: Pick that up, and be quick about it.

FIRST: Yes, your Highness.

THIRD: Now you know what it's like to be nothing but a pair of hands, a household object. To be no one, to own nothing, to beg for every last mouthful from those you serve.

FIRST: Yes, your Highness. What must I do now?

THIRD: Why don't you go into the kitchens and count the grains of rice, and divide the brown beans from the black?

FIRST: I am very tired.

THIRD: Tired? You lazy heap of dirt. You bag of nothingness.

MAN: Does your maid not please you, my dear?

THIRD: Perhaps she could be set to some simpler task?

MAN: We do need a goose girl.

THIRD: Perfect. She can mind the geese in the field.

She snaps her fingers at FIRST, who leaves.

THIRD: But I'm still afraid, even though the girl is banished to the fields, and too scared to breathe a word of the truth. I won't feel safe until the wedding's over. The great palace seems too small. I've paced the corridors till I know them by heart; my feet itch to get out of here. I've never eaten such good food in my life, but my stomach is a knotted rope. All night I dream of the goose girl.

FIRST: I sit in the long grass all day. I keep so still that even the rabbits don't notice me. Swallows trace out secret messages across the sky.

THIRD: I dream that the girl picks up a stick and draws pictures in the mud of the palace courtyard, illustrating my crime for all to see. I wake with my knees under my chin, as if I've been packed in a barrel like a thief.

MAN: Will the Queen your mother be coming to our wedding, my love?

THIRD: Impossible, sadly. She can't take the risk of leaving her kingdom unguarded, even for a few days. We women are so defenseless…

She shelters in his embrace.

THIRD: In the dreams that line up along my bed at night, the Queen points at me across the royal dining table and slaps the crown from my head. She rips the glove from my hand and holds up my finger, pressing it to her blade till the tablecloth is stained with dark drops of my commoner's blood. I wake doubled up. As if they're driving long spikes through the sides of the barrel, into my skin.

FIRST: I sit so still, two ladybirds mate on my knuckle, and a shrew nibbles a hole in my stocking. These fields are teaching me that we're all – princess or maid – equally tiny under the eye of the sky.

MAN: My love, a messenger has arrived from the land of your birth. The Queen your mother –

THIRD: Not here?

MAN: – has fallen in battle.

THIRD lets out a peal of hysterical laughter, then tries to disguise it as tears. MAN comforts her, then slips away.

THIRD: So I'm safe. I wonder who'll tell the goose girl? What I fear is that now she has nothing more to lose. Tonight at dinner, when I'm sitting at the King's right hand, will she run into the great hall to denounce me? I catch sight of her walking her flock of geese through the fields in the usual way. How strange.

MAN: Our wedding day is set at last. Tomorrow!

THIRD: This is what my mother would have wished.

She runs from the palace to the river, and retrieves the handkerchief.

THIRD: Yes, there they are still, the three faint brown marks of her royal mother's blood. The dew and the sun couldn't bleach them out.

She rushes off to find the goose girl.

FIRST: Your Highness.

THIRD: Don't mock me. It'll be tonight, won't it? You're waiting till the very last minute before the wedding, so my hopes will be at their highest just before the guards come to drag me away.

FIRST: Are you afraid of me?

THIRD holds out the handkerchief. FIRST reaches for it, but THIRD pulls back.

THIRD: If I give you back your mother's handkerchief, will you let me run away from court before you tell them?

FIRST: Tell what?

THIRD: Your fear of me will die away as the years go by. Your need to speak the truth will swell inside you. You'll whisper to the geese, and they'll honk it aloud.

FIRST: Give me the handkerchief.

Warily, THIRD does.

FIRST: I'll never tell what's not true.

THIRD: But –

FIRST: By the open sky, on my dead mother's name, I swear I'll never tell what's not true.

THIRD: But you are the royal princess, the royal bride.

FIRST: No, not anymore.

THIRD: What do you mean?

FIRST: I've grown accustomed to this life. I've found that the fields are wider than any garden.

THIRD: Have the geese stolen your wits?

FIRST: You hunger for attention, but I dread it. You want to be queen, but I was always nervous in case I'd forget what to do. You wear the dresses better; you know how to play the part.

THIRD: Can you possibly be choosing not to marry the King, not to wear the crown?

FIRST: It's yours.

THIRD: As I hear her, the barrel I feel always about my ribs seems to crack open, its hoops ringing about my feet.

FIRST: Go home, your Highness. Tomorrow's your wedding day.

MAN leads THIRD away by the hand, formally.

SECOND plays the Witch.

SECOND: They're not as different as they think, those women. They've both strayed away from the paths mapped out for them by their mothers and their grandmothers before them, and who's to say whether it'll bring them more or less happiness in the end?

FIRST speaks as the Witch too.

FIRST: The goose girl might forget she was ever a princess.

THIRD speaks as the Witch too.

THIRD: The Queen might even come to love the King in the end, once the crown is secure on her head.

SECOND: That's what usually happens to ordinary women: love creeps in like a thief in the night.

FIRST: But not to me, the Witch.

THIRD: No.

SECOND: No.

FIRST/SECOND/THIRD: Never to me.

SECOND: Nothing happens to a witch that's not of her choosing.

FIRST: A witch doesn't choose a crown, or peace of mind, or love.

THIRD: A witch chooses power.

SECOND: I need nothing.

FIRST: I fear nothing.

SECOND: That's why you all need me.

FIRST: That's why you all fear me.

THIRD: That's why you'll always come back for more.

ACT TWO

FIRST, SECOND and THIRD come on as the Witch.

SECOND: Power? Oh I've got power all right. Power that comes not from my own body or mind, but that's been invested in me by a village.

FIRST: A village like any other.

THIRD: A village of idiots.

SECOND: Power I've had to learn to pick up without getting burnt.

FIRST: How to shape it –

THIRD: And conceal –

SECOND: And use it –

FIRST: And when to use it –

SECOND: And when to flaunt it –

THIRD: And when to still my breath and do nothing at all.

SECOND: Power that these scaly-fingered fishwives and their wiry husbands could use themselves, if they only knew how.

THIRD: But instead they tell themselves how helpless they are, and how terrible the Witch is, and they come and lay power at my feet.

FIRST/SECOND/THIRD: Fools!

THIRD: But once in a while it's different.

SECOND: One time comes someone I won't forget.

THIRD: Once upon a time there's a girl with a voice.

SECOND/THIRD: It's a tale of a voice.

THE TALE OF THE VOICE

FIRST comes on as Fishgirl, singing as she mends a net.

FIRST: Sprinkle him with lavender / Gird his throat with gold / For her lover rides to see her / On his stallion so bold...

THIRD plays Fishwife, working alongside her daughter.

THIRD: Such nonsensical songs you sing, for a fisherman's daughter!

FIRST: They pass the time while we're mending the nets.

THIRD: But they put no bread on the table.

FIRST: Weave his shirt in one piece / Polish his silver horn / For he comes to bring ease / To his lady all forlorn...

THIRD: Hope for too much in this life, child, and you'll surely be disappointed. Keep your heart small enough and sorrow will never spy it and plunge down like an eagle on a lamb.

FIRST: I'm just a fisherman's daughter / I own nothing and no one owns me...

MAN plays a handsome Merchant.

FIRST: Who's that young man walking through the market?

THIRD: No one we know.

FIRST: But who is he?

THIRD: A merchant from the city, by the looks of him.

FIRST: What I don't tell my mother is that I think he's an angel come to earth. His hands are pale; mine are scored red with the scales of fish. His boots look like they've never touched the ground, while my toes are caulked with mud. He's as strange to me as satin to sackcloth, feathers to lead, a heron to a herring.

He smiles briefly at her as he goes.

THIRD: Wake up, daughter! It's past sunrise.

41

FIRST: Next day I'm sick to my stomach. I'm in love. All the signs say this must be the real thing.

THIRD: Cold porridge? Pickled cod?

Fish rejects both with revulsion.

THIRD: Sing us a song, then, daughter.

FIRST: Not today.

She rushes back to the market.

FIRST: I'm looking for a man. No, a particular man! A young merchant with the face of an angel. I don't know, he was here yesterday. Tell me where he's gone!

She sets off up the steep cliff.

FIRST: I know what I'll have to do: go to the Witch. That's what desperate girls do, if they're desperate enough. Everyone knows where her cave is, even if no one will admit to going there. They say her eyes are like oysters in their shells, and her voice has the crackle of old nets. They say she gives you one long look and your life hangs in the balance; if she takes against you, she'll reach out one hooked finger and magic you into a gull, to wheel and scream for all eternity. But they say so many things about her, they can't *all* be true.

SECOND appears as the Witch, startling FIRST.

SECOND: Is he worth it?

FIRST: Worth what, the climb?

SECOND: What climb? I meant the price.

FIRST: What price? How did you know about him?

SECOND: There's always a him. A girl comes up here for one of three reasons: to catch him, to quicken his blood, or to bring on her own, if she's late.

FIRST: He's not a fish, to be caught.

SECOND: So that's it.

FIRST: I love the man.

SECOND: Love!

FIRST: What would you know? You're old enough to be my mother.

SECOND: I'm the Witch. I see everything. I know everything.

FIRST: How can you see anything or know anything without love?

SECOND: I manage. So what sort of man is he, your beloved?

FIRST: His collar gleams like a halo. His arm is a drawn bow. He smells like apples stored in the dark all winter.

SECOND: I've known wormy apples with shiny skin. I've glimpsed rotten teeth behind a handsome beard.

FIRST: His smile sets me stuttering and my knees buckle like straw.

SECOND: That proves your weakness, not his worth.

FIRST: He makes me think of trumpets, and horses, and the flash of high gates. He's everything I'm not, everything I haven't, everything I can't.

SECOND: Tell me, now, what would you do to win him?

FIRST: If he was drowning, I'd jump in the sea to save him. I'd forget father and mother for his sake. I'd... I'd weave nettles with my bare hands.

SECOND: Not particularly useful in this case. I suppose there's no point my telling you he's not worth it?

FIRST: You've never even seen him.

SECOND: I don't need to see him, little girl. I've seen enough men in my time. I can tell you this much: whoever he is, he's not worth what you'll pay.

FIRST: He's worth any price.

SECOND: Love's a common delusion. If the man's as ugly as Lucifer, you'll still see the stars in the leavings on his plate.

FIRST: I have to have him or I'll die.

SECOND: Good. A girl who knows what she wants. Tell me now, how big a job will this be? Does the man like you, at least?

FIRST: I think so.

SECOND: I've got a ring on my finger that tells me if it hears a lie.

FIRST: I haven't actually spoken to him yet.

SECOND laughs.

FIRST: You've no ring on your finger!

SECOND: Well, this must be love indeed, if you know nothing about him. This must be the real thing, if there's not a pinch of truth in the brew.

FIRST: This is the truth, old hag. I want to walk where he walks, in his world. I want his eyes to rest on me when I'm dancing.

SECOND: Go dance for him then, what's stopping you?

FIRST: They say he's gone back to the city.

SECOND: So follow him.

FIRST: No fisherfolk I know have ever been to the city. They say bad things happen there.

SECOND: Bad things happen everywhere. Now what do you want of me?

FIRST: Even if I went to the city, what could I say, what could I do? What would draw his lips down to my salty skin?

SECOND: Your chance is as good as the next girl's.

FIRST: No! You must change me first. Make me better. Make me a woman a man like him could love.

SECOND: What's wrong with you, girl, that you'd make yourself over again?

FIRST: Everything.

SECOND: Change for your own sake, if you must, not for what you imagine a man will ask of you.

FIRST: I'm doing the asking now. I know you can do it; I've heard about your transformations. One girl, they say she had the face of a pig till you laid your spell on her and made her beautiful.

SECOND: They say a lot of rubbish.

FIRST: Take pity on me, Witch.

SECOND: I save my pity for those who need it. Folks who've got something wrong with them. Not beautiful girls who sing like larks.

FIRST: What good is a sweet voice to me now?

SECOND: What good is anything to a fool? That's all that's wrong with you: stupidity. You're fooling yourself that a man is all the future you need.

FIRST: But it's true.

SECOND, giving up, turns back to her cave.

FIRST: Will you do it? Will you change me? I've no money today, but if you'll give me a little time –

SECOND: It'll cost you your voice.

FIRST: My voice?

SECOND: You said it was no good to you. It's all the pay I'll ask. If you make this bargain, you won't be able to laugh or answer a question, to shout when something spills on you or cry out with delight at the full moon. You'll neither be able to speak your love nor sing it.

FIRST: But –

SECOND: But you will be changed, and you will win him.

FIRST: I'll get what I want?

SECOND: Girls like you always get what they want. But there'll be pain too. Like a sword cutting you in half. You will bleed for this man.

FIRST: Yes.

SECOND: Well done.

FIRST: I've chosen right?

SECOND: Not at all. But I have a weakness for brave fools.

She turns to go.

FIRST: Wait. Don't you – isn't there something we have to do?

SECOND: What, should I make you vomit up your voice and bury it at the base of the cliff?

FIRST: All I want to know is, when will it happen?

SECOND mimes yanking the voice from FIRST's throat.

SECOND: It already has.

FIRST walks home, getting excited as she realizes she can't speak.

THIRD: Daughter, where have you been? What are you packing that bag for?

FIRST mouths 'I'm sorry'.

THIRD: Where are you going? Are you leaving your mother without a word? What have I ever done to you, that you'd break my heart?

FIRST blows her a sad kiss and walks off.

As she travels she cheers up. She washes her face in the water and sees that she's becoming beautiful.

Reaching the city, she sits down and waits till MAN walks by.

MAN: Don't I know you? Haven't we met before? Was it here in the city, or on my travels, I wonder? Surely I'd remember if I'd ever laid eyes on one so beautiful. Can't you answer me? Never mind. What need of words has a girl like you? Your power works silently, and your loveliness speaks for you. Tell you what, I'll give you a name. I'll call you Silence. Will you come into my house, little Silence?

He leads her in.

MAN: My adorable little foundling! My sweet little Silence! Is there anything you need? But you can't tell me. Never mind. You can answer all my questions with kisses. Tonight I'll take you to a feast in a castle, then to a ball on board a great ship. Never mind if the ladies laugh behind their fans; they'll just be jealous. I'll always be dancing with you, or watching while you dance.

They dance. Then he lies down on top of her. She cries out soundlessly.

MAN: I never meant to hurt you. Rest, now. Have some wine. Some cakes. Oh my love, you look like some strange seaweed, washed up on that cushion. You're mine now, aren't you? You're really mine.

SECOND: Every day she wakes up a little altered. She'd like to ask her lover when they're going to be married. Surely it won't be long now? Her eyes put the question, but he just kisses them shut. For the first time, she's beginning to feel the lack of a voice. But he takes her out to another ball, and she forgets her fears. The night is scented with blossoms. On such a night she wishes she could sing her love aloud.

FIRST dances for the Merchant's eyes, then turns to find him, but he's not there.

THIRD plays a Lady, lying down under MAN, both of them laughing with pleasure. FIRST reels back in shock.

SECOND: What a fool she was to trust a witch's bargain!

MAN: There you are, my little Silence. I've been looking for you everywhere. Time I took you home.

They go home and lie down together. Man falls asleep.

SECOND: How can she blame him? His sweet, dumb foundling seems to ask so little. In this life we get, not what we deserve, but what we demand. Without a word from her, how can he tell that her heart is cracking?

FIRST searches through his clothes and finds a knife. She holds it over him.

SECOND: If he were dead, would he belong to her at last? If she drank from his throat, would it give her back her voice?

FIRST drops the knife and runs away.

SECOND: The city isn't even as kind as he was. How can she stay here? But where else can she go? She reels from one day to the next like a mermaid on dry land, gulping as if each breath will be her last. She's betwixt and between, a monstrous hybrid, spoiled for every life she could have lived. Always she'll be restless now. Always she'll remember what she's missing. Her tears taste of the sea. All she knows is the way home.

THIRD, as the Fishwife, rushes to embrace the Fishgirl.

THIRD: Daughter! You came back!

FIRST notices her mother's head is wrapped in a scarf.

THIRD: I went to the witch. I paid her with my hair.

FIRST protests mutely.

THIRD: You're worth any price.

FIRST runs up to the Witch's cave. Unable to shout, she throws a stone.

SECOND: I said you'd catch the man; I never said anything about keeping him. There's no spell lasts long enough for that.

FIRST mimes hair being cut off.

SECOND: It was your mother's idea. I told her to weave it into a shawl to keep me warm this winter, in return for my bringing you home and giving you back your voice.

FIRST points to her throat.

SECOND: I don't have it, you know. I've never had it. Wish to speak and you'll speak, girl. Wish to sing, and your songs will rise on the wind. Wish to die and you can do that; wish to live, and here you are.

FIRST: I don't understand.

SECOND: Your silence was the only transformation.

FIRST: It was a trick?

SECOND: Silence made you the kind of girl such a man would want. Didn't he like you that way? Didn't it suit him?

FIRST nods.

FIRST: Why did you let my mother think you had my voice? Why did you have to take her hair?

SECOND: People never value what they'll get for free. Having paid so dearly for you, she'll treasure you now.

FIRST: Monster! Carrion crow!

SECOND: There's not a name you can call me that I haven't heard before.

FIRST spits at her, and turns to go.

SECOND: When I was as young as you are now, I had to learn how to save my own life. You thought that merchant would save you, but it's not something anyone can do for anyone else. He did teach you a lesson, though.

FIRST: He betrayed me.

SECOND: But you're stronger now, aren't you? You know not to believe in magical transformations. You've remembered the power of your voice.

FIRST: How did you do it? Save your own life?

SECOND: The details don't matter. The thing is to take your own life in your hands. A tiny, frail bird; you have to cup it to your breast, feed it, love it, if you ever want it to grow strong enough to carry you away.

FIRST: Tell me.

SECOND: I'm the one who asks the questions.

FIRST: Please. Tell me your own story.

SECOND: I've never told it to a soul before.

FIRST: Has anyone ever asked for it?

SECOND: What do you want to know?

FIRST: Who were you before you came to live in a cave on a cliff?

SECOND: Ah, that's a strange story. It's a tale of a witch.

THE TALE OF THE WITCH

SECOND, as the Witch, tells her story to FIRST, the Fishgirl, who remains an active listener throughout the story.

SECOND: Half a lifetime ago, I'm an ordinary girl.

FIRST: Ordinary? You?

SECOND: No better or worse than other girls, except that I've a little wit in my head, so I find I'm not content to be nothing but a girl. And there's another difference: I don't bleed like other girls. The blood comes only meagerly, and after a few years it doesn't at all. Once my parents are in the grave, I have to consider my future. A barren woman earns nothing but hate; she's grudged every crust she can snatch. Without sons to honour her in her old age and daughters to clean her, what'll she become but a rag tossed in the corner? Well, I'm not going to end up an old rag, when every hair I have is still red as a lobster in the pot. So after they bury my mother, I pack up all the herbs in her cupboard and walk away.

FIRST: Where are you going?

SECOND: I don't care, so long as it's a long way away from everything I've known. I walk and walk till the bones show through the skin of my feet.

FIRST: What are you looking for?

SECOND: I don't know: a weapon, a refuge, a life of my own.

FIRST: What do you find?

SECOND: A cave, high on a cliff. I think it's empty. There's an old blanket, and a water bag, and a dip in the floor hollowed out by many small fires. This is it. I can taste freedom like salt on the breeze.

> *THIRD, as the Dying Witch, comes out of the cave and lies down with a moan.*

SECOND: Who's there? What's your name, old woman? Will I bring you food? Water? Fire? Will I fetch someone from the village?

THIRD: Waiting.

SECOND: You're waiting? Waiting for what?

THIRD: You.

SECOND: You've been waiting for me? Wake up, old woman! Don't you dare die before you tell me what you mean.

THIRD: You know herbs?

SECOND: Yes. What of it?

THIRD: You can bear scorn?

SECOND: I've known it all my life.

THIRD: One last question.

SECOND: What is it?

THIRD: Can you live…without love?

SECOND: I suppose I'll have to.

THIRD: Then it's you all right.

SECOND: What's me?

THIRD: The next one. I didn't want to leave the cave empty.

SECOND: The next what?

THIRD has died.

SECOND: I don't like it. Feels like a trap.

FIRST: Why don't you run away?

SECOND: I'm curious. Besides, this is a good dry cave, and once I've buried the old woman, it doesn't belong to anyone but me.

FIRST: So you stay.

SECOND: It takes me months to learn how to keep hunger at bay and disease from the door. I try out every herb I brought and every herb that grows on these cliffs, till nothing can shock my stomach. I have all I need. Rock to my back and the sea to my face, driftwood to burn and the odd fish to fry. I have time to wonder, now, time to unpick the knotted ropes of my thoughts, time to dream by the fire like a cat. There's no one to nurse, no one to feed, no one to listen to but my own self. Perhaps nobody will ever bother me again, and I can live out my life as peaceful as a gull, a weed, a drop of water.

She laughs at how ignorant she was.

FIRST: What's so funny?

SECOND: What I find instead of peace is power.

FIRST: What kind of power?

SECOND: The worst kind: power over people. I don't go looking for it; it's laid out for me to trip over. One day I step outside my cave and find a clutch of eggs. I think for a moment some extraordinary chicken has flown up to bring me dinner. The next day, a slab of roasted meat, juicy and still warm.

FIRST: They're gifts?

SECOND: That's what I assume: food freely given, to keep a stranger from starving over the long winter. The truth is, they're fees, paid in advance. It's a boy who tells me.

MAN plays Village Boy.

MAN: What happened to the old one?

SECOND: The old what, boy?

MAN: Witch.

SECOND: There's no witch here.

MAN: There must be. The eggs are gone, and the meat too. If you're not the Witch – have you got her shut up in the cave, or did you boil her in the pot?

SECOND: There's no one here but me, boy. This is my cave now.

He runs off.

SECOND: So it's a witch they're wanting!

FIRST: But you're only an ordinary girl.

SECOND: Have you learned nothing yet? What do you think a witch is? A woman who's stumbled across a bit of power, that's all. It doesn't take me long to learn to be what the villagers need, the witch of their dreams and their nightmares. Most days they leave me alone with my herbs and my thoughts, but every few months, one of them creeps up the headland after sunset and calls out.

THIRD plays Village Woman.

53

THIRD: Are you there?

SECOND: The cave throws their words back at them: Are you there?

MAN plays Village Man.

MAN: Will you help me?

SECOND: Help me?

THIRD: I've brought you something.

SECOND: And only then, when they're sweating cold as dew, do I emerge, step by slow step, a black scarf over my head to hide the awkward fact of my youth. Not that they ever look at me properly; as if they fear my eyes will scald them.

MAN: I think I'm dying.

THIRD: Nothing makes it any better.

SECOND: To the sick I give potions that will do them no harm and might even make them well if they want it enough.

THIRD: I've got a terrible secret.

SECOND: To women in trouble, I give herbs to shake that trouble loose and shed it.

MAN: What do I owe you?

THIRD: How can I pay you?

SECOND: I accept their eggs, and their meat, and their new-baked bread, and even gold coins, sometimes, if I judge it'll take a fearsome price to make them really believe in their cure. As for the guilty, I think at first that it's forgiveness they're after.

MAN: I know it's my fault.

THIRD: I've always hated her.

MAN: He made me do it.

THIRD: What choice had I?

SECOND: Listen to me. Your crime is done. Drop it and walk away.

MAN: I haven't slept right in ten years for thinking of what I did to my daughter.

SECOND: Then sell all your cows to make up her dowry.

THIRD: I'm a bad girl.

MAN: I'm a bastard.

SECOND: But at last I come to the conclusion that the guilty don't want forgiveness. It makes them uncomfortable. Punishment is what they're after. What they crave are my curses.

MAN: I'm damned for this.

THIRD: I'm going to burn in hell.

SECOND: May you burn on earth first! May weeds spring up where you walk! May a tail grow in the middle of your chin!

MAN and THIRD run off.

FIRST: So the whole village has come to need you.

SECOND: So they believe.

FIRST: What would they do if you went away?

SECOND: Curse each other, I suppose. Maybe cure each other too.

FIRST: Your story wasn't what I was expecting. You weren't always a witch, then. You pretend to be what you're not.

SECOND: Or you could say I've become what I once had to pretend.

FIRST: If the villagers stopped coming up here for help, would you miss them?

SECOND: Not at all. I prefer the solitary days. I can recognize the cry of every bird.

FIRST: And the nights?

SECOND: My bones have grown like iron from sleeping on stone; it no longer feels hard to me. In the dark, nothing touches me except the occasional spider. Every year I need less.

FIRST: Is it true, then, what you told the old witch when she was dying? Is it true that you can live without love?

SECOND: I've lived this long without it, haven't I? Now go home, Fishgirl.

FIRST: What have I done to make you angry?

SECOND: You have your voice back, sweeter than before, and I gave you the story you asked for too. I've nothing else for you.

FIRST: It's I who owe you.

SECOND: No you don't.

FIRST: I have to pay you for the lesson you taught me.

SECOND: I don't need anything.

FIRST: But I need to give you something. A pat of butter?

SECOND: I don't care for butter.

FIRST: I churn it myself.

SECOND: I can't stomach the stuff.

FIRST: A nice fresh fish?

SECOND: I've had enough fish for several lifetimes.

FIRST: What'll you have of me, then?

SECOND: A kiss.

Startled, FIRST laughs.

FIRST: Is that all? Why are they all so afraid of you, if your price is so easy to pay?

SECOND: I don't believe you'll do it. Kissing a witch is a perilous business. Everyone knows it's ten times as risky as letting her touch your hand, or cut your hair. What simpler way is there than a kiss to give power a way into your heart?

FIRST kisses SECOND on the lips and exits.

SECOND: I've lived in this cave since before that fishgirl was born. But I can't sleep a wink tonight. No matter which way I lie, stones poke me awake. The blankets are heavy with damp. The wind whines in the cave mouth. If I took a fever and lay tossing here, who'd know? The villagers would still leave the odd bit of food outside, and the birds would pick it clean. Only the wind would hear the people's petitions, and maybe its answers would be wiser than mine. I could die and rot here alone. Oh, it was a bad idea, that kiss I asked for! I try to get on with doing all the same things I've done day after day for years on end, but I can't remember why I've ever done them, or whatever brought me up here to live alone in a hole like a wild animal. I wake one night and the moon is full in the mouth of the cave. All at once I know I need that girl like meat needs salt. What can I do? Is there a witch in the world who could help me now? And what if I do go down there, into the village? The children will scream. Their parents might throw stones. Besides, the fishgirl could be gone away already. Will her mother tell me where she is? Will I ever be able to find her? But if I do, I swear to myself, I swear on the perfect disc of the moon, I won't let pride stop up my mouth. I'll beg to go with her and teach her all I know and learn from her all I don't know. I'll give her my heart in a bag and let her do what she likes with it. I'll say the word love.

FIRST appears.

SECOND: You again. What do you want now?

FIRST: I'm not sure.

SECOND: You were sure enough last time.

FIRST: This is different. What if I were to say I wanted another kiss?

SECOND: Then I'd say, get away from here. I'd tell you, witches are trouble.

FIRST: I've seen trouble already in my life and I'll see it again.

SECOND: Not like this. I'm the rock that splits the river. I'm a crack in the road before you. I'm a cliff crumbling under your feet.

FIRST: I know what you are.

SECOND: I'm old enough to be your mother.

FIRST: But you're not my mother. I'm old enough to know that.

They kiss.

THIRD comes forward as the Witch.

THIRD: The best authorities on the matter are inclined to agree that a witch should not kiss. Some go further and say it's the not being kissed that makes her a witch. Perhaps the source of her power is the breath of loneliness around her.

SECOND: She who takes a kiss can also die of it.

FIRST: Or wake transformed into something unimaginable.

THIRD: Some new species.

FIRST: But if a beast can be a woman –

SECOND: – and a princess be a donkey –

THIRD: – and a maid be a queen, then perhaps –

FIRST/SECOND/THIRD: – witches can kiss.

FIRST: It's strange.

SECOND: No doubt about it.

FIRST: But stranger things happen every day.

THIRD: Don't worry about it.

SECOND: These are only old stories.

FIRST/SECOND/THIRD: Like kisses passed from mouth to mouth.

Curtain.

TRESPASSES

Scenes

Act One

Graveyard

Wednesday

Wine

Touch

Pipe

Deposition of Mary

Education

Chamber Pot

The Lord's Prayer

Deposition of John

Tests

Act Two

Confession

Friday

Native

Fit

Blame

Away

A Wee Favour

Wolf Hunt

Trespasses

Set over three days in 1661 in the prosperous County Cork port of Youghal (pronounced to rhyme with *bawl*), *Trespasses* is a free fictionalization of the judge's own account of one of the tiny handful of witch trials that ever took place in Ireland, published in Joseph Glanvill's *Sadducismus Triumphatus* in 1681.

Adapted by Emma Donoghue from her radio play of the same name for RTE, 1996.

First produced by Cirencester College at Cheltenham Festival of Literature Youth Drama Festival, 11–19 October 1997.

Dramatis Personae

FLORENCE NEWTON an old Irishwoman
(i.e. in her 40s/50s) who scrapes a living from
cloth-making and charity

MARY LONGDON a 'New English'
(i.e. immigrant from England)
maid-of-all-work in her late teens

DONAL O'DARE an Irish boy, fourteen

JOHN PYNE a New English widowed merchant

MAYOR an 'Old English'
(i.e. descended from English immigrants) educated man

VALENTINE GREATRAKES an Irish 'stroker' (healer)

CLERK the Mayor's New English secretary

NED PERRY an Old English merchant and bailiff
(can double with CLERK)

TURN-KEY an Irish jailer (can double with MAYOR)

GUARD 1 an Irish guard
(can double with GREATRAKES)

GUARD 2 an Irish guard
(can double with CLERK/PERRY)

ACT ONE

GRAVEYARD

MARY LONGDON runs in and hides among the graves, high above the town of Youghal. Then slips to the ground and has an epileptic fit.

She comes back to consciousness, bewildered.

MARY: It comes out of nowhere. No warning. It spills out of my head like a wind. I had a chance to make something of myself. 'You only get one,' my mother said, 'so grip hold of it and don't let go.' I were ready, Mother. I said yes. And now that old woman's torn it all apart. What was it about me? Why did I draw down the hex, and not some other girl? Haven't I done my best ever since I had to leave my mother? Didn't I say my prayers? I thought I were cured, this morning. I woke up and thought, 'It's all over.' But now I see the fit rides me still. That old woman in the gaol below still has me by the throat and she won't let go. Why me? Maybe it's a punishment. When I first came to Ireland I were so lonesome I wanted to die. Sometimes I used to run up here to the graveyard, and stand with my back against the walls of the church, and I thought of bringing up a rope to make myself a swing I'd not come down from. God forgive me!

She runs off.

WEDNESDAY

DONAL O'DARE sleeps in a prison cell that looks out onto the High Street of Youghal. Off-stage, the TURN-KEY bangs a spoon in a saucepan.

TURN-KEY: *(Off-stage.)* Rise and shine on a windy Wednesday!

DONAL wakes. Notices a bundle of rags in the corner: a new prisoner. He crawls over and discovers FLORENCE NEWTON, curled up in terror.

DONAL: What are you in for? I'm Donal O'Dare from over Imokilly way. I was fourteen last summer. Come on, Gammer, give us your name even.

FLORENCE: I'm saying nothing.

DONAL: You just said something.

He moves over to the tiny window.

DONAL: It passes the time, watching the feet go up and down the High Street. I can nearly always tell who it is, now, just by the shoes. Don't have a pair, myself. Not that we've much call for shoes in here.

FLORENCE starts to sob.

DONAL: Ah stop, I was only skitting! If you lie on your chain like that, you'll get a sore, Gammer. I was in irons too, the first week, but once you're good and quiet they'll take them off. Here, I'll shift your chain for you.

But she kicks out savagely when he tries.

DONAL: What was that for?

FLORENCE: I don't care what they say.

DONAL: Nor I. What do they say?

FLORENCE: It's lies, damnable lies. Why me? I'm sitting in my hut, minding my own business, and they come out of nowhere.

DONAL: Who?

FLORENCE: How should I know? With their sticks and their irons and their terrible words. Who am I to be called such names?

DONAL: Who are you?

FLORENCE: I'm a god-fearing Protestant soldier's widow. I'm Florence Newton and I've done nothing. D'you hear?

DONAL: Never said you had.

FLORENCE: Nothing!

DONAL: I did. I stole a salmon.

FLORENCE: Were you hungry?

DONAL: Me and six sisters.

She nods.

DONAL: At least this cell has a window. I was in the dark one at the back for the winter, but come spring they moved me to put a girl in that smothered her babby. She'll be in Hell by now.

FLORENCE: Will you ever shut that gob of yours and let a body get a bit of rest?

DONAL: Of course, you're heading there yourself, being a Protestant.

FLORENCE: And what about you, you nasty little thiever? If they hang you with that on your conscience, you're coming down with me.

DONAL shakes his head.

DONAL: I'm confessed and absolved already.

FLORENCE launches herself at him and they fight.

DONAL: I wouldn't want it on my conscience that I ever struck a woman and an old one.

FLORENCE: Don't fret, you won't get the chance. Popish brat!

She bangs his head on the floor.

DONAL: Dirty old witch!

Stricken with fear, she lets go of him and backs away.

FLORENCE: You believe it too.

WINE

JOHN PYNE is drinking wine with his guest, NED PERRY.

JOHN: 'Good neighbours,' I said, 'this Gammer Newton is a menace to the whole town of Youghal. If she could throw my maid Mary into such grievous seizures, what could she not do to the rest of us?'

NED: True for you, John.

JOHN: Shall we stand by while this fine port succumbs to satanical sorcery?

NED: Indeed and we won't.

JOHN: It cannot be said that I came to this land an innocent lamb. The works of all the learned authors warned me that the Celtic race are idle, filthy, sensual, drunken and deceitful, and have ever been given over to sorcery. *(Remembers that NED is of Irish stock.)* No offence to your forefathers, Ned.

NED: None taken.

JOHN: My hope was that settlers of good Saxon blood could civilize this rebellious country. Crusaders: bearers of the good news. How was I to know that even wellborn Englishmen degenerate here, and are soon rolling in the muck with the natives.

> *NED nods, enjoying his wine.*

JOHN: This whole island wallows in a mire of superstition. Can you credit it, Ned – some still leave out milk for the fairy folk.

> *NED squirms, because he does that.*

NED: I heard tell the Newton woman's only the second witch every found out in the whole island of Ireland.

JOHN: There's plenty more walk the land unpunished. God requires us to keep our eyes open as wide as gates.

NED: I'll drink to that.

JOHN: Will you take another cup?

NED: Ah no.

JOHN: Mary! More wine for my good friend Ned Perry.

NED: Just a drop, then, since it was my ship that brought it in.

MARY comes in with a jug and serves them both.

NED: And are you feeling right in yourself now, girl?

JOHN: I'll tell you this for a wonder, Ned – her fits calmed yesterday the instant, the very instant Gammer Newton was clapped into irons.

NED: Is that so?

JOHN: If you ask me, vagabones should be cleared from our streets before they trespass against person or property.

NED: I've said the same to the Mayor in council, but will he hear it?

JOHN: I think he will now.

NED: Business calls me. Good day to you, John. And to you, Mary.

She curtseys stiffly.

Once NED has left, MARY turns to go, but her master stops her.

JOHN: Mary. Are my daughters safe at home?

MARY: They are, sir.

JOHN: We'll have the pigeon pie for dinner.

MARY: Very good.

JOHN: You are fully restored?

MARY: *(Lying.)* I swear it.

JOHN: No need to swear.

MARY: I'm sorry.

JOHN: Now you have your strength back, this afternoon you're to see the Mayor himself for him to take down your deposition.

MARY: Must I?

JOHN: What sort of question is that?

MARY: Only, I thought it were all over. Now she's locked up, and I'm cured. I thought you and I could –

JOHN: *(Interrupts.)* Oh Mary, it's only beginning.

TOUCH

MARY hurries down the street. She is stopped in her tracks by VALENTINE GREATRAKES.

GREATRAKES: Do you know me, Mary Longdon?

MARY: Mr Greatrakes, sir.

GREATRAKES: Do you know why they call me the stroker?

She nods and tries to slip by.

GREATRAKES: Stand still now one moment. Let me look in your eyes till I see are you well now after your awful fits.

MARY: I'm quite well.

GREATRAKES: Are you sure? Let me have a feel of your palm.

MARY: I'm late.

GREATRAKES: Are you a Christian, Mary?

MARY: What else would I be?

GREATRAKES: And have you never heard of the laying on of hands, by which Our Saviour performed so many miracles? And by which his humble servants carry on his healing mission, to this day?

MARY: I'm healed already. The witch is locked up.

GREATRAKES: But as long as she lives, you'll be within reach of her dark powers.

MARY evades him and flees.

PIPE

FLORENCE: Curse my hands to be shaking so I can't even redden my pipe.

DONAL, still wary, considers this overture.

DONAL: Will I see could I light it?

She extends her tinderbox. He comes over and lights her pipe.

FLORENCE: Take a draw, Donal O'Dare?

DONAL: I won't, but thank you.

FLORENCE: 'Tis a very healthful habit. *(Racking cough.)* Purges the lungs of damp. Wasn't it Youghal itself where Sir Walter brought home the first pipeful of tobacco?

DONAL: *(Ironic.)* Aye, 'tis a fine town.

FLORENCE: Bugger Sir Walter. Bugger them all.

DONAL: Hard to credit it that up above our heads sits the Mayor.

FLORENCE: I'd wipe my nose on him, and all his bailiffs. John bloody Pyne that never had a civil word for anybody that wouldn't have shoes of Spanish leather.

DONAL: That's the same merchant I whipped the salmon from. I was passing by his door and it was lying there on the table as long as my leg, like a gift from God.

FLORENCE: That's blasphemy.

DONAL crosses himself regretfully.

FLORENCE: Ah, thieving's the only way the likes of us'd ever get bit, bite or sup from John Pyne.

DONAL: I never stole a thing before. Never even begged a meal.

FLORENCE: *(Bristling.)* Aren't you the great wee mannie?

DONAL: But my sisters hadn't eaten flesh in half a year. They had the salmon sweetly roasted when the bailiffs came to the door. I'd just touched my thumb to it and had a wee lick. Never tasted anything so fresh in all my life.

FLORENCE: Stop it, you're making me hungrier.

DONAL: I suppose John Pyne and his household had it for dinner.

FLORENCE: I wonder when they'll bring us something?

DONAL: Not till dark.

DEPOSITION OF MARY

The MAYOR sits at his desk rapidly dictating to his CLERK.

MAYOR: 'That on this twenty-third day – '

CLERK: Twenty-fourth, your worship.

MAYOR: ' – twenty-fourth day of March in the year of Our Lord sixteen hundred and sixty-one, I, as Mayor elect of the town of Youghal in the County of Cork in the kingdom of Ireland, do commit to prison one Florence Newton – ' How did she pick up such an English name?

CLERK: Widow to one of Cromwell's soldiers.

MAYOR: Has the physician seen the Longdon girl yet?

The CLERK plucks out the relevant paper.

CLERK: He has purged the girl, bled her, cupped her, and administered a poultice, a vomit and an enema.

MAYOR: God help her. Let her come in.

CLERK: Mary Longdon!

MARY comes in, very nervous.

MAYOR: Now Mary, there's nothing to fear if you have a clean conscience.

MARY: Aye sir.

CLERK: The Mayor should be addressed as 'his worship'.

MARY: Aye, his worship.

CLERK: 'Your worship.'

MARY: 'Your worship.'

MAYOR: When you go to the Assizes in Cork to testify against the witch, the judge will be asking you many a question, such as, when did you first set eyes on Florence Newton?

MARY: I misremember.

MAYOR: Try.

MARY: Three, four years back, maybe.

MAYOR: Was it on the road you met her?

MARY: In the pasture, in the summer. She asked for a sup of fresh milk out of my pail.

MAYOR: And did you give it?

MARY: *(Guiltily.)* I did.

MAYOR: Why?

MARY: Her mouth were cracked with the thirst. Would you have no pity on a body when the day was as hot as coals?

CLERK: It is for His Worship to put the questions, and for you to answer them.

MARY: I beg pardon.

MAYOR: Someone saw you in the pasture and told your master.

MARY: Told Ned Perry, and he told my master, who beat me for it.

MAYOR: Do you bear a grudge against John Pyne?

MARY: *(Shocked.)* Who am I to bear a grudge against my master?

MAYOR: How often did you see Florence Newton again after that?

MARY: *(Evasive.)* Only the odd time. We'd share a pipe and watch the swallows.

MAYOR: Did she ever give you anything?

MARY: Just a length of frieze that she'd wove herself. That was for the beating I took on her account. And I gave her a twist of baccy once.

MAYOR: Your master's?

MARY: My own. Then one windy day I were up on the bell tower, and –

She breaks off, remembering that attempted suicide is a crime.

FLORENCE stands up in her cell beside the sleeping boy, joining in the memory.

FLORENCE: Is that you, Mary Longdon?

MARY: There she was down below, with her dirty black shawl over her head.

FLORENCE: What are you doing up in that belfry?

MARY: Nothing!

FLORENCE: You might fall to your death.

MARY: But no one could prove I did it on purpose.

FLORENCE: Come down off of that, child, you're too young for such thoughts.

MAYOR: Mary? What's all this about the bell tower?

MARY: Down in the chapel she showed me the nine little stone children, and the wish stone where they wash the holy vessels.

FLORENCE: Rub your finger there, on the wish stone. What do you want most?

MARY: Home.

FLORENCE: Try something smaller, for now.

MAYOR: Did you meet her on any other occasion?

MARY: One May Day she showed me how to tie ash stems around the udders to ward off the little folk. Unless that were witchcraft too? Oh sir, your worship, how could I have known any better? She said that's how things were done in this country.

MAYOR: Let's come to the mutton.

CLERK: Beef, your worship. *(Checking his notes.)* You were salting the beef in the tub a month ago when Florence Newton came to the door.

MARY: I was. She said –

FLORENCE/MARY: God be with the work.

FLORENCE: Would you ever give me a strip off the side of the beef, Mary, only for the eyes do be popping out of my skull with hunger?

MARY: My master says I've no right to give away his vittles to vagabones.

MAYOR: Did she utter any curse or threat, then?

MARY: She only…grumbled.

FLORENCE: It might have been better for you if you'd spared me the wee scrap of meat that was in it.

MARY: And then John Pyne came down and said he'd set his wolfhound on her, so she ran off.

MAYOR: Did you meet with Gammer Newton again after that, but before last Monday fortnight?

MARY: Sometimes we laid eyes on each other, about the town.

MAYOR: Did she make any signs against you with her fingers, or scowl as if she meant you harm?

MARY: No sir, your worship. We just looked away, because of the beef.

MAYOR: Then last Monday fortnight…

CLERK: You were going to the river with a pail of clothes.

MARY: She were there before me, washing her linen, and she came up and lifted the pail down from my head –

MAYOR: Did she throw it down violently?

MARY: No. She said, 'Mary, I pray – '

She breaks off with a sob.

MAYOR: To what power did she pray?

FLORENCE: Mary, I pray we be friends again.

MAYOR: Was it then she gave you the kiss?

FLORENCE: No quarrel too ill / For the kiss of goodwill.

She kisses the air. In the MAYOR's office above, MARY's hand flies up to her cheek.

MAYOR: Why would you let a beggarwoman kiss you?

MARY: I didn't let her exactly. My master says a witch's kiss allows the evil jump out of her and into you, but I didn't know that then, to be afraid of her.

MAYOR: Did the kiss pain you, at the time?

MARY shakes her head.

MAYOR: Any taste of venom or gall?

MARY: No. She were –

She can't speak.

MAYOR: She was what? What was she?

MARY: She were the only person that ever gave me any mark of affection in this country.

MAYOR: What, is there no affection in John Pyne's house?

MARY: No marks of it. My master says the only thing proper for kissing be the Good Book, and that but sparingly.

MAYOR: After the kiss, did Gammer Newton speak any words?

MARY: *(Lying.)* None that I remember.

FLORENCE: Girl, I bear you no ill will and I pray you bear me none. Wasn't it me talked you down, the time you were up on that tower?

MARY: Only to look at the sea!

MAYOR: What?

FLORENCE: I'll not tell a soul. Let yourself and myself be friends again.

MARY: My master calls you a vagabones.

FLORENCE: I'm no woman of the roads. I have a little turf hut, would you come and see it?

MARY: My master says I must stop at home.

MAYOR: Mary? Are you ill?

With an effort, MARY returns from the memory.

MARY: I'm perfectly well.

MAYOR: So Florence Newton was like a friend to you, is that what you're saying?

MARY: No! When the fits came on me I knew it must have been no affection, but spite, that made her kiss me. I woke up in my bed where my master had carried me, and he were asking could anyone have put a hex on me, and I thought of her. And that night in my dream I saw a woman with a veil over her face, and she lifted it up and it were her.

79

MAYOR: Florence Newton?

MARY: Must you keep on saying her name?

The CLERK slides his notes over, tapping a significant spot.

MAYOR: The judge in Cork may ask you, Mary, had you ever been troubled with fits before Gammer Newton kissed you. Because some say you've always been given to strange turns.

MARY: I have sometimes been a bad servant since John Pyne brought me to this country. I can't seem to wake up in the morning, and when I'm churning butter my mind sometimes goes astray and I forget to turn the handle, or I might weep without good reason. But not fits. Fits be from witching, my master says.

MAYOR: Never mind your master. What do you say?

MARY: With fits, there's a smell like bad eggs.

MAYOR: Brimstone?

MARY: Then my hands prickle, and I fall down.

MAYOR: Do you taste anything in your fits?

MARY: Fish, maybe.

MAYOR: And hear anything?

MARY: My mother's voice.

MAYOR: What's that?

CLERK: Speak up.

MARY: My mother's voice.

MAYOR: And when you wake?

MARY: I find the sun's moved on, or the moon. And, and also…

MAYOR: Yes?

MARY: Let him not write it down in his book, but.

The MAYOR nods at the CLERK, who puts his quill down.

MARY: When I wake after a fit, my skirts do be…wet through. And sometimes I choke up all manner of stuff. It seems there are needles stuck in my arms, and I have to pluck them out. And a feeling like many small stones falling on me as I go from room to room.

MAYOR: Small stones. Can you pick them up?

MARY: I try, but they vanish away.

MAYOR: Thank you, Mary.

She stumbles out.

MAYOR: Poor eejit.

EDUCATION

FLORENCE: When I get out of this cell, I'll never kiss man, woman nor child again. I'd be safer spitting. Donal? Are you listening?

DONAL: Sure what choice do I have?

FLORENCE: Why don't you fear me?

DONAL: I fear you'll bang my head on the floor again.

FLORENCE: I said I was sorry. But you don't shrink from me like everyone else in this turd of a town.

DONAL: I have some education, Gammer. I know that the devil has more important things to be doing than laming cows or sending silly maids into fits.

FLORENCE: She wasn't silly, just homesick. How was I to know there was such capacity for malice in her?

DONAL: Just ignorant, I'd say.

FLORENCE: So where does a pauper Papist get all this education?

DONAL: We have schools of our own.

FLORENCE: Not in Youghal you don't.

DONAL: It's not walls that make a school. The priests teach us in a barn, or behind a hedge even.

FLORENCE: And were you a good scholar, squatting in the mud?

DONAL: Good enough to be headed for Belgium.

FLORENCE: Belgium? To be priested?

DONAL: There's no law against it anymore. *(In a low voice.)* They say King Charles is a Catholic on the sly.

FLORENCE: You're talking through your hole! He's as good a Protestant as I am.

DONAL: What would you know, anyway, you ignoramus? Bet you can't even sign your name.

FLORENCE: Much good your reading and writing will do you in here!

DONAL: Well, that's the truth.

FLORENCE: The wind's on the rise. And the rain with it.

DONAL: Aren't we God's favoured creatures, now, not to be out in all that?

FLORENCE: Oh, aye. Snug as lice.

Sound of a tile crashing down off the roof.

FLORENCE: What in the name of Jesus was that?

DONAL: Maybe the roof's coming down in the storm. *(Joking.)* Maybe the holy angels are coming to smash the gaol and take me out.

FLORENCE: Maybe your brains are leaking out your nose.

CHAMBER POT

Knocking at JOHN PYNE's door. He looks out the window.

JOHN: Who knocks at this hour?

GREATRAKES: John Pyne, let me in out of the rain for one minute.

JOHN: I can see you well enough from my window, Mr Greatrakes, and there's none here has any need of your fondlings.

GREATRAKES: I come in a neighbourly spirit –

JOHN: You won't play Jesus here, you quack. Has my household not been interfered with enough?

GREATRAKES: I would never have disturbed you on such a wild night except for what God has put here in my hand.

JOHN: Looks like a lump of slate to me.

GREATRAKES: It's a tile off the roof of the gaol, Mr Pyne, fortuitously falling by my feet as I was passing. And if you'll let me have your maid to make water on it, then –

JOHN: What new sacrilegious nonsense is this?

GREATRAKES: It is well known to those of us versed in matters occult that if the afflicted person's water falls on a tile off the roof where the witch is housed, the witch will be grievous tormented, and that will be a sure sign.

JOHN PYNE: Mary is asleep in her bed, and no member of my family will be making water anywhere but in their pot tonight. The matter of Florence Newton is in the hands of the Mayor, and there's no call to poke your nose in further.

GREATRAKES: Is this the tone of a Christian who has nothing to hide? I ask nothing that'll cost you – just a cup of your maid's water.

JOHN: If piss is all you're after, here's a whole potful.

He empties a chamber pot out the window.

GREATRAKES: It's God's work you're defiling here.

JOHN: Get away from my house.

THURSDAY

FLORENCE lies awake in the cell beside the sleeping boy. Spoon bangs in a saucepan.

TURN-KEY: *(Offstage.)* Rise and shine on a cold Thursday!

FLORENCE: Would you look at the wee mannie snoozing as if he hasn't a care in the world?

DONAL: *(Waking.)* I was dreaming of the court-room.

FLORENCE: What do you want to dream of that for? You'll see it waking, soon enough.

DONAL: We can't help our dreams. Do you know the Lord's Prayer, Florence?

FLORENCE: Of course I do.

DONAL: My cousin was at a trial for witchcraft once, and they made the woman say it right through, to see if she'd stumble. Can you do that?

FLORENCE: It's often I've said it.

DONAL: Go on, so.

FLORENCE: Don't rush me.

DONAL: The judge might rush you.

FLORENCE: Our Father which art in heaven, hallowed be thy name, thy kingdom... What cause have you to be peering at me like that?

DONAL: The crowd at the Cork Assizes will peer at you.

FLORENCE: Thy kingdom come, thy will be done, on earth as it is in heaven. Give us this day our daily –

DONAL: Speak up, old woman!

FLORENCE: Don't fluster me, ye cur.

DONAL: Won't the judge try to fluster you in Cork?

FLORENCE: Give us this day our daily bread and lead us not into temptation…

DONAL: Missed a bit.

FLORENCE: I did not. Did I? Thy kingdom come…

DONAL: After that.

FLORENCE: And lead us not into…

DONAL: Before that. Give us…

FLORENCE: Give us this day our daily bread and lead us not into temptation…

DONAL: Try again.

FLORENCE: I'm old. I misremember.

DONAL: And forgive us our trespasses!

FLORENCE: I never did her any harm. Is a body not allowed a friend in the world?

DONAL: Forgive us our trespasses as we forgive… Come on. What comes next?

FLORENCE: I don't care.

DONAL: That's blasphemy.

FLORENCE: Does that gob of yours ever shut?

DONAL: We're nearly finished.

FLORENCE: Listen, me boyo, if I could get this chain off my ankles I'd throttle you with it.

DONAL: I'm only trying to save your skin.

FLORENCE: Better look to your own, thief. All your book-learning won't save you from the noose.

For the first time, we see DONAL's fear.

FLORENCE: I'm sorry. D'you hear me? I take it back.

DONAL just stares out the window.

DEPOSITION OF JOHN

MAYOR: I'm sorry to keep you from your business, John Pyne.

JOHN: No business is greater than the rooting out of evil, your worship.

MAYOR: Tell me, when the girl first named Florence Newton –

JOHN: It was on the third day after the witch kissed her, as I learned afterwards. Mary was folding the linen when a fit took her with such frenzy that myself and my two daughters could not hold her.

MAYOR: Yes, all this is noted down already.

JOHN: And I laid the Good Book on her breast, and she flung it clear across the room! What clearer sign of the devil's agency can there be than the casting down of Holy Writ?

MAYOR: This vomit, John –

JOHN: She puked up all manner of wickedness that my younger daughter swept up off the floor after. There were crooked pins in it, and straw, and splinters of wood, and wool all daubed with bile –

MAYOR: But when did the girl name and blame the Newton woman?

JOHN: Right after her fit, I asked was it Florence Newton that had put a hex on her, and she nodded.

MAYOR: But why did you mention that particular name? Why did you put Florence Newton into her head?

JOHN: She was in my maid's head already, like a canker in a bud.

MAYOR: But how could you know it was her?

JOHN: The woman's notorious – hanging around begging or worse, pretending friendship for honest maids just to line her pockets. I've seen her drunk on a Sunday!

MAYOR: That doesn't make her a witch.

JOHN: It was the devil her master made her that. And he's made many more who walk the roads of this heathen country.

Instead of answering that, the MAYOR consults the CLERK's notes.

MAYOR: Straw. Splinters. Pins. Is it within the bounds of possibility that such things were on the floor already, before the girl vomited?

JOHN: We keep a clean house, your worship!

MAYOR: I'm sure. But did you yourself see such rubbish fall from the girl's mouth?

JOHN: Not with the eyes of the body. For now we see as through a mirror, darkly…

MAYOR: Indeed we do. Thank you for your deposition, John Pyne.

JOHN: I know I am not alone in this time of trouble. I have assured my fellow bailiffs that you'll do your utmost to prosecute this case.

MAYOR: *(With irony.)* I appreciate your trust.

JOHN: Youghal is God's outpost in a strange land, your worship. United we stand.

JOHN PYNE exits.

CLERK: A message has arrived from the Lord Attorney-General, your worship. He is travelling to Cork to try Florence Newton's case himself.

MAYOR: I should never have sent word to Dublin so fast, on Pyne's request. Between you, me and this wall, I'm convinced the girl is troubled by nothing more than the falling sickness.

CLERK: But a Mayor of this town could be considered not so much an individual as the combined voice of its citizens. So perhaps the question is not whether you believe the old woman guilty.

MAYOR: *(Nodding.)* My duty is only to report to the judge. Who'll most likely dismiss the case as superstitious foolery.

CLERK: If I might just add, your worship: Valentine Greatrakes has been back, claiming that John Pyne cast ordure upon him. He states that if he is not let bring the girl into the gaol to test the witch, he will write to the Lord Attorney-General himself.

MAYOR: Let him have half an hour after dinner and be done with it.

TESTS

In the cell, FLORENCE is trying to scratch underneath her fetters.

DONAL: Stop that. It does no good.

FLORENCE stops.

FLORENCE: I'd love a breath of fresh air from the hills. These damp walls close in about a body, don't they? A smell like death. That white thing over in the corner, d'you think it's a bone?

DONAL: Indeed it is.

FLORENCE: Horrible!

DONAL: I should know the ham-bone I had for my own dinner last Sunday.

FLORENCE: You maggot! When I was young and yellow-haired, I thought I'd rather die than grow old, but now it's come upon me, I want to live as long as the Old Countess of Desmond.

DONAL: Who's she?

FLORENCE: Lived a hundred and forty year, till she climbed up a tree for some cherries she was craving and fell down on her head.

DONAL: *(Skeptical.)* Oh, aye.

FLORENCE: You young ones don't know enough to fill a spoon. Do they teach the childer nothing these days?

DONAL: Nothing only Latin, and Greek, and French, and Geometry, and Divinity.

FLORENCE: That's some learning.

DONAL: I'd barely begun. If I'd got to the college in Belgium… I imagine it has white shining walls, every book ever written and all the time in the world to read them. The only sound, the bells calling you to Mass.

FLORENCE: Beautiful!

DONAL: Says you, a Protestant?

FLORENCE: Ah, that was a big fat lie. I'd no English soldier husband no more than you, nor any kind of husband.

DONAL: Then why did you let on you –

FLORENCE: *(Interrupts.)* Time was there seemed great protection in a name. When the good Protestant soldier's widow Florence Newton came to Youghal, no one looked crooked at her.

DONAL: And now?

FLORENCE: Vagabones is vagabones, no matter the name. I've been keeping my head down, the length of my life, and this is where it's brought me.

DONAL: So who are you, then?

FLORENCE: Fionnuala. Fionnuala Ní Neachtain.

TURN-KEY: *(Offstage.)* I was in the middle of my dinner!

GREATRAKES: *(Offstage.)* We come on the Mayor's own authority, and Mr Perry here is a bailiff of this town.

The TURN-KEY lets VALENTINE GREATRAKES and NED PERRY (holding an awl, and chisel and a hammer) into the cell.

NED PERRY: Here's for your trouble.

TURN-KEY: Let you not stay long.

He accepts the tip and exits.

NED PERRY: I don't much like this, Mr Greatrakes. John said no one –

GREATRAKES: *(Interrupts.)* John Pyne knows nothing of matters occult.

NED PERRY: No more do I.

GREATRAKES: Now, Gammer Newton, we are here… This is a boy!

DONAL: She's over there.

GREATRAKES spins around and addresses FLORENCE.

GREATRAKES: Gammer Newton. Tell us the truth of your witchcraft, which will save time and trouble for all concerned.

FLORENCE: I never bewitched a soul.

GREATRAKES: Then let us try the test of the awl. Sit down on that stool, woman.

FLORENCE: Why?

GREATRAKES: Because it will go very ill with you if you don't.

FLORENCE sits on the stool.

GREATRAKES: Now I will endeavour to stick the awl into the stool.

DONAL: What are you doing to her?

GREATRAKES: Hold your whisht and bear witness.

FLORENCE: I'll not stay.

GREATRAKES: You'll not move.

He smashes the awl against the stool just behind her, making her jump.

GREATRAKES: Mark how it will not go in, Ned Perry. Note it down.

NED PERRY: I didn't bring paper or pencil.

GREATRAKES: In the book of your memory, you great galoot.

He tries again.

GREATRAKES: This time, see how it's stuck fast! Ned, let you try and take it out.

NED PERRY: I'll not go near her filth.

FLORENCE: I'm cleaner than your mother!

GREATRAKES: Now let us try the test of the chisel. Ned, put the witch's right hand flat against the floor.

NED PERRY: But –

GREATRAKES: It is your bounden duty to the town council, Ned.

NED seizes FLORENCE.

FLORENCE: Get off me.

He twists one arm behind her, and forces the other hand flat against the floor.

GREATRAKES: Mark the mole there, on the flap between finger and thumb? That's a sure sign.

He strikes it with the chisel, and FLORENCE screams.

DONAL: You've no right to be tormenting her.

GREATRAKES: Bear witness, all of you, I drove the point into the skin full half an inch, and it does not bleed! That proves it's a devil's mark.

FLORENCE: Why do ye put me to such pains?

GREATRAKES: *(Shocked.)* Pains, woman? Under English rule no witch, however foul, is put to the pains, she is only questioned and tested.

The TURN-KEY leads in JOHN PYNE and MARY LONGDON.

GREATRAKES: John Pyne the blasphemer, at last!

FLORENCE: Mary!

DONAL: Mr Pyne, sir, about your salmon…

JOHN PYNE ignores DONAL.

JOHN PYNE: I've brought my maid by order of the Mayor. Ned, what do you do here?

GREATRAKES: Mr Perry is lending me assistance as is his duty as a bailiff.

FLORENCE: Can't you look me in the face, girl?

MARY: I want to go home.

FLORENCE: Tell them you were mistaken and we can all go home.

NED PERRY: Stop up that gob, now, or I'll stop it for you.

GREATRAKES: Mary Longdon, do you know this woman?

JOHN PYNE: Of course she knows her.

MARY: I wish I didn't.

She weeps.

GREATRAKES: The deponent weeps. Mark that down for a sign.

FLORENCE: I never meant you any harm, Mary.

MARY: You must have done. What of my fits?

FLORENCE: You'll live through worse. I've had many an ague and a palsy in my time, and here I stand.

MARY: But where did they come from, if not you?

FLORENCE: Where did the storm come from last night? Would you blame the weather on me too?

MARY: *(To JOHN PYNE.)* I want to go home.

He holds her.

JOHN PYNE: Very soon.

FLORENCE: If ever there was affection between us, Mary, stop spouting these lies.

MARY: There never was.

FLORENCE: Then damn you for a sniveling little bitch.

GREATRAKES: Hark at her now!

FLORENCE: Curse your hand and may it never wear a ring.

MARY nurses her hand as if it hurts.

GREATRAKES: Out comes the poison.

FLORENCE: Curse your belly and may it never bear fruit.

MARY doubles up as if struck.

FLORENCE: Curse your life and may it ever be lonesome.

NED PERRY grabs FLORENCE by the face.

NED PERRY: Hold your tongue, old hoor of Babylon.

GREATRAKES: Now the test of the hammer. Girl, take this hammer and strike at the woman's head with it.

MARY: Why must I?

GREATRAKES: To please the Lord your God.

NED forces FLORENCE onto the stool again. MARY takes a halfhearted swing at her.

JOHN PYNE: She can't do it.

GREATRAKES: Exactly! Something twists her hands away.

MARY tries again, even more feebly.

JOHN PYNE: Let her go.

NED PERRY: I'll take a turn.

GREATRAKES: 'Tis the girl must do it, Ned.

MARY throws the hammer on the ground instead.

MARY: I can't!

JOHN PYNE: I'll watch no more of this foolishness. Mary, come with me. And you, Ned.

He hurries them both out.

GREATRAKES: Aye, so the rats run. No matter. Though I be left to stand alone in the company of felons and sorceresses, my knees will never shake, my fist will be of iron.

DONAL: You bully!

GREATRAKES steps up to DONAL and kicks him in the stomach. Then squats beside the moaning FLORENCE.

GREATRAKES: Sh. I feel for you, woman. All you want in the world is to go home. Am I right? I'm no enemy of yours, only of the devil in you. Time was, I was a creature of Satan myself. None knows better than I his hairy grip. But 'tis time now to harry him out of you. You must heave him out of his heart, and choke him up, and give us his stinking name.

FLORENCE shakes her head.

GREATRAKES: Your confession is not a matter of whether or what, but only of when. Tonight's your last chance to speak free. Sure don't I have McGinley the smith working this

minute on a bridle for you? Tomorrow, instead of breakfast,
you'll be biting down on iron. Two spikes against your cheeks,
and a long one to hold down your tongue, and there'll be no
words after that.

FLORENCE: No!

The MAYOR strides in.

MAYOR: Valentine Greatrakes, how can I conduct the town's
business with all this caterwauling going on?

GREATRAKES: Ah, your worship, this is indeed an honour.

DONAL: Mr Mayor, sir, I'm the boy who stole the salmon. If I
could just explain…

MAYOR: Where's the maid?

GREATRAKES: Her master insisted on taking her home, but
the evidence is mounting up nonetheless. Mark this chisel.

MAYOR: I am not concerned with chisels. Gammer Newton?
Let me put it to you plainly. Did you at any time put any spell
on Mary Longdon?

FLORENCE: I did not.

MAYOR: Then you need have no fear.

She looks up at him in relief and gratitude.

MAYOR: Tomorrow's the very last test.

FLORENCE: What test?

MAYOR: You're to be swum.

GREATRAKES: Glory be.

FLORENCE: Swum?

MAYOR: According to the best authorities, the test of the water
is the only real proof of innocence.

FLORENCE: No.

MAYOR: You'll be rowed out into Youghal Harbour and dropped over the side. If the water – God's own baptismal element – rejects you and the devil keeps you afloat, we'll know you're a witch. But if the water takes you in and lets you sink down, you've be proved innocent –

DONAL: And sunk.

MAYOR: And the men will pull you out and bring you home to your little hut. Do you understand? I'm doing you a kindness.

FLORENCE only weeps.

MAYOR: Time to go, Mr Greatrakes.

GREATRAKES: God bless you, your worship.

The men leave FLORENCE and DONAL in the cell.

WHEN

JOHN PYNE and MARY LONGDON are at home, holding hands, speaking in whispers.

MARY: What she said.

JOHN: Sh. The ravings of a lost soul. Wipe them from your memory.

MARY: She said I'd never marry, never bear a child, always be lone.

JOHN: Satan's lies.

He kisses her forehead.

MARY: But are we still… Will we still… When are we to be wed? You hesitate!

JOHN: I don't. I only consider the matter carefully. As soon as all this is over –

MARY: When will that be?

JOHN: As soon as they take the witch away to Cork. Then I'll talk to my daughters, and the parson, and set a date.

MARY: Soon?

JOHN: As soon as we know for sure.

MARY: Know what?

JOHN: That you're cured of your fits.

MARY: *(Lying.)* Of course I'm cured!

JOHN: I need to know for certain that this shadow has been lifted from our house.

MARY: She has no power over me any more. I mean to make you a good wife, John Pyne.

JOHN: It won't be long now.

MARY: And we'll be happy.

JOHN: If God wills it.

ACT TWO

CONFESSION

In the cell, FLORENCE is hyperventilating in panic.

DONAL: Florence?

With a mighty effort, she gets control of herself.

FLORENCE: I've made up my mind: I'd rather hang than drown.

DONAL: Don't say that.

FLORENCE: Quicker and drier.

DONAL: You won't drown.

FLORENCE: I won't let them throw me in the Harbour. There's not a man in Youghal I'd trust to pull me up fast enough.

DONAL: Sh. I'm cold. Let me in under the edge of your blanket.

FLORENCE: Is that what your mammy used to do?

DONAL: Unless I was bad, then she'd say 'Say your prayers, boyo, or Old Ironsides will come for you in the night.'

FLORENCE: I saw him once, you know.

DONAL: Oliver Cromwell?

FLORENCE: He was lodging down there in the High Street in the winter of Forty-Nine, when you must have been just a baby. It was a bad time then, but not as bad as this. Between marching and fighting and drunkenness and burning, who was to notice a bit of a female? There were more trees back then: the whole county of Cork was thick with them like hair on a man's thigh. But they chopped them down for the Earls' ironworks, and to shake out the rebels, and to feed their ovens. They'll leave this country as bald as an old fellow's head. Nowhere to hide, these days; no cover or shelter or shade.

DONAL: Try would you sleep a bit now.

FLORENCE: I'll never waste time sleeping from this night out.

FRIDAY

Sound of a spoon banging in a saucepan.

TURN-KEY: *(Entering.)* Rise and shine on a clear Friday!

FLORENCE: Mr Turn-Key?

TURN-KEY: I've no food for ye yet.

FLORENCE: Would you take a message upstairs to the Mayor for me?

TURN-KEY: I would not.

FLORENCE: Tell him Gammer Newton is ready.

TURN-KEY: The boatmen aren't here yet.

FLORENCE: Ready to confess.

DONAL: Don't!

TURN-KEY: I'll bring him down this minute.

He rushes out.

FLORENCE: I'll tell how I hexed the girl up down and sideways. I'll confess the sky's red and the river's black, and the devil comes riding past my hut with a nanny goat on his back!

DONAL: What did you do that for?

FLORENCE: To be done with it.

She picks up dust from the floor and smears her face with it.

DONAL: What are you at? Florence?

FLORENCE: I'm not Florence anymore.

DONAL: Fionnuala, then.

FLORENCE: Not her neither. I'm the Witch of Youghal.

NATIVE

JOHN PYNE talks to the MAYOR in his office.

JOHN PYNE: She swears she's cured.

MAYOR: If the girl's fits don't come back, would you think of letting the matter drop?

JOHN PYNE: I would not! Have you seen all this, and still you won't believe?

MAYOR: I can believe that evil sometimes walks the land in supernatural form, but not in the form of Gammer Newton.

JOHN PYNE: The Good Book says, 'Thou shalt not suffer a witch to live.'

MAYOR: What if you're wrong? What if your maid is not hexed but merely epileptic, and Gammer Newton is only an old beggar? What if all the rest is invention?

JOHN: Lies, you mean?

MAYOR: Fancies. Nightmares. I believe that in all good faith you do believe it, but –

JOHN: *(Interrupts.)* Have you gone native?

MAYOR: This has nothing to do with Irish or English.

JOHN: It's your equivocating Irish mind that opens the gates to these feeble scruples. It's the Irish blood seeping through your veins that leaves you too weak to rule this town.

MAYOR: I am the elected Mayor of Youghal.

JOHN: Not for long, maybe.

MAYOR: Oh, would you be my successor then? Another little Cromwell, throwing human beings like sticks onto bonfires?

JOHN: Whatever it takes to cleanse this country. Wherever we find the devil's fingerprints.

MAYOR: Even if it was one of your own daughters?

JOHN: Whatever God demands.

MAYOR: I called you in to tell you, Florence Newton has confessed.

JOHN: *(Excited.)* To what, exactly?

MAYOR: To everything.

JOHN rushes off.

FIT

At home, JOHN hurries up to his sleeping maid and gathers her into his arms.

JOHN: Mary! Wake up, Mary. She's confessed. It's over. Praise be to His Holy Name.

Shock sends MARY into another epileptic fit. At first PYNE tries to hold her, but her bucking is so violent that he lays her down and backs away. MARY calms, and gradually comes to consciousness, forgetting the last few minutes. PYNE starts to leave.

MARY: Master?

JOHN: Yes, child.

MARY: I'm no child.

She holds out her arms seductively.

MARY: Help me sit up. I feel so weak this morning.

JOHN: You had a fit.

MARY: Just a little one, surely?

He helps her sit up, then disengages himself from her arms.

JOHN: That must be the last time. No more touching. It pains me more than I can say –

MARY: You said you wanted me for your wife. You gave me your word.

JOHN: That was when you were well.

She tries to hit him, but he evades her.

JOHN: I must think of my children.

MARY: What about mine?

JOHN: Them too. We mustn't risk passing on the taint.

MARY: I did nothing wrong.

JOHN: You're a good girl. You'd have made a good wife.

MARY: I'll end up a lone woman in a little hut: just like her.

BLAME

CLERK: I've made four copies of the confession, signed and sealed.

MAYOR: Marked with an x, all raggedy from lack of sleep. Put any of us to such tests, and what wouldn't we sign? Lord God, what have I done?

CLERK: Your duty.

MAYOR: My duty is to defend the town of Youghal and keep peace within its walls. A petty quarrel over a lump of beef, and look what it's come to. Through my fault, my own most grievous fault.

CLERK: The guards from Cork are here to take the prisoner.

MAYOR: You've been my clerk how long, five years? And in all that time, have you ever known me to follow my conscience?

CLERK: Inasmuch as your worship's conscience has been compatible with the judgment of those men who elected you to such high office.

MAYOR: Five years, I've been a puppet on this wretched little stage. I might as well pull off these golden chains and toss them into the Harbour. Let the waves govern Youghal; let the fish decide.

CLERK: You have been, if I may say, no worse a Mayor than any I've served under, and better than some. We all do our jobs.

MAYOR: Then we are all to blame.

AWAY

DONAL looks out the window of the cell.

DONAL: There's the guards saddling the cart up for you. I can smell the horse from here.

FLORENCE: You'll have both the blankets now.

DONAL: Stop it! You're a terrible stupid woman. What did you tell them that heap of codology for? You might have sat tight and come safe through the trial.

FLORENCE: With the learned men of Ireland ranged up against me? I could say Our Fathers till my jaw broke off and they'd never let me go.

DONAL: They'll hang you for sure.

FLORENCE: Sure I'm older now than my mother ever was. And I still have my powers.

DONAL: Which powers would those be?

FLORENCE: If the whole town fears my forces, then they must be considerable. I could turn you into a flea, maybe, with a flick of my finger.

DONAL: Set me free, then, why don't you?

FLORENCE: How'd you like that, Donal, to wake up tomorrow with the doors swinging wide?

DONAL: That'd be lovely, thank you.

FLORENCE: I could do it, and all. The right words in the right ear.

DONAL: That's enough of your nonsense now.

FLORENCE: Wouldn't you like to go home to your sisters?

He breaks down in tears.

DONAL: There's no going home.

FLORENCE: If you make it over to your darling Belgium, and get priested, would you say a mass for me?

GUARD 1: Here she is.

DONAL: *(Trying to joke.)* Are you sure one mass would do?

FLORENCE: Maybe you'd better say a dozen.

GUARD 2: Florence Newton, let you come quiet or we'll carry you out.

FLORENCE: There's no one of that name here.

The GUARDS exchange a puzzled glance.

GUARD 1: You are to be taken to –

FLORENCE: *(Interrupts.)* I'm not who ye think me.

They pick her up.

FLORENCE: Ye don't know me from Eve!

They carry her out.

A WEE FAVOUR

GUARD 2: Let's put her in the cart.

In the street, FLORENCE sees JOHN PYNE watching her being hauled towards the cart. This is her chance.

FLORENCE: John Pyne.

JOHN: Keep your distance.

The GUARDS fasten her hands behind her back.

FLORENCE: I want you to do me a wee favour.

JOHN: Why should I?

FLORENCE: Did you leave your daughters safe when you left home this morning? Is it sleeping they were, in their beds?

JOHN: The rats of Lucifer will gnaw you in hell.

FLORENCE: One little favour, that's all, and I'll turn my evil eye away from your household.

JOHN: Why should I listen to a woman who'll be dangling from a halter in Cork before too long?

FLORENCE: Very well. I'll see your daughters go by in coffins before me. *(To the GUARDS.)* Let's be off.

JOHN: *(Whispers to her.)* What would you have, then?

FLORENCE: That boy.

JOHN: Which boy?

FLORENCE: Donal O'Dare, in the gaol. Don't you even know his name?

JOHN: What need have I of a fish-thief's name?

FLORENCE: For telling the Mayor that he's to go free.

JOHN: It's the judge who'll decide.

FLORENCE: I'll take more than salmon from your house if you thwart me, John Pyne.

JOHN: I won't stoop to bargain with a witch.

FLORENCE: Then you'll stoop to pick up your daughters' bodies.

He capitulates.

JOHN: He can walk free for all I care, so long as you swing.

FLORENCE: Give me your word on that Bible you carry.

JOHN: You dare to speak of the Good Book!

FLORENCE: Swear, or your daughters will sicken by nightfall.

JOHN: I swear. *(To the GUARDS.)* Get her out of this town.

FLORENCE: Donal! Can you see me through the bars, Donal?

DONAL: *(Shouting from the window.)* Clear as day.

FLORENCE: You'll be let out tomorrow.

DONAL: *(Joking.)* Oh, aye.

FLORENCE: The walls will fall! The walls will fall!

The GUARDS carry her off.

WOLFHUNT

MARY is up in the graveyard, hiding behind a headstone.

MARY: If I stay up here in the graveyard I won't have to see them taking her away. Maybe I'll never go back down. Who'd mind? John Pyne could hire a sturdy maid come market day. There's to be a wolf hunt tonight. There were no wolves where I came from. I thought they were just stories, like unicorns. But they're real: I've heard them howling, some nights. Anything can come true in this country. I've been puzzling and puzzling to think when it began, the badness. There was no evil in the old woman that day at the belfry, I'm sure of it. So when did it all go sour, like milk left too long in the churn? What moment was it the devil wriggled in? I need to be watchful, for next time. For ye know neither the day nor the hour. I should have asked her. I should have made her tell me, where did all the badness come from.

She mimes choking and shaking FLORENCE NEWTON.

MARY: Tell me. Tell me! Was it me?

Curtain.

I KNOW MY OWN HEART

I Know My Own Heart

This play was inspired by the early diaries of Anne Lister, edited by Helena Whitbread as *I Know My Own Heart: The Diaries of Anne Lister, 1791-1840* (London: Virago, 1988). It takes considerable liberties with the facts of Lister's life, for instance combining several of her inamoratas into the single character of Marianne. Heartfelt thanks to Helena Whitbread for all she has done to decode Anne Lister and her writings.

This two-act version of *I Know My Own Heart* was first produced by Glasshouse Productions, directed by Katy Hayes, at Andrew's Lane Theatre, Dublin, November 1993.

First published in *Seen and Heard: Six New Plays by Irish Women*, ed. Cathy Leeney (2001).

Dramatis Personae

ANNE LISTER a Yorkshire heiress-in-waiting

MARIANNE BROWN a farmer's daughter

NANCY BROWN a farmer's daughter, Marianne's younger sister

ISABELLA (TIB) NORCLIFFE a woman of independent means

ACT ONE

ANNE LISTER is at her desk, murmuring as she writes.

ANNE: 'Anne Lister of Shibden Hall, Halifax, Yorkshire. *Miss* Anne Lister. Wednesday the third of April, in the year of our Lord 1811.'

She addresses the audience.

ANNE: My friend Tib brings me a present whenever she comes to stay. This time it's a journal.

She reads the inscription.

ANNE: 'In the fond hope that through a thoroughly honest account of your days, you might come to know yourself.' I am acquainted with myself already, of course, but that is merely the skin. I intend to probe down to sinew and bone. And I have devised the most cryptic of codes to protect my journal from any prying eyes – even Tib's.

MARIANNE BROWN writes a letter in her family's parlour, beside her sister NANCY BROWN.

MARIANNE: 'Dear Miss Lister.' Do help, Nancy.

NANCY: Go on, thank her for the book.

MARIANNE tries out the words without writing them.

MARIANNE: 'Kindly allow me to take this opportunity to offer you my most humble appreciations…'

NANCY: No, no, keep it graceful and simple, Marianne.

MARIANNE: 'Dear Miss Lister, thank you for the book.'

NANCY: Too simple. She'll think you a child.

MARIANNE: I may not have attended your fancy boarding school, Nantz Brown, but I am still your elder by eighteen months.

NANCY: No need for peevishness. I'm only trying to be of use.

ANNE is still writing in her diary.

ANNE: 'The lecture on electromagnetism lasting longer than usual, and I staying on afterwards to look at the apparatus – or rather, at that girl with skin the colour of fresh cream – I did not get home till near midnight. Though I woke at six I lay dozing till eight, remembering her. According to my aunt, the girl's name is Miss Brown. Elder daughter of Mr Copley Brown, of West Farm. Oh dear.'

NANCY: Try this. 'My dear Miss Lister, allow me to thank you for your most kind gift of Miss Seward's *Poetical Works*. My sister and I read aloud from the first volume after supper last night, and we particularly enjoyed – '

She flicks to the contents page and scans it.

NANCY: '– the "Ode to Content".'

MARIANNE: Did we?

NANCY: They all seemed pretty much alike to me, but the important thing is to make you sound like a woman of discernment.

MARIANNE: Oh indeed. Carry on.

ANNE: 'Considering her low station in life, Miss Brown is quite wonderful. What does she think of me? She must be flattered. What girl would not be? My attention to her at church yesterday was certainly marked enough to attract her notice. Tib had to give me a great jab with her elbow when it came to Holy Communion. I fear I never received the sacrament with less reverence, Miss Brown being directly opposite me at the altar rails. My Euclid class with the vicar made not a whit of sense to me this afternoon. Somehow Miss Brown steals my wits away. Was it going too far, to send her that book of Miss Seward's poetry? Well, let me dream and scheme what I may, I shall never permit myself to do anything beyond exchanging a civil word with her in the street. Now and then. When our paths happen to cross.'

NANCY: What else is there to say?

MARIANNE: What do you think she'd like to hear?

NANCY: You forget that I've never met Miss Lister.

MARIANNE: But you must have remarked her at church, on your visits home.

NANCY: Is she so remarkable?

MARIANNE: Oh yes. Tall, strong, distinguished. She wears a great black cloak, and rides a horse called Lord Byron.

NANCY: Pretty?

MARIANNE: Handsome, more like.

NANCY: And her manners, are they similarly mannish?

MARIANNE: Her manners are…softly gentlemanlike.

NANCY: Speaking of manners, how shall we end this letter? 'My family would be charmed to welcome you to our…'

MARIANNE: 'Humble abode'.

NANCY: You've been reading too many sentimental novels again. The correct phrase is 'modest home'. 'My family would be charmed to welcome you to our modest home, should you happen to be passing on the way to town. Your kind gift has won you the eternal gratitude and esteem of your servant, M. Brown.'

MARIANNE: She'll know I didn't write that. I don't speak a bit like that.

NANCY: Nor do any of us. It's merely a polite code.

MARIANNE: You make a fair copy, Nantz – your hand is so much neater than mine.

NANCY: But what if she sees your scrawl somewhere else and notices the difference?

MARIANNE: You're right, as usual.

NANCY: Why this timidity, Marianne? She may be Squire Lister's niece but she's unlikely to bite you.

MARIANNE: You don't know her.

NANCY: Is she so frightening?

MARIANNE: Oh yes.

ISABELLA (TIB) NORCLIFFE enters ANNE's room without knocking.

TIB: Anne, your lady aunt says Betty is busy helping her make plum jam, so you must mend your leather stays yourself.

ANNE: Oh Tibs, it's all so small.

TIB: If you find my company tedious…

ANNE: You're always touchy before luncheon. The fact is, I didn't sleep at all well last night.

TIB: I knew those walnuts would give you wind.

ANNE: Nonsense, I can digest anything. In fact I was fast asleep at half past three when Betty came rapping at my door to say there was a shabby looking man interfering with the hens.

TIB: Why didn't he wake your uncle?

ANNE: My aunt will not have him disturbed. That inflammation of the bowel is troubling him again. Besides, I'm the one with a pistol.

TIB: A pistol?

ANNE: Surely I mentioned it before. Perhaps it slipped your memory.

TIB: You are the most outrageous –

ANNE: *(Interrupts.)* Calm yourself, Tibs. I bought it in Halifax on Tuesday, because that same man – or some similar vagrant – had been seen snooping round our stables the night before. I haggled it down to sixteen and six.

TIB: I don't care what it cost, Anne. What matters to me is that my dearest friend is becoming more eccentric by the day.

ANNE: My hens needed protection. When the tramp came back last night, I leaned out the parlour window and shouted, 'If you do not go about your business immediately, I will blast out what few brains you possess.' But he paid me no attention, so I fired off the pistol.

TIB: *(Ironic.)* And shot him dead?

ANNE: I'm afraid not. The pistol bounded through the window and broke the lead as well as two panes of glass. My hand felt stunned for some time.

TIB: No doubt the shabby looking man was equally stunned. Tell me, my dear, have you heard that the townsfolk have taken to nicknaming you Gentleman Jack?

ANNE: Oh, that's an old one. Have they invented nothing new?

TIB: Does it not discomfit you?

ANNE: Why should it?

TIB: Well, the fact that your somewhat…masculine demeanour has provoked disapproval even in the lowest ranks.

ANNE: Disapproval is too strong a word. I'd call it affectionate mockery. They know I'll be their master as soon as my uncle…passes on.

TIB: And is that how you want to spend your prime of life, Squire Lister – overseeing farmhands?

ANNE: On the contrary. After the…unhappy event, I intend to get things into shipshape order here, then convert half my fortune into francs and set off for Paris.

TIB: Will I never cure you of your dreaming habit?

ANNE: You went to Paris. And Brussels, and Rome, and Athens.

TIB: I had independent means. Your uncle could live for thirty years more. You feed on hypotheticals.

ANNE: Because nothing ever happens in Yorkshire.

She walks down the street, and narrates for her diary.

ANNE: 'I offered Miss Brown my arm at the bottom of the High Street. I regretted it the moment I did it. Think what damage this acquaintance could do to my dignity, my social standing. I offered her my arm; a slight readjustment of the muscles, no more. Such a small gesture to bear so much weight.'

MARIANNE: Oh, Miss Lister.

ANNE: I spotted you by your drooping ribbon, Miss Brown. It is quite the prettiest I have ever seen.

MARIANNE: I thought you didn't notice such feminine fripperies.

ANNE: Not in general. Other girls might have sacks around their heads, and I wouldn't notice, but there are some whose ribbons I could recall in detail after seven years. You never do respond to a compliment, Miss Brown. I missed you at church last Sunday. I hope you were not unwell.

MARIANNE: A feminine complaint.

ANNE: Ah. After the service – you must excuse the impertinence, but as I was passing the pew where you sit, I peeped into your prayerbook.

MARIANNE: Whatever for?

ANNE: Simply to discover your first name, but it was not on the flyleaf.

MARIANNE: It's Marianne. You're very kind to take an interest.

ANNE: Marianne. I must fill the name in the blank in my diary.

MARIANNE: What did you write about me?

ANNE: Several things that would make you blush.

MARIANNE: For shame?

ANNE: For pleasure.

MARIANNE: That journal of yours frightens people. At the lecture I overheard Miss Caroline Greenwood say she dreaded to open her lips in front of you, for fear of your pen.

ANNE: I record only those remarks that are worth remembering, so Miss Caroline Greenwood need have no fear.

MARIANNE: I believe you have an exquisite garden at Shibden Hall, Miss Lister. I love to walk around our little kitchen garden by moonlight. It makes me deliciously melancholy.

ANNE: Ah, so I've found you out: you are a romantic. Yes, I should have had great pleasure in inviting you to see Shibden, were it not that, my uncle being old and sickly, we scarcely ever make new acquaintance.

MARIANNE: But my mother would be delighted to have *you* call on *us*. That should not trouble your uncle.

ANNE: I have not said I will never call.

MARIANNE: Indeed. Good day, Miss Lister.

ANNE: Good day.

   MARIANNE leaves.

ANNE: 'The impertinent little baggage. How dare she adopt such pettish manners with her betters? Presuming and demanding and sulking and waving her creamy neck about like a constipated swan. Well, the townsfolk will have nothing to gossip about now. I will waste no more nights dreaming of Farmer Brown's daughter. I will keep out of the girl's way as much as possible, and devote myself entirely to the study of great literature.'

TIB: Have you see anything of your little friend from the lecture recently?

ANNE: Miss Brown is only an acquaintance, not a friend. I did pass her on the street today, as it happens, but she returned me only a cold little nod.

TIB: Why so?

ANNE: Well, perhaps I am being fanciful, but it occurs to me that she is hurt because I haven't called on her.

TIB: Surely a girl of her station would not presume to expect a call from you.

ANNE: But I may have – unintentionally – led her to hope for one. Over the past few months, we, Miss Brown and I, we have met once or twice accidentally at the library. And occasionally walked together on the moor.

TIB: How nice for you.

ANNE: I'll not have you mock me.

TIB: But I'm more than glad that you've found a congenial friend in this 'wretched little town'!

ANNE: Oh Tib, you are all that I require in a friend. But with Marianne...

TIB: Do you like her as you liked Eliza when you were at boarding school?

ANNE: Much more. She fills my head the way the scent of a bowl of roses fills a room. One does other things, one occupies oneself...

TIB: And one's thoughts drift back to one Miss Brown.

ANNE: You *are* mocking me.

TIB: God help me, I'm not. I remember just how addlepated I was when I first knew Charlotte.

ANNE: The thing is impossible. I cannot understand how I have such feelings for a girl completely outside my social sphere.

TIB: There are more important things than understanding yourself, you know.

ANNE: Such as?

TIB: Happiness. Why don't you call on the girl?

ANNE: Because she expects me to. Besides, that family!

TIB: I believe they're worthy folk.

ANNE: Oh yes, very worthy and obliging, but low, Tibs, the Browns are undeniably low. From the hue of her nose one might even suspect Mrs Brown of a taste for spirits.

TIB: You're so intolerant of those of us who drink the least drop more than you do.

ANNE: Tipsiness is undesirable in any woman, Tib, but quite unacceptable in the mother of the girl I...have a growing regard for. Besides, my aunt would never permit me to call.

TIB: Then don't ask her.

ANNE: It's out of the question. I have far too much respect for the family name.

Despite her best intentions, she follows MARIANNE into the Browns' parlour.

MARIANNE: Pray sit down, Miss Lister. Oh, I expect you'll find that one more comfortable.

ANNE: I would much rather sit here beside you.

MARIANNE: You look most distinguished today, Miss –

ANNE: *(Interrupts.)* You promised to call me Anne.

MARIANNE: Anne.

ANNE: Will I tell you a secret? I have made up my mind always to wear black.

MARIANNE: Oh, do. It brings out...it suits you.

ANNE: What does it bring out?

MARIANNE: It brings out the fire in your eyes.

ANNE: You think it's the colour of my clothes that does that, Marianne?

MARIANNE: Nancy would mock me for my flowery language.

ANNE: Nancy is your little sister, I take it – the one at school.

MARIANNE: Yes. When she comes home on visits, she shows me no mercy.

ANNE: Tib and I are just the same. Our letters are courteous, but whenever we meet the sparks fly.

MARIANNE: So your friend Miss Norcliffe – Tib – does not actually live at Shibden Hall?

ANNE: Certainly not. We've been exchanging visits for years now, but as to living together…how could you have thought that?

MARIANNE: You seem so well matched. Comfortable.

ANNE: Oh, Tib and I jog along well together, all things considered. But only after my uncle's death will I be finally free to choose.

MARIANNE: Choose what?

ANNE: A companion. As long as my uncle lingers I am his dependent. You seem to think me rich, Marianne, but I am obliged to beg and wheedle for every guinea. Sometimes I mend my stockings over and over again because I have too much pride to crawl to him for the money.

MARIANNE: So if he passes away…

ANNE: When he dies, a small but comfortable fortune will be mine. And I will choose someone to share my life at Shibden. Someone who touches my heart far more deeply than Tib ever will.

MARIANNE: I see. I was so surprised when you knocked on the door this afternoon.

ANNE: So was I.

MARIANNE: I'm sorry about my mother. She's always been that way.

ANNE: It does matter. Truly. I'm so glad to be here, to see where you eat, where you sew, where you…wake.

MARIANNE: If you'd not called today you would have missed me. I go to stay with my cousins in Sheffield tomorrow.

ANNE: Ah yes, a little bird told me that you are expected to make a good match there!

MARIANNE: Well…

ANNE: You mean it's true?

MARIANNE: Oh no. There is a gentleman – a Mr Charles Lawton – but nothing has been said. In all likelihood nothing will come of it. Why would he stoop to me when he could have his choice of fine ladies with fat dowries?

ANNE: Lawton Hall is a prosperous estate. I seem to recall seeing it as a child. I should rejoice at such a marriage for you.

MARIANNE: Would you?

ANNE: I said should, not would. I ought to rejoice at it, and I would certainly seem to. And you?

MARIANNE: I am not sure whether I want to be anyone's wife just yet.

ANNE: Well then. Bring your heart back safe from Sheffield.

MARIANNE: What must I do with it?

ANNE: Just don't throw it away. I must go. My aunt expects me. *Au revoir*, Marianne.

MARIANNE: Aw… Awvwah.

ANNE writes in her diary.

ANNE: 'Seven weeks she's been gone now. Received a letter from Tib, suggesting I go to hers for Easter, but I haven't the heart. Oh, my daily routine keeps me busy enough, from going to check Lord Byron's been well groomed, at six in the morning, through Greek, French, overseeing the workmen if my uncle's unwell, paying a tedious call or two, then dinner and smoking a hookah with my aunt before retiring at ten. If I have any difficulty in sleeping, I lie on my back and practise arithmetic.'

ANNE and MARIANNE, reunited, walk on the moor.

MARIANNE: I love the wind in my hair.

ANNE: So do I.

MARIANNE: But you've got a hat on.

ANNE: I mean I love the wind in your hair.

MARIANNE: How long have I been gone?

ANNE: Seven weeks and four and a half days. I hope you received all my letters.

MARIANNE: They made me pine for a walk on the moors. The air tastes so sweet after the grime of Sheffield.

ANNE: Why did you stay away so long?

MARIANNE: Mama has scores of friends there. And I suspect she kept delaying our departure in the fond hopes that Charles would – as she put it – speak.

ANNE: And did he not? I notice that you are on first name terms.

MARIANNE: I gave him no chance to speak. Whenever it seemed that we were being left tête-à-tête, I fetched my cousin Lucy to play duets.

ANNE: That must have pleased your mother.

MARIANNE: Oh, she's worse than ever. I had to promise to be home by five o'clock today. My time is never my own.

ANNE: My aunt never interferes directly in my life, but I can sometimes sense her disapproval.

MARIANNE: You mean because of me.

ANNE: No, not in particular. She'd always been made uneasy by my 'takings-up', as she calls them; the way I set my heart on a friend at first sight and feel for them…more than is quite correct.

MARIANNE: So there have been others.

ANNE: Never like this. I had a friend at boarding school: her name was Eliza Raine. We used to dream of running off to Paris together when we were of age. I invited her to Shibden for the holidays twice a year, and my aunt became increasingly irritated. She used to refer to the friendship, even in front of the servants, as 'Anne's little infatuation'.

MARIANNE: Where is Eliza now?

ANNE: In York, being taken care of by relatives. She was always a nervous girl, but now she has completely lost her wits.

MARIANNE: Do you visit her?

ANNE: On occasion. Sometimes I think she recognizes me. Once we had five minutes of lucid conversation, till she shattered the illusion by addressing me as Mr Smith and bursting into tears.

MARIANNE: Poor girl.

ANNE: Am I boring you?

MARIANNE: Never. I'm honoured that you confide in me.

ANNE: Oh Marianne. Confidences are the least of what I'd like to offer you.

MARIANNE: You know, I thought of you so much last night that it prevented me from sleeping. It almost gave me a pain.

ANNE: A pain? Where?

MARIANNE: I don't know exactly. Above the knees.

ANNE: Oh dear. You must never think of me after going to bed in future.

MARIANNE: And I have strange thoughts. Sometimes I cannot help wishing that you were somehow…a gent.

ANNE: A what?

MARIANNE: A gentleman. Rather than a lady.

ANNE: Your strange thoughts are no stranger than mine.

MARIANNE: But on the other hand, if you were a gentleman we could never have become such friends.

ANNE: Can you bear me as I am?

MARIANNE: Oh Anne, what a thing to say!

ANNE: Will you take me as I am?

Slowly she pulls MARIANNE close and kisses her throat.

Now MARIANNE is lying in ANNE's arms on a sofa, after the seduction.

MARIANNE: I shall have to find a different name for you now, my beloved. You see, my mother calls me Mary-Anne.

ANNE: And we can't have two Annes on one sofa.

MARIANNE: Would you like a long name or a short name?

ANNE: Short. Anything but Bartholomew.

MARIANNE: A feminine name or a masculine name?

ANNE: You choose.

MARIANNE: Hmm. Stop that at once, I can't think. I know: Freddy!

ANNE: That is the most undignified name I've ever heard.

MARIANNE: But I've always loved it. I mean to christen my first son Freddy. It sounds so gentle and trustworthy.

ANNE: Well then, I must live up to my new name.

MARIANNE: You will. This should all feel so frightening, but I know I'm safe in your arms. Are we sinners, Anne?

ANNE: We are all sinners.

MARIANNE: But is this…an unnatural sin?

ANNE: Surely our conduct is natural to us, because it is not taught, but instinctive.

MARIANNE: I suppose so. Certainly, if I didn't believe us bound together in heart and soul, I would never think it right to, to…

ANNE: Kiss me?

MARIANNE: Is that the word for it?

ANNE: One of them. Do you know what I want?

MARIANNE: What?

ANNE: I want to bite your left breast exceedingly gently. I want to slip my hand under your petticoat and slide it between your knees.

MARIANNE: Stop, I can't bear it.

ANNE: I want to kiss your soft thighs.

MARIANNE: My mother might come in. Where did you learn such language?

ANNE whispers in her ear.

MARIANNE: You didn't!

ANNE: I did.

MARIANNE: At fourteen?

ANNE: Only above the waist. But do you know what I want most?

MARIANNE: What?

ANNE: One whole night with you. No petticoats, no listening out for mothers or aunts. I want to peel you like a grape.

MARIANNE: Oh. Let's.

ANNE: It's impossible. We've aroused enough suspicion already.

MARIANNE: But Freddy, it wouldn't occur to my mother. The generality of people don't suspect that such a thing exists. I'd never heard of it myself till…till I did it.

ANNE: Didn't you always, even in childhood, have a vague imagining of what you longed for?

MARIANNE: No. I shared beds with my friends as girls do, that's all. This sweet intercourse between us must be the best kept secret in the history of womankind!

ANNE: You may be right: if we are moderately discreet, and carry it off with confidence, I see no reason why we should ever be found out.

MARIANNE: Unless my mother takes it into her head to bring me a cup of broth…

ANNE: Oh, it's intolerable to have no place we can call our own. Now I have found you, all I want to do is fall asleep with my head pillowed on your breast.

MARIANNE: Think of a plan.

ANNE: Lord Byron could carry both of us. Would you elope and marry me in disguise at Gretna Green? I'd look rather dashing in a moustache.

MARIANNE: Perhaps. If there were no other way.

ANNE: I love to watch you struggle with your timidity. Don't fret, I'll think of something else.

MARIANNE: All we need is a cottage and a hundred pounds a year.

ANNE: You couldn't buy many ribbons on a hundred pounds a year.

MARIANNE: I don't need ribbons. I need to you take me seriously.

ANNE: I do! If you'd married that Lawton fellow in Sheffield, all our problems would be solved. A married lady is never suspected of anything. We could pay each other endless visits, and in a couple of years he'd die of gout and we could set up home together.

MARIANNE: It sounds wonderful. But would you still want me as a widow, perhaps with a child or two? You might be disappointed in my looks, having watched me grow old and fat and wrinkly in the service of another.

ANNE: I would drown all your children like puppies, and kiss every inch of your body till it was beautiful again.

On impulse, she fishes a ring on a chain out of her bodice.

ANNE: This belonged to my great-grandmother.

MARIANNE: It's much too fine.

ANNE: Nothing's too fine for my wife.

ANNE puts it on MARIANNE's little finger.

MARIANNE: Should it not go…

ANNE: If I put it on your ring finger, my love, people might talk.

MARIANNE: Of course, how stupid of me.

ANNE: Tell your mother it's tin, with gilt on.

MARIANNE: I'll say I won it at the hoopla at Midsummer Fair.

ANNE: And now nothing can part us.

MARIANNE: When we've taken Holy Communion together, then we'll be truly married.

ANNE: If only we could be. I'd drive you to church in our own carriage; I'd take you to Paris for the month of May. I'd ravish you on our own dining-room table and no one could call it a sin!

MARIANNE: What would we live on?

ANNE: Air. And kisses. *(Puts on a yokel's accent.)* There do be fine feedin' in kisses, Mistress Lister.

MARIANNE: Call me that again.

ANNE: Mistress Lister, giver of the longest, wildest kisses.

MARIANNE: Freddy, I'm frightened.

ANNE: Of what?

MARIANNE: The future. I can't see it. My mother is talking of sending me away to Cornwall to help my aunt with her inn.

ANNE: Tell her you'd pine for the Yorkshire moors.

MARIANNE: What I pine for is some security.

ANNE: The day I inherit Shibden I'll send a carriage for you.

MARIANNE: But the world would talk.

ANNE: What does the world ever do but talk?

MARIANNE: Would you not care?

ANNE: Not unless you did.

MARIANNE: All I care about is this. But I dread it might all slip through my fingers.

ANNE: Not if I hold them tight.

TIB looks up as ANNE runs in disheveled and panting.

TIB: What in God's name has happened to you?

ANNE: I have been grossly insulted.

TIB: How?

ANNE: I was walking quietly along the river bank when a little man in a black coat came up beside me. We exchanged a few remarks on the inclement weather, and then he stepped closer and said, 'Aren't you the lass they call Gentleman Jack? I'll warrant you could do with a sweetheart to make a real woman of you.' What stinking breath he had too. Well, I rounded on him, I said 'I'll have you horsewhipped.' But the next thing I knew, the brute was trying to put his hand up my skirt. Thank God for my umbrella. I was aiming a blow at the fellow's privates when he ran off as fast as he could.

TIB: You must have been terrified.

ANNE: Not in the least. I knew I could knock him down if it came to a fight. I shouted, 'Damn you for a craven cur,' but he was already out of sight in the bushes.

TIB: 'A craven cur'?

ANNE: It was the only phrase that sprang to mind in the heat of the moment.

TIB: I mustn't laugh. You're a heroine.

ANNE: I blame myself for speaking to him in the first place, but being so near home I was off my guard. What if my conversation encouraged him?

TIB: What had you said?

ANNE: Only, 'I think it may thaw soon.'

TIB: That could hardly be deemed encouragement.

ANNE: Well, it'll be a lesson to me to take care to whom I speak in future. One cannot keep people at too great a distance in this wretched town.

TIB: I hear you haven't been keeping a certain young farmer's daughter at too great a distance since my last visit.

ANNE: Tib, I have endured more than a year of teasing from you on that subject, not to mention my aunt's pursed lips, and snide remarks from the vicar's wife. I think you should refer to my friend politely as Miss Brown or Marianne, or leave Shibden by the window.

TIB: Yes, Master Lister. There'll be no more teasing. I'm just glad to see you happy.

ANNE: Is it so obvious?

TIB: Let's hope the infatuation lasts till Christmas.

ANNE: You've got such a shriveled old heart, you don't remember what it's like to be in love.

TIB: Too true.

NANCY comes into the Browns's parlour where ANNE waits.

NANCY: Miss Lister, I presume? Oh, no need to rise. I'm Nancy Brown.

ANNE: I'm delighted to make your acquaintance at last. I seemed to keep missing your visits home.

NANCY: Marianne has been delayed at the milliner's. She sent me on to reassure you that she had not forgotten the time.

ANNE: Your presence will be quite sufficient compensation for the loss of your sister's company.

NANCY: She warned me you were gallant. I feel as if I know you intimately, Miss Lister, since Marianne's letters mention little else.

ANNE: There is little else to mention. Halifax does not provide much that is newsworthy. You do well to live elsewhere.

NANCY: Ah, but my time at school must soon draw to a close. My mother insists on my coming home to help her and generally replace Marianne.

ANNE: Replace Marianne?

NANCY is angling to discover how much ANNE knows.

NANCY: On the occasion of her marriage.

ANNE: I was not aware…

NANCY: Of course nothing has been quite decided yet. I only mention the matter because you are a close friend of the family.

ANNE: Of course. And when exactly…

NANCY: I have no idea. My father only received the letter from Mr Lawton a week ago, and as for Marianne, she's too bashful to allow it even to be whispered of in her presence.

ANNE: But you think she has given her consent?

NANCY: Let me put it like this: I do not think her refusal has been too strenuous. Will you take a stroll in our little garden, Miss Lister?

ANNE: With pleasure.

ANNE has told TIB the news, hiding her hurt feelings.

TIB: Engaged? Since when?

ANNE: She sent off her formal consent yesterday. The wedding will take place on Tuesday fortnight.

TIB: How very odd. Did you know about it?

ANNE: Oh yes, in fact the idea came from me. I suggested that the only way to free herself from her impossible family and wretched circumstances was to accept a good offer, such as Mr Lawton's. He's an old man.

TIB: Barely five and fifty.

ANNE: Old enough not to be a trouble to her for too many years. As the widowed mistress of Lawton Hall, Marianne will be elevated almost to my social level, and then I defy anyone to sneer at our friendship.

TIB: Are he and she…in love?

ANNE: God, no.

TIB: Mutually attached?

ANNE: Enough to marry, so she says.

TIB: And what do you feel?

ANNE: Well, I really… I don't know.

TIB: Poor girl.

ANNE: But she is most fortunate.

TIB: I meant you. Come here to me.

ANNE: I'm very well where I am.

TIB: As you please. I cannot believe what you've done.

ANNE: What have I done? I'm only the friend. I'm offstage. I have no role to play in this particular drama.

TIB: You could have. Do you think I'd have let Charlotte slip through my fingers?

ANNE: But she never had to marry.

TIB: She came close.

ANNE: When?

TIB: It's all so long ago.

ANNE: Go on.

TIB: It was in her second-last year on earth, if you must know. Her parents received and offer for Charlotte from a rich man of business. They knew full well that she was ill, so they bullied her to accept him before her 'fading charms' might change his mind.

ANNE: And did she?

TIB: Charlotte was not made of such stern stuff as you and I. She could never bear to displease anyone. I pulled her one way, Mr and Mrs Threlfall another. Between us all we reduced her to silence, and her health worsened. Well, finally I went to her suitor myself, though we had not even been introduced. I told him bluntly that bearing a child would kill her. And when he expressed some fond hopes about an improvement in her health, I said, 'Sir, you may not realize that Miss Threlfall and I enjoy a sincere and tender friendship – a marriage of souls – '

ANNE: Delicately put.

TIB: '– and that to force us to live apart would be the greatest sin you could ever commit.'

ANNE: What did he say?

TIB: Not a word, poor fellow. He sent a regretful note to her parents, and left for the colonies a week later.

ANNE: So you and Charlotte…

TIB: We had eighteen more months together. She left me her entire fortune in her will. Her parents were incensed.

ANNE: I thought you lived on family money.

TIB: Oh no, if it were not for Charlotte's legacy I'd be a governess by now.

ANNE: And you never regretted what you'd done?

TIB: Regretted? She died in my arms. It was what we wanted. So you see, sometimes life has to be seized with both hands.

ANNE: But your romance depended on money.

TIB: And nerve.

ANNE: What have I got to offer Marianne?

She pins on MARIANNE's bridal veil.

MARIANNE: Why don't you say something?

ANNE: What would you like me to say?

MARIANNE: Tell me you're not angry.

ANNE: I'm not angry.

MARIANNE: Well, what do you feel?

ANNE: Nothing. I feel nothing.

MARIANNE: You do understand that this will make no real difference to us?

ANNE: I understand nothing about this.

MARIANNE: Freddy, I'm your wife. Remember that.

ANNE: Yes.

MARIANNE: I wore your ring first, and I'll never take it off.

ANNE: Yes.

MARIANNE: And I'll see you at Lawton Hall in fourteen days.

ANNE: Yes.

MARIANNE: Say it!

ANNE: What?

MARIANNE: Say you don't want me to marry and I shall call it off.

ANNE: Five minutes before the ceremony?

MARIANNE: I'll run away with you. I'll do anything you want. Just tell me what to do.

NANCY calls from a distance.

NANCY: Marianne, your groom awaits.

MARIANNE: Just one moment!

ANNE: Go to your wedding.

MARIANNE: I won't lose you?

ANNE: No.

MARIANNE: We shall be together.

ANNE: We shall.

MARIANNE leaves. ANNE collapses. TIB comes in.

TIB: Girl, girl, control yourself.

ANNE: I cannot.

TIB: You have no choice.

ANNE: The cold, worldly little bitch. To wait till the very last moment, then offer to run away with me. To make me do the refusing.

TIB: If the wedding guests see you cry, they will think you jealous.

ANNE: Am I not?

TIB: Of course, but of him, not of her! As one withered old maid to another, I advise you not to let them think you mind.

ANNE: You're right.

TIB: Now let's join the bridal party. Head high.

Another day, NANCY, TIB and ANNE walk together.

NANCY: Have you heard from my sister since her last visit?

ANNE: Oh yes, a letter arrived yesterday. All goes on swimmingly.

TIB: Charles sounds highly devoted.

ANNE: Indeed. He gives her strengthening medicines and washes her back with cold water every morning. All this in hopes of a son and heir.

NANCY: I believe he's taking her to the sea for three months this summer.

ANNE: She didn't mention that.

TIB: Of course he may have reformed, but I did hear that Charles Lawton was rather gay in former years.

ANNE: Gay?

TIB: A womanizer. A bit of a rake.

ANNE: Why didn't you mention this before the wedding?

TIB: It was only a rumour.

NANCY: I heard it too.

ANNE: But I would never have let her marry except that I trusted the man would treat her with the utmost care and respect.

TIB: As, it seems, he is.

ANNE: All is well, then. Marianne is adequately happy. Isn't she?

NANCY: I suppose.

ANNE: We are all happy.

TIB: Do you miss her, Nantz?

NANCY: One expects to lose a sister if she receives a good offer.

TIB: I don't suppose you're the kind of girl who'd refuse a good offer.

NANCY: It would have to be as good as Marianne's, or better.

ANNE: You mean you intend to refuse any suitor whose income is less than Charlie's?

NANCY: Don't look so shocked. I haven't seen you leaping into marriage.

ANNE: My reasons are rather different.

NANCY: Yes, but in both cases it's a kind of pride. I won't stoop to a farmer, and you –

ANNE: I won't stoop to any man at all.

NANCY: Perhaps we three should form a sisterhood of Yorkshire spinsters.

ANNE: I'm not sure whether you have the stuff of spinsterhood in you, my dear.

NANCY: What do you mean?

TIB: It takes considerable strength to defy the world, when all the time the world will pity you for having missed your chance in it.

NANCY: And you think me lacking in this unconventional strength?

ANNE: You have not proven otherwise.

NANCY: I may surprise you yet.

ANNE: Please do.

ANNE writes a letter to MARIANNE.

ANNE: 'My darling Marianne, I can scarcely believe what you tell me about Charles and the chambermaid. Married less than a year to the loveliest woman in England, and already he's stooping so low! Forgive my bluntness. I meant to soothe your woes, not aggravate them. If only you were here beside me. Of course you were right to dismiss the girl. I advise you to inform Mr Lawton that if you discover any more such goings-on in your own home, you will leave on the instant. Sometimes I fear there will be no peace for you and me, my love, as long as that man lives.'

MARIANNE: 'My dearest Anne, Charles has been in a foul temper all week. The dreadful thought occurs to me that he may have gone rummaging through my bureau and come across your last letter. He has made some sarcastic references to 'you and your mannish friend', and congratulates himself on his health in a rather insinuating manner. I need hardly remind you that if I fail to produce a male heir, the entire estate will go to Charles's cousins after his death. Unless I stay on the best of terms with him, I cannot expect a penny in his will. Till his jealous fit subsides, I will expect to hear from you only every second Tuesday – and perhaps we could use the cryptic code you devised for your diary. Our future depends upon discretion.'

ANNE: 'Beloved, I enclose my secret alphabet as requested. But I'm growing weary of discretion. I want to publish our love, Marianne, to have it celebrated in church, to announce it in ecstatic notes to all our friends and neighbours. Aren't there times when you sicken at the thought of sneaking down another corridor, stealing a few hours together, playing at being romantic friends?'

ANNE comes into a bedroom to find MARIANNE pretending to be asleep.

ANNE: Boo! I know you're awake, so stop shamming.

MARIANNE: I've been waiting for you for an hour and a half.

ANNE: But darling, you said you were going to bed early to take some laudanum for your toothache. I didn't want to disturb you.

MARIANNE: Then why come in to me at all? You could have sat up cozily chatting to Nantz all night.

ANNE: Oho, is that it? Don't tell me you're jealous of your own little sister.

MARIANNE: She's an incurable flirt.

ANNE: We weren't flirting, only…agreeableizing. Nancy needed help with her Hebrew exercise.

MARIANNE: What else did you and she talk about?

ANNE: You, of course.

MARIANNE: Love, I wasn't so much jealous as concerned. I know you never mean to flirt, but your eyes do mislead people. You have all the civility of a well-bred gentleman, which confuses these girls. They cannot understand why you make them feel such excitement.

ANNE: Do you speak from experience?

MARIANNE: You know I do. But seriously, now: Miss Caroline Greenwood told me the other day that you looked 'unutterable things' at her in church.

ANNE: Miss Caroline Greenwood has an overheated imagination.

MARIANNE: But won't you alter your manners a little, Freddikins, to please me?

ANNE: Very well, then, I'll try to be less gallant. But I can't help pleasing girls.

MARIANNE: Pleasing is allowed, but nothing more. The rule of your conduct should be: what would a married man do?

ANNE: That gives me a long rein. Married men are not exactly models of fidelity.

MARIANNE: Must you remind me?

ANNE: I'm sorry. But you mustn't upset yourself over nothing; I was only talking to Nancy.

MARIANNE: Yes, but she lives just down the road, and you gossip with her anytime. Whereas I have only a very few precious days with you.

ANNE: I'm hardly to blame for that.

MARIANNE: Of course not. I only meant, let's make the most of our time.

ANNE: I quite agree.

MARIANNE: And now I want to fall asleep in your arms.

ANNE: You might sleep better if you lulled to rest by something tenderer.

MARIANNE: I'm afraid I'm far too fatigued for any of that. And my toothache is bad again.

ANNE: Oh, I'm sorry. You must try to sleep.

MARIANNE: In most respects, Charles is an excellent husband. He made no objections to my paying another visit to Shibden so soon after the last.

ANNE: Very sweet of him. How is his health?

MARIANNE: Not good.

ANNE: I wonder if he'll drag on into his sixties. Not more than five years, surely.

MARIANNE: Oh Anne, don't be so indelicate.

ANNE: It's what we want. Isn't it?

MARIANNE: All in good time.

ANNE: So here I am wasting my life in expectation of a time which you are too delicate to calculate.

MARIANNE: You know I long for the freedom to spend the rest of my life at Shibden Hall. But it would be sinful to wish my own husband dead. He's not a bad man. You always think the worst of him.

ANNE: On the contrary, I rarely think of him at all. The other day, though, I was wondering, just as a matter of interest: how often are you two…connected?

MARIANNE: I'm not sure.

ANNE: Twice a month? Three times?

MARIANNE: About that.

ANNE: About which, twice or three times.

MARIANNE: Several times a month. It would be indelicate to keep account. What's the matter?

ANNE: Nothing.

MARIANNE: Don't let's quarrel, Freddy. You know how my nerves are at this time of the month.

ANNE: Don't tell me, tell your lord and master. Has it occurred to you that this is adultery? You are, after all, another man's wife.

MARIANNE: What do you mean, another?

ANNE: What do you mean, what do I mean?

MARIANNE: You said 'another man's wife'. But you're not a man.

ANNE: Do you offer this as some kind of consolation?

MARIANNE: All I mean is, I am one man's wife, and one woman's...beloved.

ANNE: I fail to see the distinction. You can't gloss over your oddity as glibly as that.

MARIANNE: What oddity?

ANNE: Your feelings for women. The same oddity as mine.

MARIANNE: Oh, but *I'm* not – you're the only woman I could ever love in that way.

ANNE: Why, what is unique about me?

MARIANNE: Well, you're a sort of...female gentleman. If you had been of a feminine nature, I would have been quite content with platonic relations.

ANNE: How you deceive yourself.

MARIANNE: I'm not –

ANNE: *(Interrupts.)* Look, you and I and Tib and the late Queen of France and God knows how many other wives and spinsters were simply born this way.

MARIANNE: What makes you say that about Tib?

ANNE: I've told you about her and Charlotte Threlfall.

MARIANNE: Just that she lived with a friend, who died young, not that they were...as we are.

ANNE: I thought that much was obvious.

MARIANNE: Only to you. Most women never go beyond holding hands, you know.

ANNE: How can you be so sure? There might be millions of us.

MARIANNE: Don't be silly. Well now, Tib and Charlotte, who'd have thought it? Just as long as she never finds out about us. Anne, you didn't!

ANNE: She's known since it began.

MARIANNE: How could you put us in such danger?

ANNE: Who am I meant to talk to when you're away at Lawton Hall? Besides, she won't breathe a word of it.

MARIANNE: Who knows what she'll let slip when she's on her seventh glass of wine?

ANNE: Tib is no drunkard. She's the best friend I have.

ANNE writes in her diary.

ANNE: 'It is strange that the kisses are always best after we have quarreled. Saying goodbye in the downstairs hall yesterday morning, while me aunt was looking out the front door for the carriage, Marianne let me gently pull her to me, with her right leg a little between mine. I could feel the heat of her thigh through my petticoats. My whole frame shakes as I think of it. This morning before breakfast I locked the chamber door and tried on my new waistcoat with the braces over my drawers. The effect was striking, if I say so myself. Spent half an hour in foolish fancies about dressing entirely in men's clothes, driving my own carriage, being my own master. Then Betty knocked, wanting to empty my chamber pot, and again I was the shabby spinster of Shibden Hall. I pray it will not be many months before I take Marianne in my arms again. Deprived of this intercourse, I am prey to every passing fear and irrational rage.'

TIB reads aloud from Emma, *while ANNE darns her clothes.*

TIB: 'Harriet was a very pretty girl, and her beauty happened to be of a sort which Emma particularly admired. Emma was so busy in admiring those soft blue eyes that the evening flew away – ' Are you listening?

ANNE: Mm. Something about blue eyes.

TIB: You particularly asked me to bring Miss Austen's new novel.

ANNE: I'm sorry, I can't settle to anything this afternoon. Do you realize we haven't put a foot out of doors in six days? If this weather doesn't improve by Saturday, I shall gallop out on Lord Byron and let the storm do what it will with me.

TIB: I suppose Marianne is holed up in Lawton Hall serving spiced wine to Charlie and his friends. How long has it been now?

ANNE: Two months. Almost three.

TIB: What prevents her from visiting?

ANNE: She fears to provoke her husband's suspicions again. So she says.

TIB: Any hint that she's…in an interesting condition?

ANNE: No, thank God. I begin to doubt whether Lawton is capable of siring an heir.

TIB: Her letters must be some comfort.

ANNE: They're full of local gossip and they bore me to tears. We lead such separate lives. She does love me, but she also loves her house, her fine dresses, her social standing.

TIB: What about you? Don't you love anything or anyone apart from her?

ANNE: I feel barren, these days. No love, just need and bitterness. In her last letter Marianne complains that I am growing more 'mannish' by the year. She used to say I was 'gentlemanly'.

TIB: People call you masculine simply because you are more upright and confident than ladies are supposed to be. We all tease you, but we wouldn't want you to be different.

ANNE: I'm not so sure. For the sake of female company, I'd almost consider taking to frills and bonnets.

TIB: How very unnatural that would be.

ANNE: Don't joke, Tibs. I long for a companion, and I long for an establishment of my own, but by the time I control my fortune I may be too old and odd to attract anyone.

TIB: You will never be anything but irresistible.

ANNE: You're mocking me.

TIB: I'm not.

ANNE: I can't bear much more waiting. Marianne is teaching me to live without her.

TIB surprises her with a long kiss.

TIB: Then let her be answerable for the consequences.

Later, ANNE groans in exhausted pleasure.

ANNE: Where did you learn to do that?

TIB: Paris, of course. You taste better than wine. And coming from a lady who likes a fine vintage, that is no mean compliment.

ANNE: You're a wicked seductress.

TIB: You provoked me to it. When you hung your head and said you'd soon be too old to attract anyone… I couldn't resist.

ANNE: I used to suspect that perhaps you had a slight partiality for me, but no more than that.

TIB: So there I was, hungering after your smooth limbs, and you never noticed.

ANNE: Why didn't you tell me?

TIB: I've been hinting at it for ten years. But you've had other things on your mind.

ANNE: I suppose so.

TIB: No sad faces tonight; I feel like champagne bubbling over. Do you realize that no one has laid hands on me since… 1804?

ANNE: Poor Tib, you have been sadly neglected.

TIB: You were worth the wait. Do your aunt and uncle have any idea?

ANNE: God forbid.

TIB: Your uncle must have some knowledge of such things. His library is full of Lucian and Juvenal.

ANNE: Yes, but he's not a thinking man. My aunt, on the other hand, is a thinking woman, but reads nothing but recipes.

TIB: Tell me seriously, though, as a fellow sinner, does your conscience never prick you?

ANNE: No, I cannot say it does. Don't you think our connection with the ladies must be more excusable than, say, self-pollution, which has no affection to justify it?

TIB: That is an attractive argument.

ANNE: In any event, I mean to repent at five and thirty and retire with dignity. That gives me nine more years. I shall have had a good fling by then.

She hears a sound.

ANNE: Is that a carriage, at this time of night?

TIB: Take a look out the window.

ANNE: God help us. Get up, Tibs. It's the Lawton crest on the side.

TIB: What in heaven brings her over the moors this late?

ANNE: Quick, the butler must have let her in already.

TIB: I'll be in my room.

ANNE: Tib? I'm so sorry. I'll try to come to you later.

TIB: Don't trouble yourself, I'll be asleep.

After TIB leaves, ANNE neatens herself. Then MARIANNE rushes in.

ANNE: What is it, my love?

MARIANNE: Charles.

ANNE: What has he done?

MARIANNE: I've left him.

ANNE: You can't.

MARIANNE: Why not?

ANNE: I mean – I can't believe it.

MARIANNE: I gave him five years of my life. And now he's killing me. He's killing us both.

ANNE: Sit down and tell me calmly.

MARIANNE: It's so shameful. I paid a visit to the doctor this afternoon on account of a hot, itching sensation in my… down there. And he said it was…venereal! It must have been Charles and that dirty hussy of a cook.

ANNE: Damn him to hell for this.

MARIANNE: I wouldn't mind so much for myself, but what if I've passed the taint on to you? I'll not forgive him this time. Oh, it's a relief to be safe at Shibden. I'll send the carriage back for my things tomorrow.

ANNE: What do you mean?

MARIANNE: Well, I'll need my medicine, and some clean linen…

ANNE: But dearest, you're not thinking of staying here? My aunt would never permit it, what with my uncle bedridden and your husband likely to ride up at any moment with a brace of pistols.

MARIANNE: I shall send Charles a note informing him of my decision.

ANNE: He'd toss it in the fire. Think, Marianne. Even if you did manage to run away and hide in London, you'd lose all you call precious: your house, your friends, your reputation, even.

MARIANNE: But not you. You're the most precious thing I have, and I wouldn't lose you. We can leave in the morning.

ANNE: With what? Seven pounds and ten shillings, that's the sum total of my worldly wealth. So don't taunt me with impossibilities.

MARIANNE: I thought you loved me.

ANNE: I do. That's why I must save you from your own recklessness. Charles is rich enough to divorce you by act of parliament, and your name would be mud.

MARIANNE: Oh Freddy, you must trust my courage. I'm not a little girl anymore.

ANNE: Come here, you're frozen. We'll make our plans in the morning.

ANNE writes in her diary.

ANNE: 'She's gone. It's as if she never came. Just a ghost in the night. Well, what else could I do? A surprisingly humble note arrived from Charles before breakfast; he must be afraid we'll spread the news of his disease and damage his prospects with the young ladies. There was no need for the note. I had already persuaded Marianne to go home. I never asked her to leave him! I wanted only a fair share of her: a little more time together; a little more hope. Some reassurance that this is not some elaborate game for her. Less discretion and patience and respectability. A little more courage… What am I talking about? Last night she came to me full of courage – and I sent her back. Tib patted me on the back before she left this afternoon. She says I did the only sensible thing. But then, she wants a fair share of me too. What a mess I'm making of our lives.'

ACT TWO

MARIANNE writes to ANNE.

MARIANNE: 'My dearest, truest husband, here I am back in Lawton Hall. I shrink from sharing a house with Charles, but your will be done.'

TIB writes to ANNE.

TIB: 'My very dear Anne, I hope this letter finds you well and recovered from the shock of Marianne's little escapade. Since my last night at Shibden, I have been finding it impossible to banish your image from my mind.'

NANCY writes to ANNE.

NANCY: 'Dear Anne, I am sending this note up to the Hall by Billy the butcher's boy to say a thousand thanks for lending me Miss Edgeworth's novel. This is proving such a bleak midwinter that any company, even that of fictional characters, is welcome…'

ANNE writes in her diary.

ANNE: 'The weather continues cold and muddy. I spent the afternoon translating Rousseau. It occurs to me that I may have thrown away my only chance to escape from all this.'

She flicks through two letters before sealing them.

ANNE: 'Darling Marianne, keep your spirits up…enclosed is a little sketch I did of Lord Byron…the nights are long without you.' 'Dear old Tibs…the weather…the lecture on fossils…my aunt's rheumatism…with undying friendship, as ever…'

ANNE and NANCY walk on the moors.

NANCY: Oh, it's delightful to snatch a mouthful of fresh air.

ANNE: I thought it would never stop raining; I can't do without my daily walk.

NANCY: I've often seen you striding towards the town, and longed to put on my cloak and join you.

ANNE: And why didn't you?

NANCY: My mother always manages to find something useful for me to do instead.

ANNE: So how did you elude her today?

MARIANNE: Well, we've had no letter from Marianne in several weeks, so when we spotted you through the kitchen window I told Mother that I'd run after you to get some news secondhand.

ANNE: And was that not indeed why you ran after me?

NANCY: I usually have more than one reason for whatever I do. Will your aunt be angry to see you walking with another farmer's daughter?

ANNE: I am at perfect liberty to walk with a chimney-sweep if I choose. Not that the cases are alike. In that pretty gown you'd be an ornament on any arm. I hope the rain holds off, though, or you'll be soaked to the skin.

NANCY: Oh I dare say someone might shelter me under her cloak.

ANNE: If you asked very nicely.

NANCY: But as it is presently not raining, there is no need. Tell me, *do* you have any news of my sister?

ANNE: None at all. Her last letter was three weeks ago.

NANCY: I used to think Marianne and you very silly about each other, but that seems to have blown over.

ANNE: Silly in what way?

NANCY: Passionate about the slightest things. Remember the time you two had a tiff, and you tried to make your peace with a bag of barley sugars? She refused to even taste one, and you burst into tears on the spot.

ANNE: I had quite forgotten. So it's your impression that Marianne and I have outgrown all that?

NANCY: There has been some improvement. I suppose it's a side effect of age.

ANNE: Age?

NANCY: Well, twenty-eight is hardly young. Marianne is settled in married life, and you are almost the mistress of Shibden Hall.

ANNE: Master, please. They stare at us as we pass, you know.

NANCY: Who do?

ANNE: The townsfolk.

NANCY: Oh, they're nobody.

ANNE: Once in Leeds I was waiting by the mail coach, and two bad women took it into their heads that I was a man. One of them gave me a knock on the breast and tried to follow me. Her friend shouted out – can you guess what she said?

NANCY: No.

ANNE: She shouted, 'Does your cock stand?' Have I shocked you?

NANCY: Nothing shocks me.

ANNE: You see, Nancy, I am used to being stared and jeered at in the street, but you are not, and it could happen to you too if you walk with me.

NANCY: That is a risk I will have to take.

ANNE: Will you not be ashamed of me?

NANCY: People like you make their own rules.

ANNE: You're not answering my question.

NANCY: You won't take to wearing trousers, will you? The occasional hat or cane, and your splendid cloak, they can be carried off with style, but trousers would be –

ANNE: *(Interrupts.)* No trousers. You have my word on it.

NANCY: Then I will walk with you again, if I may.

ANNE: The pleasure is all mine.

NANCY: Not all.

ANNE writes in her diary.

ANNE: 'Slept with Tib again on this visit. I had three very good kisses. She had…not a very a good one. She assured me it was not important. In the middle of the night, Tib leaned over and whispered in my ear, 'Do you love me, Anne? Do you love me, damn you?' I pretended to be asleep. Well, what else could I do?'

TIB comes in.

ANNE: I called on Dr Simpson today…

TIB: The whites?

ANNE: How – don't say I've passed it on to you?

TIB: No, but I have noticed you scratching madly whenever you thought I wasn't looking, and you left your uterine syringe in the bureau.

ANNE: I didn't want to worry you until I was sure.

TIB: Its source is that lecher Charlie Lawton, I presume.

ANNE: I hope his privates rot away.

TIB: Anne!

ANNE: The doctor's examination was so humiliating. He averted his gaze and poked his hand up my skirt as if opening a drain. Then he asked if I was married, and I said 'No, thank God,' without thinking. So I told him that I must have caught the infection from a married friend whose husband was dissipated, because I remembered visiting the water closet just after her.

TIB: Oh dear. I believe it's a tedious business.

ANNE: I must take sulphate of zinc twice daily, the doctor said, and rub mercury into my skin. I have tried to take precautions, Tibs, the times I've been with you.

TIB: I noticed. Don't fret, love, we shall be as careful as we can. And speaking of illness, how was Nantz Brown this morning?

ANNE: Oh, not half so unwell as I had heard. I think she simply wanted a visitor.

TIB: I spotted the pair of you stealing away after tea the other afternoon.

ANNE: We only went to the drawing room for a game of chess.

TIB: Ah, but a lot of coquetting can get done over a chess table.

ANNE: So you've noticed? I thought it was just my tainted imagination, but no, the girl is making a dead set at me.

TIB: To which you return no encouragement, of course.

ANNE: Well, one must be civil.

TIB: One must.

ANNE: And she is rather delicious. And she sometimes makes me think of…what I should not.

TIB: It's understandable. Is she a forward girl?

ANNE: Let's put it this way: she has an instinctive grasp of how to play her part. She draws me out, she leads me on…she asks me to tie her ribbons, for God's sake. If I chose to persevere, I think I could have her on what terms I pleased.

TIB: And she wouldn't run blubbing to Mama?

ANNE: Never. She has too much pride for that.

TIB: Well then, you should take the first opportunity of giving the girl a little kiss to see how she likes it.

ANNE: I already have.

TIB: When?

ANNE: When we were playing chess, I let her buy her queen back with a kiss. A quick one, but moist.

TIB: Was it like this?

Halfway through the kiss, ANNE turns her face away.

ANNE: No, it wasn't a bit like that. It was a little soft one with our teeth closed.

TIB: You'll have to educate her.

ANNE: All this is a joke, isn't it? Tib?

TIB: That depends on your sense of adventure.

ANNE: But you would mind, wouldn't you, if anything did happen with Nantz? You mind about Marianne, even though you try to hide it.

TIB: Nancy is an amusement. Nothing worth being jealous of.

ANNE: Well then, if anything were to happen, you would be more to blame than I. But nothing will, because my life has been made complicated enough by just two beautiful women.

ANNE enters the Browns's house.

ANNE: Nancy, your mother said I'd find you here.

NANCY: Come in. I've been packing my trunks for Sheffield.

ANNE: Bridesmaid again?

NANCY: One more time, and you shall have to acknowledge me as an old maid.

ANNE: Will it be long before you return to Halifax?

NANCY: Why, would anyone miss me?

ANNE: Very possibly.

NANCY: What are you staring at?

ANNE: Your frill, it's a little crooked. There, that's better.

NANCY: Thank you.

ANNE: Do you think me rude, Nantz?

NANCY: A little.

ANNE: Odd?

NANCY: I'm used to you by now.

ANNE: Would you prefer me to be different?

NANCY: Never. I like you as you are. I don't think you have ever fully remarked how much I like you.

ANNE: Well, you have always been assured of my esteem and high opinion.

NANCY: I don't want your esteem and high opinion. I would rather another word.

ANNE: You're swimming out of your depth, Nantz Brown.

NANCY: Then hold out your hand.

ANNE: You're too cold for my kind of life.

NANCY: Cold, am I? This is just a mask. I could drop it at any time and show you my true face.

ANNE: No doubt you could, did circumstances not forbid it.

NANCY: Which circumstances?

ANNE: All of them.

NANCY: There is only one circumstance in our way, and it begins with an M. And she is far away and need never know.

ANNE: It is a circumstance I cannot forget.

NANCY: For one night you could.

ANNE: I suppose…for one night, I could forget anything.

ANNE writes in her diary.

ANNE: 'It was the sheets that upset me. The last time I slept in that bed was with Marianne, over a month ago. She had bad cramps: her sobs woke me in the middle of the night, and I remember rubbing her belly with my palm until the pain went away. Today I woke at five, and found myself on the left side of the bed, where Marianne usually sleeps. I looked down at the sheet just beside my hip, and it bore the faint, brown mark of her blood. I could feel Nancy's warmth behind my back, but I got out of bed without looking at her and dressed in the next room. What a paltry, lust-ridden creature I am, that I cannot wait a few more years for the woman I love. God have mercy on me and clean my heart. I had expected to feel low today, but not that low. Strictly speaking, I know the word 'incest' is not appropriate, there being no link of marriage or blood. Nor does 'infidelity' fit, exactly, since I never made Marianne any vows. And why should I worry about Christian taboos when according to the best authorities I am damned for all eternity anyway?'

ANNE, in bed with TIB, gets out and starts dressing.

TIB: Oh, my head. What time is it?

ANNE: Late.

TIB: What's the day like?

ANNE: Chilly.

TIB: Come back to bed, Master Lister, it's warm in here. What are you putting your boots on for?

ANNE: I have to interview a new farmhand.

TIB: I've seen practically nothing of you all week. I might as well have stayed at home and written you a witty letter.

ANNE: I'm sorry you feel neglected, but I have been busy.

TIB: If you choose to fritter away your time on petty chores and parish duties, what can I say?

ANNE: Well, Tib, lying in bed all day reading last year's *Ladies' Almanack* and taking vast quantities of snuff has never appealed to me.

TIB: How is it that you are constantly finding fault with me, and never with darling Marianne?

ANNE: It's different when one is in love.

TIB: So did you enjoy her sister?

ANNE is thrown by that. Then regains control.

ANNE: Not particularly. She made me do all the work.

TIB: The girl's a little inexperience. Give her time.

ANNE: It won't happen again. Tib, why did you push me into it?

TIB: Don't blame me. You're a grown woman. I did hope it might make you a little more realistic. Sometimes your romantic dedication to the unattainable Mrs Lawton turns my stomach.

ANNE: You're jealous!

TIB: I'm ten years past being jealous. As you friend, I hate to watch you waste your life on a fantasy. Marianne is a happily married woman, and her husband is not going to drop dead on request.

ANNE: However long it takes, I shall wait for her. What else can I do?

TIB: Oh, run away to Paris. Become a lion tamer. Come and live with me.

ANNE: I am grateful for the offer, but you and I don't suit.

TIB: How can you be so sure? You've never really looked at me.

ANNE: What do you mean?

TIB: Every time you turn your gaze in my direction, a kind of fog intervenes. All you can see are the many ways in which I am not, and never will be, like Marianne.

ANNE: Tibs, that's not true. You've always been very dear to me.

TIB: I could get that kind of affection from a lapdog.

ANNE: Not affection, then. Love.

TIB: How unwillingly you drag the word to your lips. Let's just call it friendship, shall we?

ANNE: You must agree that we're better off living apart and paying frequent visits. This arrangement keeps boredom at bay.

TIB: No doubt you've discussed the matter fully with Marianne. Does she know about us?

ANNE: I hope not. She thinks of you simply as my oldest friend.

TIB: A fairly accurate description.

ANNE: No, it's not that I'm ashamed of our connection, but I would rather Marianne was kept ignorant of it.

TIB: If we can bear the truth, I fail to see why she needs protection from it.

ANNE: She's more fragile than we are.

TIB: Fragile? Marianne?

ANNE: You must never take it upon yourself to enlighten her without consulting me.

TIB: Oh, I wouldn't. I know my place, Freddikins.

ANNE: I beg your pardon?

TIB: It's your pet name, isn't it? It suits you.

ANNE: How did you learn it?

TIB: Could I have seen it on a scrap of paper you left lying around? I think the phrase went, *(Putting on a lisp.)* 'Darling Freddy, I miss you so dreadfully.'

ANNE: You opened my bureau and read Marianne's letters.

TIB: Only the top few. They soon palled. Epistolary eloquence is not the girl's forte, is it?

ANNE: You interfering old hag.

TIB: Well how else do you suggest I pass my days on this godforsaken estate?

ANNE: I'm not listening.

TIB: You're out all morning harassing foxes, and at night, if I'm lucky, I get one halfhearted kiss before you're snoring –

ANNE storms out.

Writes in her diary.

ANNE: 'Passing near Lawton Hall, I stayed the night. We all behaved uncommonly well. Charles has been most civil to me ever since I prevented Marianne from leaving him. He retired at ten. My room was next to theirs. Marianne came in and we had three kisses each, very quietly. Through the wall we could hear Charles snoring all the while. Then she got dressed again and went in to her husband. He is in the best of health, he says. Unlike my uncle, who is not to have any more solid food, and doesn't know us, these days, after his half pint of laudanum. What an ungrateful cub I am, that I can feel no love for the poor old fellow. Today I got the gardener and five boys to cut the last of the elms into logs, which kind of work always excites my manly feelings. When I saw a pretty young maid go up the lane, I had a foolish fancy about taking her into a shed on Skircoat Moor and being connected with her. I was supposing myself in breeches and having a penis. Just a small one. A parcel has arrived from Tib, bearing a little alabaster cupid from London. I got her picture out of the bureau and looked at it for ten minutes with considerable emotion. I almost managed to persuade myself that I could settle down and be happy with her. I thought of several reasons: Tib's social connections are good, her fortune considerable, her affection beyond doubt, and in bed she is excellent. But my heart has never listened to reasons.'

MARIANNE looks up guiltily as ANNE comes in.

MARIANNE: I didn't mean to pry. I was just looking for some writing paper and I stumbled across it.

ANNE: An old diary of mine.

MARIANNE: On my wedding night, you wrote about my selfishness, infidelity, the waste of it all.

ANNE: I was distraught. I don't even remember what I wrote. You can't be angry with me now.

MARIANNE: I'm not angry. I just never knew till now how much my marriage cost you.

ANNE: What would have been the use in ranting and raving? Your mother was already sewing your trousseau.

MARIANNE: If I'd known all you felt, I couldn't have gone through with the wedding.

ANNE: What else could we have done?

MARIANNE: Eloped together, like those Irishwomen in Wales.

ANNE: I told you, the Ladies of Llangollen had family money as well as a faithful servant. We couldn't even have rented a cottage.

MARIANNE: I'd have lived with you in a coal hole.

ANNE: Let it go, love. I'm sorry about the diary.

MARIANNE: I don't think I deserved some of the comments. 'Utterly self-absorbed and worldly' – that's a little harsh.

ANNE: I'll tear the damned page out, there. After all these years, can you doubt how much I love you?

MARIANNE: When we go to church, you ogle every girl in sight.

ANNE: I do not ogle. I merely observe.

MARIANNE: How can I be sure you don't pay court to all the local ladies when I'm out of the way at Lawton?

ANNE: Because you know me.

MARIANNE: You never promise, though I have often vowed fidelity to you.

ANNE: Promising comes easy to you, Marianne. Remember the day you promised to love, honour and obey Charles Lawton? I'm sorry, the words just slipped out. It's the damned itching, it sets my nerves on edge.

MARIANNE: I don't mind your hurting me if it does anything to comfort you.

ANNE: It doesn't. You have to forgive me.

MARIANNE: Always.

ANNE: Do you remember what today is?

MARIANNE: No.

ANNE: The eighth anniversary of our first night together.

MARIANNE: Eight years? I'm getting old.

ANNE: And more beautiful by the day. Listen, tonight I'm willing to promise anything to make you happy.

MARIANNE: I don't need promises. Just love me.

ANNE; I think perhaps I can manage that. Where would Milady like to be loved?

MARIANNE: You know.

ANNE: I haven't the faintest idea. On your ear perhaps? Your elbow? I know, your knee.

MARIANNE: The place.

ANNE: What place? I know nothing about a place.

MARIANNE: Don't tease me, Freddy, not tonight.

ANNE: But I am perfectly willing to touch any lady who specifies where and how she wishes to be touched.

MARIANNE: You know I hate it when you make me ask.

ANNE: Ask for what? What is the word you're looking for?

MARIANNE: There is no word for it.

ANNE: Well say please then.

MARIANNE: Oh take your hands off me!

NANCY and TIB sit outdoors.

NANCY: How can you let the sun full in your face? I should be afraid of getting freckled.

TIB: At your age I was equally vain, but nowadays I have no complexion to protect.

NANCY: I'm all bones, though. I'd swap my complexion for your figure any day.

TIB: You don't see to be doing too badly with the one you've got.

NANCY: Anne told you, didn't she?

TIB: She didn't need to tell me.

NANCY: You're one too, I suspect.

TIB: One what?

NANCY: One of her ladies.

TIB: You make it sound like quite a crowd. There are only three of us.

NANCY: Three that we know of.

TIB: I think I know Anne pretty well by now.

NANCY: Were you and she – was it always that way between you, even before my sister?

TIB: No, just the last year or so.

NANCY: I suppose, between you two, it is more a matter of friendship than of love.

TIB: I have loved Anne Lister since the day she strode into my parlour bearing a large, muddy clump of white heather. And that was ten years ago. So yes, it could be called a matter of love.

NANCY: I didn't mean to offend you. I didn't know.

TIB: She's snobbish, and deceitful, and sometimes cruel, but I don't expect I'll ever grow out of loving her.

NANCY: I quite agree about the snobbery. I could scarcely believe my ears the other evening when she had the family pedigree brought down and read aloud.

TIB: It was not directed at you. She does that on the first Sunday of every month.

NANCY: I am not exactly sorry for what I did – with Anne – but I do hope I haven't hurt you.

TIB: Not in the least. Only love arouses my jealousy, and there was none of that between you.

NANCY: I suppose not.

TIB: You simply wanted to steal a slice of your big sister's cake.

NANCY: Is that all it was?

TIB: Don't ask me, I wasn't there. Anne was your first, I presume?

NANCY: Oh yes. And my last, I expect.

TIB: Was it so disappointing?

NANCY: Not at all. But it shook me. I felt as if I were being gently dragged towards the edge of a cliff.

TIB: I know that feeling.

NANCY: I think perhaps I may marry after all. It would be so comfortable. Sam Waterhouse would have me at the bat of an eyelid. What do you advise?

TIB: Oh, I never give advice, having made too many mistakes of my own. But I do wish you luck.

ANNE is having a multiple orgasm as quietly as possible.

ANNE: Oh. Oh my good God. Oh. Oh. Oh Marianne.

MARIANNE: Sh, you'll wake your aunt.

ANNE: I don't care if I wake every horse in the stable! Do you think she heard?

MARIANNE: She couldn't have, all the way down the end of the passage.

ANNE: No one else ever gave me a kiss like that.

MARIANNE: What do you mean?

ANNE: What?

MARIANNE: You said no one else.

ANNE: No love, I said no one.

MARIANNE: You said no one else ever gave you a kiss like that. Well, what kind of kiss have they given you then?

ANNE: Love, you know I used to kiss Eliza when we were at school.

MARIANNE: Not that kind of kiss. You meant body kisses, down there.

ANNE: I didn't. You're confusing me. I don't know what I meant.

MARIANNE: You said I was the first ever.

ANNE: You were, I swear it. You were the first woman who ever did that to me.

MARIANNE: And since?

ANNE: Since what?

MARIANNE: Since me, during me. Have you been with another woman?

ANNE: No.

MARIANNE: I don't believe you. It's Tib, isn't it?

ANNE: Of course it is.

MARIANNE: So you've been betraying me all along.

ANNE: Oh wake up, Marianne. For the first time in your life be frank with yourself. I've been no more unfaithful than you.

MARIANNE: I never did.

ANNE: What do you call your marriage? Any binding engagement between us was cancelled when you walked up that aisle.

MARIANNE: It's different with a man.

ANNE: It is not.

MARIANNE: How would you know? You've never been with a man. You don't know how…nothing it is. A damp fumble in the dark. An insignificant spasm.

ANNE: Insignificant?

MARIANNE: It never really touched me. You know that, and yet you've let a woman inside you, the place I thought belonged to me.

ANNE: It's my body. It belongs to none of you.

MARIANNE: Then I don't want it.

ANNE: I never deliberately lied to you, except by omission. You never asked. I thought perhaps you knew.

MARIANNE: Did you really? And what else was I expected to know? How many more women are there?

ANNE: No more. Not any more.

MARIANNE tugs off her ring.

MARIANNE: You had better have this back.

ANNE: Don't.

MARIANNE: Consider yourself quite at liberty. You are not mine and I am not yours.

ANNE snatches the ring. Then softens, and reaches for MARIANNE's hand, and puts it back on.

ANNE: Yes you are.

MARIANNE: Yes. Yes I am. It's myself I should blame. If we had our time over again, I swear I'd never marry. I'd not leave you on your own, to be tempted by other women. I was a mere girl when I walked up that aisle. I knew nothing of my own heart.

ANNE: Sh. You could still have all my love, Marianne, if you asked for it.

MARIANNE: I've not been a very good wife to you, Freddy, have I?

ANNE: Don't say that.

TIB writes to ANNE.

TIB: 'My dear Anne, the best thing to combat the smell of sickness in a house is dried lavender, sprinkled in the fire. Yes, I did see Nancy's bulging diamond on my last visit. As you say, that Sam Waterhouse does not deserve her, but she tells me she's made him promise her an extraordinary sum of pin money. Can Marianne really not contrive to visit you for another three months? You write that you are "worn out from pining for the unattainable", which is quite understandable. The important thing is to know exactly what you want. As a woman who has for many years known what she wants, and known too that she will never get it, I am, I think you will agree, in the best position to give advice. Yours, as ever, Tib.'

ANNE wakes, curled around MARIANNE. She pulls the blankets back to admire her.

ANNE: So that's why you blew out the candle!

MARIANNE starts to wake.

ANNE: I should have known you were hiding something. I've never known you to want to do it in the dark. How many months?

MARIANNE pulls the blanket around her.

MARIANNE: Five gone, four to go. You always knew it could happen.

ANNE: It had been so many years, I'd stopped fearing it. Twenty-eight is far too old for a first child, everyone knows that.

MARIANNE: I'll be all right.

ANNE: And I'm not going to stand around watching you swell up like a brood mare.

MARIANNE: What on earth can we do about it?

ANNE: I can go.

MARIANNE: Don't make any rash decisions, my love. This doesn't have to come between us.

ANNE: You don't understand me at all, do you? Sharing you with Charles is bad enough. Do you think I'd stoop to compete for your attention with a puking infant?

MARIANNE: I was going to ask you to sponsor it.

ANNE: Oh, were you? What kind of fairy godmother would I make, grudging the child every soft glance from its mother?

MARIANNE: I don't know. I never expected you to take it to heart so. After all these years…

ANNE: That's the whole point. The years have worn me out.

MARIANNE: Am I altered in your eyes?

ANNE: You're all you ever were. But you're not just you now, are you? You'll be choosing a name soon. Another little Charlie, perhaps? A royal George?

MARIANNE: Stop.

ANNE: Just promise me it won't be Freddy.

MARIANNE: I…

ANNE: Promise.

MARIANNE: I can't promise anything. It's the father's right.

ANNE: He has no right to any of this.

MARIANNE: You and I have come through so many storms, I don't see why we can't weather this one.

ANNE: If you don't see, I can't explain it.

MARIANNE: Well, whatever we christen it, it can't be more of a baby than you! Whining, griping, that's all there's been these last few years. I am sick of feeling like the rope in a village tug-o'-war. At last I have a chance of giving Charles what he wants: here it is, it's simple, it's right inside me. But you – I'll never be able to give you what you want.

ANNE: All I want is you.

MARIANNE: That's a damn lie. You want money and freedom and a wife and a mistress, a string of mistresses. You want me, and Tib, and Nancy, and every pretty servant you lay eyes on.

ANNE: Nancy?

MARIANNE: I wasn't going to say anything. I was going to be a good wife and not stir up trouble. But what am I to think when my sister, my own little sister, has to go to the doctor with a mysterious infection?

ANNE: Oh God forgive us. Did she tell you she was sick?

MARIANNE: My mother told me. Nancy convinced her it's easily caught by drinking out of someone else's glass.

ANNE: I'm sorry. For everything.

MARIANNE: Do you think we're being punished?

ANNE: I don't know.

MARIANNE: Sweetheart, I don't think I can do this any longer. I'm coming apart.

ANNE: Perhaps you'll find it easier to love me a few hundred miles away. It can't be more than a few weeks now.

MARIANNE: Do you intend to go right after the funeral? Paris?

ANNE: Of course. Then, who knows.

MARIANNE: I promise I won't let the baby be called Freddy. Nobody else is Freddy.

ANNE, wearing a mourning veil, writes in her diary.

ANNE: 'It takes a surprisingly short time to pack away thirty years of living. A bare week since my uncle's funeral, and my whole life has changed. Who knows but there may be women in Paris like myself? At any rate, I am determined to have a gay old time, and feel young before I have to be old. I've left a forwarding address with my aunt, and insured my life in favour of Marianne in case I should die on my travels. I wonder if I will miss my aunt. I think she would like me to fix on a companion before she dies. I did once try to tell her of my nature, but I don't think she understood. 'Aunt,' I said one evening, 'do you know that I prefer ladies to gentlemen?' 'Quite so, my dear,' she replied; 'ladies make much cleaner guests.' These idle memories will make me late.

All I need now is a book for the journey to Dover. I could take Rousseau's *Confessions*; I never did get past chapter one. *(Reads from the first page.)* 'I know my own heart. I am made like no one I have ever seen; I dare believe myself to be different from everyone in the world.' Pompous old lecher – but I know what he means. I feel like a girl again, waiting for everything to begin. Each morning I woke up I felt myself to be poised on the blink of an adventure, a story, almost a romance. And now I'm on my own again, as I have always been.'

Curtain.

LADIES AND GENTLEMEN

Ladies and Gentlemen

Ladies and Gentlemen is a more-or-less-true story.
The time span and sequence of events have been altered,
and backgrounds invented for some of the characters,
but otherwise everything fits the play's main sources:

'Stranger than Fiction: The True Story of Annie
Hindle's Two Marriages,' *The Sun* (New York),
27 December 1891;

Franklin Graham, article on Annie Hindle under the
heading 'Dominion Theatre', *Histrionic Montreal*, 1902;

Imogen Holbrook Vivian, *A Biographical Sketch of the Life
of Charles A. S. Vivian*, 1904;

W. A. Swanberg, *Jim Fisk: The Career of an Improbable
Rascal, 1959*;

Laurence Senelick, 'The Evolution of the Male
Impersonator in the Nineteenth-Century Popular Stage',
Essays in Theatre, 1:1 (1982);

and files of clippings on the careers of Gilbert Saroney,
Charles Vivian, Tony Pastor and Ella Wesner, in the
Billy Rose Theatre Archive of the New York Public
Library.

The songs are a mixture of Victorian vaudeville numbers
adapted by, and original lyrics by, Emma Donoghue.

Ladies and Gentlemen was commissioned by Glasshouse
Productions and the Irish Arts Council, and first produced
by Glasshouse, directed by David Byrne, at Project Arts
Theatre, Dublin, 18 April to 4 May 1996.

First published by New Island Books as *Ladies and
Gentlemen*, 1998.

Dramatis Personae

ANNIE HINDLE an English-American male impersonator

TONY PASTOR an Italian-American vaudeville manager

GILBERT SARONEY an American female impersonator

ELLA WESNER an American stage dresser,
then male impersonator

PIANIST (can be replaced with recorded music)

ACT ONE

It is January 1891, in the dressing-room of a New York vaudeville theatre, several hours before show time. MUSIC: 'Could I See My Darling Again' theme plays faintly. Enter ANNIE in dress, coat and wig, carrying a quilt, carpet bag and box of letters. She puts her luggage down and takes off her coat. Rummaging through the skip, she finds a tailcoat, and holds it up against herself.

ANNIE: Ladies. Gentlemen.

> *Offstage music accompanies her softly as she sings 'Fair Irish Girl' to herself.*

ANNIE: *Talk not of damsels of sweet sunny France,*
Cool English maidens so haughty and grand,
Turkey's young daughters with dark flashing glance
Can ne'er equal those of that dear native land –
My fair Irish girl, dear Irish girl…

> *She lets the song trail off. Taking her bag over to the dressing-table, she unpacks her make-up box and hand mirror, and takes off her wig. As she puts on eyebrow stick, she addresses her reflection.*

ANNIE: It's a simple story, all told, ladies and gentlemen. Not so much 'Lost and Found' as 'Found and Lost'. Tell you the truth, I'd rather sing something else, but the Manager Upstairs won't have it. He fills in his big show book any crazy way he pleases, and he don't take advice from mere performers. What am I doing here?

> *Enter TONY, still in street clothes, holding his show book.*

TONY: You made it.

ANNIE: Weren't you expecting me to?

TONY: Of course.

> *He is not sure whether to hug her. She offers him a handshake.*

TONY: Gilbert and Ella won't be in for a few hours yet.

ANNIE: I thought I oughta give myself plenty of time.

TONY: Ah yes, now about a dresser: you wouldn't consider sharing Gretel?

ANNIE: No. I can do it myself. Really.

TONY: Whatever you like. How's the voice?

ANNIE: It'll do. How're the houses these days?

TONY: We should fill the two thousand by eight o'clock. I've put you down as the opener.

This is the hardest position, so she thanks him ironically.

ANNIE: You're too kind.

TONY: Not getting nervous, are we?

ANNIE: I can't speak for you, Tony, but I'm all right.

TONY: That's the ticket! Keep the pecker up.

ANNIE: Nailed to the roof.

TONY starts to go, then turns back.

TONY: Nearly forgot. In honor of your comeback I have composed a brand new introductory number.

ANNIE puts on a dreadful French accent.

ANNIE: *Pour moi?*

TONY: I was up all night getting it to rhyme.

He hums the instrumental opening to himself, then launches into 'Roll Up'.

TONY: *Roll up, roll up,*
You never saw such freaks!
Come see Pastor's Vaudeville Troupe
Get up to all their tricks.

ANNIE: Freaks?

TONY: You know what I mean. Novelties.

He sings on.

TONY: *We got German marches, Spanish serenades,*
Coon tunes, Oirish jamborees,
French pirouettes and military parades,
Plus tightrope cyclists if you please.
All the folk who make you laugh –
Mr Billiard Ball and the Living Corpse,
Handsome dames who get chopped in half,
The Sure-Shot Girl and the Human Horse.

ANNIE: Who's he?

TONY: Young feller, big teeth, signed up since your time.

ANNIE: My time?

TONY: The last time you were with the Troupe, I mean. Shall I go on?

ANNIE: Why not?

TONY: *Pastor's Vaudeville offers all you've*
Dreamed of on the sly...

ANNIE: Tony?

TONY: What?

ANNIE: I've got a touch of headache.

TONY: Say no more.

This time he gets almost to the exit before turning back.

TONY: I'll just show you how I'm going to key them up for you, shall I?

He reads from his show book.

TONY: 'Ladies and gentlemen! We are gathered here today to witness the return to the vaudeville stage of the ex-tra-ord-in-ary Annie Hindle, the Amazonian androgyne, described recently in the popular press as "a man's widow and a woman's widower".'

ANNIE: Cut that bit.

TONY: Now hold on just one minute.

ANNIE: I won't have her used as publicity. Cut that line or you'll be introducing an empty stage.

TONY: You've lost none of your temperament, I see.

He scores out the line.

TONY: 'As a child, little Miss Hindle broke the heart of Hertfordshire potters with her lisping rendition of "Come Into the Garden, Maud".'

ANNIE: They know all that rags-to-riches stuff already.

TONY: Not to put too fine a point on it, Annie, but there's a lot of youngsters out there ain't never heard of you.

ANNIE: It's only been five years.

TONY: That's forever in show business.

ANNIE: It doesn't matter whether they remember me or not, so long as they clap. I know how to do my job, Tony. This isn't my first comeback.

TONY: Yeah, it's becoming quite a habit. You ran off to get married the first time as well.

ANNIE: That was hardly the same.

TONY: At least this time you're back by invitation. At least this time you're not barging back onto my stage without so much as a by-your-leave.

Once he's exited, ANNIE takes off her bodice, and tries out the tailcoat and cane.

ANNIE: Miss Annie Hindle? You must have been misinformed, ladies and gentlemen. Why would I have a girl's name when I'm as hot-blooded a male as ever twirled a cane?

She mutters the first line of 'A Real Man', checking she remembers the words.

ANNIE: *I'm an elegant swell, a flash young spark…*

> *Now she sings, unaccompanied, trying to recall the gesture to go with each line, as she sang it at her first comeback, in 1880.*

ANNIE: *I'm an elegant swell, a flash young spark,*
I take snuff and I'm partial to rum.
By day a roué, a gay dog in the dark,
I can whistle as easy as hum.
So why do the ladies neglect me?
Shun my embraces, be coy?
I wish some kind female would tell me
Why I'm still a bachelor boy.

> *She rubs one eye wearily, then goes to sit down at her dressing-table. When she picks up the mirror, the smudge reminds her of a black eye. MUSIC: music-box version of 'Could I See My Darling Again' leads us back into that comeback night in 1880. Enter younger TONY (in a different suit), GILBERT (in a dress) and ELLA (in dress and apron).*

ELLA: There she is.

GILBERT: I couldn't believe my ears.

TONY: How dare you have the audacity to barge back onto my stage without so much as a by-your-leave?

ANNIE: Evening, all.

GILBERT: My favorite gentleman!

ANNIE: My best girl! *(To TONY.)* What kind of welcome do you call that?

TONY: What do you expect? Six months ago you flashed your wedding ring and kissed goodbye. I've got other star acts to top the bill.

ANNIE: I heard. Little Tich and his Miniature Poodle. Mad Murphy and his Forty Instruments. Oh, and I nearly forgot: the Bumblebee Boy.

TONY: Don't knock him till you've seen him.

ANNIE: Maybe I could work it into my act. Bzzzz! Whatcha think, El? No stings on me, but I have been known to bite.

ELLA: Get your paws off me. So where's the distinguished thespian Mr Charles Vivian, then?

ANNIE: I haven't a notion.

GILBERT: Honeymoon wasn't all it should have been?

ANNIE: Precious little honey, dear boy, and not a glimpse of the moon.

TONY: I tell you, Hindle, we've been doing just fine without you. Plenty of pants on seats. Gilbert's been wowing them with his new pirouettes, Ella hasn't been coming in to work with red eyes no more –

ANNIE: *(Interrupts.)* Heartless hussy!

TONY: You could at least have wired to ask did I want you back.

ANNIE: It was meant to be a surprise.

ELLA: Never could resist the big entrances and exits.

TONY: So will your lawful wedded let you stay the whole season?

ANNIE: I'll sign up for as long as you'll have me.

TONY: Then I'd better draft a new show bill.

He dashes off, then turns back.

TONY: Does Charles Vivian even know you're here?

ANNIE: Ask no questions and you'll hear no lies.

TONY: Well, I'm just as happy not poking into private business.

He exits.

GILBERT: I didn't think anything was private in this business.

ELLA: So whatcha do with your ring?

ANNIE: Bottom of my bag. I was going to chuck it in the Hudson, but I hate to waste good gold.

ELLA: With a bank balance like yours, you could afford the gesture.

ANNIE: Ah, but I gotta save for my retirement. So the Pastor Troupe's had the nerve to survive a whole season without me, then?

GILBERT: Barely. I've pined for our duets.

ELLA: Gilbert prefers duets because he only has to learn half the words.

GILBERT: I'd be happy to learn them if they were worth learning. My head was not designed for doggerel.

ELLA: To be honest, we've been a little short on stars. *(To GILBERT.)* You and me ought do a *pas de deux.*

She does a wobbly arabesque. He fails to support her by the waist. ANNIE looks unimpressed.

ELLA: My talent is wasted down here.

GILBERT: Most nights, Tony has to fill in himself with three encores. What I've never understood is, the man claims to know fifteen hundred songs, but he always finishes with 'Hold Your Own'.

ANNIE: I remember that one.

She plays TONY, pompous, singing unaccompanied.

ANNIE: *If the world it goes against you,*
And you're scrabbling for a bone,

ANNIE/GILBERT: *Why that's the time, me laddy buck,*
To grip and hold your own!

They clutch imaginary giant penises, and fall about laughing.

ANNIE: So has Tony been working you into the ground, poor boy? You're looking a bit shadowy around the eyes.

ELLA: Too many late nights.

GILBERT: I've been to Mr Oscar Wilde's lecture on Aesthetics twice this week.

ELLA: And he still can't spell it. *(To ANNIE.)* Speaking of eyes, that's quite a shiner you've got there.

ANNIE: Does it show?

ELLA: Only to an expert. Come here.

She takes out her powder to cover ANNIE's black eye.

GILBERT, made uncomfortable by this hint of violence, drags the dressmaker's dummy forward.

GILBERT: Say, have you been introduced to the newest member of the family?

ANNIE: Now there's a fine figure of a woman. What's she called?

GILBERT: I've been toying with Angelique.

ELLA: Like that ventriloquist in Denver with the doves that wouldn't go back in the box.

GILBERT: That was Angelina.

ELLA: All done.

She releases ANNIE.

ANNIE: I've got it: Miss Dimity.

GILBERT: 'Miss Dimity, I presume?' Maybe I could bring her on stage for a waltz tomorrow.

ANNIE pulls out a cut-throat razor.

ELLA: What do you think you're doing?

GILBERT throws himself on his knees.

GILBERT: Don't do it! If not for yourself, then live for us.

ANNIE expertly shaves her upper lip.

ANNIE: I want a moustache.

ELLA: I've got half a dozen in my box.

ANNIE: But I want one of my own.

GILBERT: For real?

ANNIE: I was talking to this barber johnny on a train the other day. He said the blade stimulates the follicles, and eventually I won't have to fake it at all.

ELLA: Urgh!

ANNIE: Did someone ask your opinion?

TONY dashes in with the new show bill.

TONY: Annie? What's going on?

ELLA: You don't want to know.

TONY: You get that veil done yet, Ella?

ELLA: How many hands have I got here? And what about an assistant? Especially now I've Annie to dress too.

TONY: All right, all right, I'll put a notice on the stage door. *(To ANNIE.)* I'm billing you in two-inch capitals as 'The Royal Return of the Monarch of Male Impersonation'.

GILBERT's face falls.

ANNIE: We can talk business tomorrow.

TONY: Not an hour in the place before she's chucking her weight around...

ELLA: So what's new?

GILBERT runs to catch TONY as he exits.

GILBERT: Tony? Tony, I thought maybe you said *I* could headline tomorrow.

> *ANNIE hears that, and is troubled. She turns to ELLA, who is busying herself with mending a bridal veil.*

ANNIE: Well. Here we are alone again.

ELLA: You're better with an audience. So how did you get the black eye, Mrs Vivian?

ANNIE: Walked into a wall.

ELLA: Right.

> *ANNIE goes on the offensive.*

ANNIE: Remember the night I seduced you on the train to San Francisco, with the two salesmen snoring in the other bunks?

ELLA: Huh! You'd never even laid hands on a woman before.

ANNIE: I was always a quick learner.

ELLA: Well, as I recall it, I was the one who did the seducing.

ANNIE: Who undid the first button?

ELLA: Who pushed your hand away and undid three of yours?

ANNIE: We should have known we were too much the same to suit.

ELLA: I knew that much before anything got unbuttoned. I knew we wouldn't last three months and I didn't give a damn.

ANNIE: Did you also know I was going to get married?

ELLA: No. But we were dead and buried by the time Charles Vivian came along.

ANNIE: I guess I just wanted a go at being ordinary.

ELLA: Fat chance.

ANNIE: Stop the damn sewing for a minute. So when I left, were your eyes all red like Tony said?

ELLA: Don't push your luck.

ANNIE: You're looking mighty perky now, I must say.

ELLA: Shows what a lot of beauty sleep will do.

ANNIE: Nah, I reckon there's somebody special in the wings.

ELLA: There might be.

ANNIE: Is it a Mister or a Miss? Presuming you still haven't made up your mind.

ELLA: I'll tell you this much: it's one or the other.

ANNIE: You're such a tease.

ELLA: Not quite forgotten me, then?

ANNIE: Could I?

ELLA starts to feel her up.

ELLA: I'd like to see you try.

ANNIE: You're outrageous.

ELLA: Just my way of saying welcome home.

ANNIE: You don't even want it.

ELLA: I always did go a long way to prove a point.

Enter RYANNY in shabby clothes, exhausted, with a carpet bag and patchwork quilt: they move apart.

RYANNY: Excuse me. Is this where I'm meant to be?

ANNIE: Depends what you're looking for.

RYANNY: I'm the new girl. To help with the clothes and such.

ELLA: I don't believe it.

RYANNY: It's true.

ELLA: How long have I been asking him for an assistant? Come in, come in. Ella Wesner.

ELLA shakes hands with her.

RYANNY: My name is Ryan, Miss Annie Ryan.

ANNIE: Oh that won't do.

RYANNY: I beg your pardon?

ELLA: You can undress Gilbert tonight.

RYANNY: Undress… Gilbert?

ELLA: I gotta finish his veil.

ANNIE: Your name, it won't do at all. We can't have two Annie's in one dressing-room. Miss Annie Hindle, at your service.

ANNIE shakes hands with her.

RYANNY: Pleased to meet you. Miss Wesner, where should I –

ELLA: Ella. Everybody calls me Ella.

RYANNY: I'm sorry.

ELLA: You've done nothing to apologize for. Yet!

ANNIE: Why don't you take the weight off your feet for a minute, Miss Ryan. You look dead beat.

RYANNY: I'm after carrying my bags all the way from Twenty-Fifth Street.

ELLA: From tonight you can lodge with my aunt Trudi just around the corner. No bugs in Trudi Wesner's sheets.

RYANNY: That's nice.

ELLA: No need to be afraid of anything here. Except me!

ANNIE: Guess it all seems sorta crazy behind the scenes, huh?

RYANNY: It's a job.

ANNIE clicks her fingers and addresses ELLA.

ANNIE: I've got it. We could put Annie and Ryan together and call her Ryanny.

ELLA: You cannot go changing the poor girl's name just like that.

RYANNY: I think it's –

ELLA: *(Interrupts RYANNY.)* Let her bully you once and she'll never leave off.

ANNIE: I make one simple suggestion –

RYANNY: *(Interrupts.)* I think Ryanny's a nice name.

ANNIE: There you go!

GILBERT storms in with tomato down his dress. He turns and bawls down the corridor.

GILBERT: Pigs!

ELLA: Don't you scandalize my new assistant.

ANNIE: Miss Ryanny – Mr Gilbert Saroney.

RYANNY struggles to understand that this is a man.

RYANNY: Gilbert?

GILBERT: Delighted, I'm sure.

RYANNY: Should I – can I be helping you out of that, sir?

GILBERT: *(To ANNIE and ELLA.)* Isn't she just the most green-eyed colleen you could imagine?

RYANNY: They're blue, as it happens.

ANNIE: Blue's much better.

GILBERT: If you could start unlacing, dear, I'll see to the damage.

He starts wiping tomato off his dress, but ELLA takes over.

ELLA: Didn't they like your new song, then?

RYANNY is unfastening his skirt, squeamishly.

GILBERT: They're animals out there. They can smell fear at the back of the stalls.

ELLA: I wouldn't be afraid of any audience.

ANNIE: Listen to her!

GILBERT: You should be.

ANNIE: So who's on now?

GILBERT: Big Belle the Contortionist, then Madame Jenny's Opera Juveniles doing excerpts from *Othello*. I passed them on the stairs and one of the little monsters stuck his sword in my knee.

ANNIE: You ever heard the Juveniles, Ryanny?

RYANNY: I've never actually been in a vaudeville theatre.

ELLA: Just the legit?

RYANNY: Not any kind of theatre really.

GILBERT: What possessed you to take this job, then? A den of iniquity is no place for a 'fair Irish girl'.

RYANNY: Neither's the workhouse.

ELLA: On what we dressers earn you'd be forgiven for mistaking them.

ANNIE: Don't start that again.

TONY comes in, smarmy.

TONY: All settled in, Miss Ryan?

RYANNY: Yes sir, thank you again sir.

TONY: Now if anyone bothers you with any rough talk, just you come straight to me. *(Showing off what he thinks is good Latin.)* I see myself as it were in loco parenthesis. Expect you could do with some wages up front, for rent and such?

RYANNY: That'd be lovely.

TONY: Come to my office.

He picks up her bag.

GILBERT: *(To ELLA.)* Did he say 'wages'?

ELLA: He told me he was broke.

GILBERT: Tony?

ELLA: Three weeks he owes me.

GILBERT and ELLA rush out after TONY and RYANNY.

GILBERT: Tony, I'm dying for a little up front!

ANNIE is left alone in the dressing-room, and it is 1891 again. She takes off her skirt, her tailcoat and her women's shoes; she's down to a sleeveless shift and pantaloons. In the skip she finds a pair of trousers with braces; as she holds them up against her she hears TONY offstage practicing the song 'Home'. She gets into trousers, socks and shoes.

TONY: *(Offstage, unaccompanied.) If home is where the heart is,*
Then my place is right here with you.
A man needs no banquets or parties
When he's blessed with a family so true.

After five years of retirement, ANNIE still remembers how to walk in trousers. She pulls up her braces over her shift and starts buttoning up her flies. She sings unaccompanied.

ANNIE: *If home is where the heart is,*
Then my place is right here with you.

Which conjures up another memory: she is in the dressing-room after a performance in 1881. MUSIC: a music-box version of the 'Home' theme. Enter RYANNY in a dresser's apron.

RYANNY: I was wondering.

ANNIE: You were?

RYANNY: Why do you pretend to be a man?

ANNIE: I don't pretend anything. I impersonate men, which is far more demanding than just being one.

RYANNY: But do you like wearing men's clothes?

ANNIE: They're only called that because the fellers got a hold of them first. You bet your sweet life I like them: they've got pockets for everything.

GILBERT comes in, catching the last few lines, with ELLA behind him.

GILBERT: I quite like them myself. You can lose a silver dollar in ten different places on your body.

ELLA: Or in your case, lose a cherry pie.

ANNIE: *(To RYANNY.)* You know in pantomimes... I forgot, you haven't been out much. Well, take it from me, when Vera Vestris goes on the drag in a pantomime, it's just to flash her meaty legs. Whereas I set out to look more man than the men do. The trick is to get the walk right.

GILBERT: Whatcha think, El – have we heard this the full thousand times yet?

ELLA: We could be here all night.

RYANNY: So how do men walk, then?

ANNIE: There you've made your first mistake, because they all walk different ways. The well-bred, well-heeled toff, he stalks along just so. The dirty little street coster, like this.

ELLA: Do a Tony.

ANNIE: Thought you weren't listening because you've heard it all before.

GILBERT: Don't make us beg.

ANNIE: The one, the only, the magnificent maestro of variety theatre, Mr Tony Pastor!

They all clap.

ANNIE: But the one thing they all have in common is that their feet are set well apart.

GILBERT: Let me try.

Walks wide-legged, till he loses his balance.

GILBERT: Oh girls, what'll I do? I'm not a real man!

ANNIE: That hasn't held you back so far.

ELLA: Enough. It's near midnight. *(To GILBERT.)* Are you planning to walk home in that?

ANNIE: Seems a shame to put him into trousers.

GILBERT: I hated it at first, you know.

ANNIE: What?

GILBERT: The whole business: dresses, bonnets, rouge, they made my skin crawl.

ELLA: No!

GILBERT: I wasn't born in a tutu. I was a regular little feller in short pants when my pa tied me into my big sister's dress and pushed me onto the stage.

RYANNY: You poor lad.

GILBERT: That first night on the boards, I wet myself.

ANNIE: Me too.

GILBERT: Luckily the petticoats hid everything. And now they're my second skin. Do you suppose my better three-quarters would object if I came home in a dress?

ANNIE: I dare you. Ten bucks.

GILBERT: It's tempting. But if I ever stepped outside the stage door in my frillies, I'd be horsewhipped out of town.

ANNIE: Never! You could pass for a society dame.

GILBERT: Tosh.

ANNIE: Twaddle.

GILBERT: Poppycock.

ANNIE: Bosh.

GILBERT: Bunkum.

ANNIE: Balderdash.

GILBERT can't think of another word for nonsense.

GILBERT: You win.

ANNIE: How is Mrs Saroney anyway?

GILBERT: Oh, fine.

ELLA: For all he knows.

ANNIE: Have you and the missus ever spent a whole week in each other's company?

GILBERT: What, alone?

RYANNY: Didn't you have a honeymoon?

GILBERT: I don't recall one.

ANNIE: And she doesn't mind your…wanderings?

She is being discreet in front of RYANNY.

GILBERT: Why, Elizabeth wouldn't know what to do with me if I hung around all day, cluttering up the house.

ELLA: Stealing her rouge.

GILBERT: I buy my own. Hers is muck.

ANNIE: It's not what I'd call a marriage.

ELLA: You should talk, Mrs Charles Vivian!

RYANNY is shocked by this.

RYANNY: Are you a married woman, then?

ANNIE: A lawyer might say so, but one wedding don't make a marriage in my book.

RYANNY: But you're still called Miss Annie Hindle.

GILBERT: It's known as a stage name, dear.

ANNIE: I'd be damned if I'd change my own name for that no-good scum of a son-of-a-

RYANNY: *(Interrupts.)* Language!

ANNIE: I beg your pardon.

RYANNY: My aunty Nora ran away from my uncle to Galway for three weeks once.

ELLA pretends to be horrified.

ELLA: No!

RYANNY: He'd gone and sold her chickens on her.

ANNIE: Did she end up going back to him?

RYANNY: Sure where else would she go?

ANNIE: The world's full of places.

RYANNY: Ah, ye that have money can marry for love.

ANNIE: No, I think I married Vivian for marriage.

RYANNY: I'm going to be married by the time I'm thirty.

GILBERT: That's nice, dear.

ANNIE: You mean in all the time you've been in America, not a single feller has had the courtesy to propose?

RYANNY: Ah stop it, you're only mocking.

GIBERT: What did you find to do with yourself before you came on the road with our happy family?

RYANNY makes up a lie on the spot.

RYANNY: I was living with my aunty Brigid in New York.

ELLA: And before that?

RYANNY: She'd been sending money home for years, and in the end there was enough for one ticket.

ELLA: Are the others going to follow you over?

RYANNY: I'm not sure.

GILBERT: Don't you write home to gladden their hearts?

RYANNY: The odd time.

ANNIE: What is this, a police station?

GILBERT: You're right, it's none of our beeswax.

ANNIE: I'm nearly twenty years away from London myself.

RYANNY: Do you miss it?

ANNIE: Can't say I remember much about it.

RYANNY: I miss our beach. They said New York would be by the sea, but it doesn't feel like it.

GILBERT: On hot days you can smell the docks, but it's hardly the same.

ANNIE: *(To RYANNY.)* Say, you got anything I could keep warm in?

RYANNY hesitates, then takes out her own patchwork quilt.

RYANNY: There you go.

ANNIE arranges it around her shoulders like an evening wrap.

GILBERT: Why Miss Hindle, I declare, I never suspected you of such ladylike shoulders!

ANNIE: *(To RYANNY.)* You make it yourself?

RYANNY: No, my mother did.

ANNIE: And she let you take it all the way across the ocean?

RYANNY: She died. In the hospital.

ANNIE: I'm sorry.

She changes the subject fast, addressing GILBERT and ELLA.

ANNIE: What do you think, could I do my act like this?

She sings, opera-style.

ANNIE: Adieu, my native land, adieu, adieu! *(Back to her normal voice.)* Sarah Bernhardt could carry it off. She wore some sort of drapery in *Camille* last year, she made me cry my eyes out.

GILBERT: You never told us what you and Vivian wore to your wedding.

ANNIE: Go to hell.

She picks a costume out of the skip.

ANNIE: This old suit is holding up well.

GILBERT: Ella looks pretty sharp in it too.

ANNIE spins around to look at her.

GILBERT: I taught her a couple of impersonator songs while you were away being Mrs Vivian. Which is your favorite, El?

ELLA is embarrassed that he's brought this up.

ELLA: I kinda like 'Frightfully Freddy'.

ANNIE: You have to get the accent spot-on for old Freddy. *(Parody of an upperclass English accent.)* 'Ey cennot kep mey eyeglass in mey ey.'

ELLA exits, jerking her head at GILBERT with a glare, which makes him trot after her.

Slightly bewildered by all that, ANNIE turns to RYANNY.

ANNIE: Say, you can help me with a new Oirish number I picked up in Boston. It's got this chorus that goes, 'Begorrah and Bejapers and Bad Cess to Ye All'.

RYANNY: I'm not aware that I speak like that.

ANNIE: Ah, don't take it personal, Miss Ryanny. Teasing's the language of the dressing-room.

RYANNY: Well it's not my language.

ANNIE: I'll teach you this one if you'll teach me yours.

RYANNY: What, the Gaelic?

ANNIE: What do they call a kiss, back in the old country? Just as a point of information.

RYANNY: Póg.

ANNIE: Pug?

RYANNY: Póg.

ANNIE: Pog.

RYANNY: Póg.

ANNIE: Póg. Thank you.

Sings, unaccompanied and parodically.

ANNIE: *Fair Irish girls, dear Irish girls,*
Where can they equaled be?
Bright Irish girl, dear Irish girl,
One fair Irish girl for me.

But when she turns back at the end of the song, RYANNY is gone.

ANNIE finishes doing up her flies and exits during the first verse of GILBERT's song, in 1883.

GILBERT is rehearsing 'The Wedding Ring' with the PIANIST.

GILBERT: *I'm very much a woman of the world,*
To every dodge I'm down.
I'm admired by all the Boston gents
And all the boys in town.
They call me their dear Nellie,
And they vow they love me true,
To gain my young affection,

But that caper doesn't do.
I've a smile for all, whether short or tall,
But the most important thing,
Is that no one gets a kiss from this little miss
Without a wedding ring!
Now I'm tired of single life,
And I wish that I could find
Some man to take this loving wife,
So gentle and so kind.
He'd find that love would beam from me
In every smile and glance,
I'm sure that many a fellow here
Should jump at such a chance!
I've a smile or a wave, for the meek or the brave
But that's the only thing,
Because no one gets a kiss from this little miss
Without a wedding ring!

    He looks around for his partner for the next song, a duet.

GILBERT: Where's Annie? We gotta rehearse our duet. Oh, let's start without her.

    The PIANIST strikes up 'Never Encourage the Men'.

GILBERT: *When in the ballroom you're dancing so gay,*
With a handsome young man by your side,
He vows he adores you and says –

    ANNIE saunters in with her jacket on over her shift and braces and
    takes up the song on cue.

ANNIE: *– Some day*
I surely will make you my bride!

GILBERT: *But if he should give you a hug that's too warm,*
Stand up for your rights there and then,
And just tell him quickly he'd better reform.
You should never encourage the men!
If your lover's pocket should ever get light,
Of course he'll explain all to you.
He may say –

ANNIE: – *Little darling, money is tight,*
Could you lend me a dollar or two?

GILBERT: *If you give him five dollars today, bear in mind*
That tomorrow he'll surely want ten.
So cling to your purse and don't be too kind –
You should never encourage the men.

ANNIE: *Don't ever be flattered with what they may say,*
Though they call you a rare little gem.
For if you allow them just one little kiss,
They surely will kiss you again.

> *By now ANNIE and GILBERT are doing an obscene mime with her cane. TONY, carrying his show book and a copy of a magazine called* The New York Dramatic Mirror, *interrupts the rehearsal and confiscates the cane.*

TONY: Hold it right there.

GILBERT: Don't holler, Tony.

ANNIE: If this rehearsal goes on much longer, my head's gonna burst.

TONY: Just to satisfy my curiosity, are you two aiming to have me arrested?

ANNIE: Ah, you're safe as long as we keep our clothes on.

TONY: That's bunkum. We're not touring the frontiers no more. Baltimore ladies won't stand for no old-fashioned dirty burlesque.

ANNIE: If he calls that dirty he should have seen what we were doing in the dressing-room last night.

TONY: Have I or have I not told you which gestures must not be made and which words must not be uttered?

> *GILBERT sings it prettily.*

GILBERT: *Liar, Devil, Damn,*
Hell, Slob, Backside,
Sucker, Jeez, Blimey,
Son-of-a-Gun.

ANNIE: Seeing as I'm not much of a reader, Gilbert sings me the list every morning.

TONY: When are you two going to get it into your skulls that we've moved uptown?

GILBERT: We're just not uptown enough for this troupe, Annie.

ANNIE: Not like Wallace the Porcupine, or Madame Carlotta's Dancing Bears – they're very uptown.

TONY: Look, I've already banned drinking, smoking, whistling and spitting. I give every lady in the audience a little sewing kit to take home.

ANNIE: You can't clean up a grubby business, Tony.

TONY: Says who? Who's the manager here?

ANNIE: Don't start again.

TONY: Just tell me, who is it? Is it you?

GILBERT: You're the boss, Mr Pastor.

ANNIE: Yeah, but who's the star?

She grabs her cane back.

TONY: Any more jaw from you and I'll tear up your contract.

ANNIE mimes terror.

GILBERT: What's the problem, Tony? The folks are still clapping.

TONY: But not enough of them. They're standing in line around the block at Koster and Bial's for Millie Hylton. Know what it says about her in the *Mirror*?

ANNIE: Nor do I care.

TONY: *(Reading.)* 'Miss Hylton's impersonation is never vulgar either in phrase or gesture. All the women who see her are charmed by her elegant – '

ANNIE: *(Interrupts.)* I've got other ways of charming women.

TONY: And that's another thing. I can turn a blind eye to performers' private peculiarities, but I don't want any whiff of scandal attached to my Grand Speciality Troupe, you hear?

GILBERT: *(Guiltily.)* I've been a good boy.

TONY: It makes me nervous as hell having Ella hang around with that Mansfield moll.

ANNIE: *(Astonished.)* Josie Mansfield?

TONY: She just won't be told.

GILBERT: Where did you hear that?

TONY: I've got my sources.

ANNIE: Doesn't Ella have more sense than to run with that crowd?

TONY: 'Miss Hylton appears as a model young man, while remaining a delicious young girl.'

ANNIE: If you wanted a delicious young girl, why did you hire me?

TONY: Because you were the best. An absolute professional who'd never let me down – unlike some prima donnas not far from here.

GILBERT: I've been eating humble pie all week.

TONY: When you sleep through a matinee and I have to bring back the Can-Canning Kittens twice to make up the time, humble pie is not enough. Whereas Annie still could be the best –

ANNIE: *(Interrupts.)* If I don't pack in the whole business and go live in my cottage on the Jersey Shore.

TONY: *(To GILBERT.)* That'll be the day, huh? She ever show you a picture of her miniature mansion?

GILBERT exits with TONY.

GILBERT: Only about a thousand times.

ANNIE: It's all ready for my retirement! Just a train ride from Manhattan and a stone's throw from the ocean.

ELLA comes in.

ANNIE: Some friend you are.

ELLA: What did I do?

ANNIE: I had to hear from Tony about you and that moll.

ELLA: Josie Mansfield is an actress.

ANNIE: And I'm a Sunday School teacher. All America knows she's a gun-moll for Big Jim Fisk.

ELLA: I like a woman with spirit, as you should know.

ANNIE: How long has all this been going on?

ELLA: A couple months.

ANNIE: You never said a word.

ELLA: I'm your dresser, not your slave. I was planning to introduce you when the time was right.

ANNIE: Afraid I'd steal her off her arm, were you?

ELLA: You're ten years too old for Josie.

ANNIE: What's she doing with a fat, aging gangster, then?

ELLA: Big Jim treats her pretty well. Better than Charles Vivian treated you.

ANNIE: That wouldn't be hard.

ELLA: She's known as the best-kept woman in New York.

ANNIE: It's not my idea of a life.

ELLA: Josie's got a four-story brownstone on the Upper West Side, full of canaries in cages and yellow velvet chaises longues.

ANNIE: Comfortable, are they?

ELLA: Very.

ANNIE: And what if Big Jim walks in and finds you lying on one?

ELLA: Oh, he wouldn't see a female as any threat. Ned Stokes, now – he's another friend of Josie's – Big Jim had him arrested for embezzlement once. No, I just sit on the sidelines and keep Josie entertained.

ANNIE: But they're a rough crowd all the same.

RYANNY comes in with ANNIE's box of letters.

ANNIE: Good afternoon, fair colleen.

RYANNY: I nearly tripped over your letters box and broke my neck.

ANNIE: It's getting heavier. In a couple years I won't be able to lift it.

ELLA: You are the most shameless lump of vanity it was ever my misfortune to powder the nose of.

RYANNY: Sit down till we do your hair.

ANNIE: Anything you say, ma'am. Vivian used to tease me, you know – say he was legit and I was just a novelty act, but the novelty's long over and the letters keep pouring in. I compared my box with Harry J.'s one year –

ELLA: *(Interrupts, to RYANNY.)* You want to part it on the left?

ANNIE: *(To RYANNY.)* You know him, Harry J. Montague, the Matinee Idol?

ELLA: Frankfurter in a tailcoat.

ANNIE: And he said to me –

RYANNY: *(Interrupts, to ELLA.)* Should I do a curl there?

ELLA: Other way around.

ANNIE: I'm talking to myself here.

ELLA: So what's new?

RYANNY: We want you to be a credit to us. Go on about Mr Montague.

ANNIE: Anyhow, my box of mash notes weighed twice what his did. He was not a happy man.

GILBERT enters with a sweet bun, singing his version of 'The Baker's Daughter' unaccompanied and lewdly.

GILBERT: *I am the baker's daughter,*
My buns are hot and firm.
Through the marketplace I saunter,
Come get them while they're warm!

ELLA: If Tony catches you changing the words again…

GILBERT: Oh, I'll sing the stuffy version. I keep my improvisations for my sweethearts backstage.

ANNIE: How's the house?

GILBERT: There's a rash of squalling infants in the front row, sucking their oranges.

He consoles himself with a big bite of bun.

RYANNY: You'll spoil your dinner.

GILBERT: The only point of dinner is the afters, which should ideally come before.

ELLA: No matter how much I ate, I never grew enough curves to stay in ballet. Madame Paree wouldn't hire any girl who weighed less than a hundred and thirty pounds.

GILBERT: Do you think she'd take me?

ELLA: We might have to make a few nips and tucks…

Chases him offstage with her scissors.

ANNIE: Wish I was on early so I'd have a chance to get warm under the lights.

RYANNY: You could always stand in the wings with Tony and watch the show.

ANNIE: Ah, but there's more to see down here.

RYANNY: When are you on?

ANNIE: Not for hours yet. Better stay moving or my joints will lock? Care for a polka?

She seizes RYANNY, who resists for a moment then enjoys the dance.

ELLA comes back in.

ELLA: *(To RYANNY.)* I never knew you could dance.

RYANNY: Neither did I. Now stop it, I've work to be doing.

ANNIE: You shouldn't have to wear out those hands cleaning and mending clothes for a living.

RYANNY: And what should I be doing with them?

ANNIE: Dunno. Whatever ladies of leisure do.

GILBERT enters, planning his act.

GILBERT: Listen. Horse goes into a bar, all right? All right?

ANNIE: All right.

GILBERT: So the landlord says to him, he says, 'Why the long face?'

None of them even crack a smile.

RYANNY: Is that all there is of it?

GILBERT: Well I won't be entering it for the Greatest Gag of All Time Championship, but will it do for a matinee crowd?

ELLA: It's too cold for jokes, Gilbo.

She exits.

GILBERT: I'm off upstairs to watch that new boy do his sword dance. He's got the dearest piping on his little jacket.

He exits.

RYANNY: C'mere, your parting's all crooked.

ANNIE: You take such care of me.

RYANNY: It's my job.

ANNIE: Who taught you to be so good at it?

RYANNY: Ella.

ANNIE: Bosh.

RYANNY: Bunkum.

ANNIE: You said a rude word!

RYANNY: Would you sit still before you get a comb in your eye?

ANNIE takes an unopened envelope out of her pocket.

ANNIE: Got another letter today.

RYANNY only pretends to be exasperated. She opens it, raises her eyebrows at the scent, and reads it aloud to their mutual amusement.

RYANNY: 'Darling Mr Hindle, please oh please oh please leave off this pretence that you are a woman only dressed as a man. When I told my mother I know you are a real true man and I intend for to marry you, she said – '

TONY: *(Calling offstage.)* Annie!

As he rushes in he trips over the box of letters.

TONY: Damnation!

RYANNY: Language.

TONY: Tarnation, then. What the – what is this?

ANNIE: I gotta bring my crush notes everywhere to remind me how legendary I am.

TONY: What you've gotta do is get on stage. I just fell over Little Tich on the stairs: he's drunk as a skunk and so is his poodle. The Siamese Twins are starting their last song now –

ANNIE: *(Interrupts.)* So tell them to make up a few more verses.

TONY: – so you gotta fill in with 'The Gentleman Actor' while I round up the Monkey Dancers.

RYANNY: She can't do the 'Gentleman Actor' in her 'City Banker' suit.

> *TONY scrabbles in the skip, pulls out a white silk scarf and top hat and thrusts them on ANNIE.*

TONY: Perfect.

> *He dashes off, and RYANNY follows.*

> *The memory of that night in 1883 fades and ANNIE finds herself alone in 1891 again. She tries on the hat and scarf. MUSIC: introduction to 'The Gentleman Actor'. She sings in a posh English accent.*

ANNIE: *I'm a gentleman actor, the king of the stage,*
As Hamlet or Lear, I can rant, I can bluster.
They tell me my talent's the talk of the age,
And the lady's not born yet whom I cannot fluster.
Two yards of necktie and gloves rather small,
Some think I'm a count from a far foreign shore.
My diction and figure eclipse them all,
Every girl in the audience comes back for more.
As thespians go, I'm so very distinguished,
When Irving sees me, he falls to his knees,
And the flame of my fame will not e'er be extinguished,
As long as sheer genius continues to please.

> *She takes off the hat and scarf. Music: a music-box echo of 'The Gentleman Actor' pulls her into a memory of a day in 1884. Enter RYANNY with a copy of the* New York Dramatic Mirror *and a crumpled photograph of Charles Vivian.*

RYANNY: Did you hear the news yet?

ANNIE: Which news?

RYANNY: About Mr Vivian.

ANNIE: Oh, that. Can't say it troubled me much.

RYANNY is dismayed by this. ANNIE comes to take the photograph from her.

ANNIE: Where did this come from?

RYANNY: I found it crumpled up in a corner one time.

ANNIE: Ever occur to you there was a reason a picture of Vivian might have been thrown out with the face powder and the hair clippings and the other theatrical trash?

RYANNY: I know you had your differences, but we mustn't speak ill of –

ANNIE: *(Interrupts.)* Differences? I was a good wife to him for six months and I have the marks to prove it.

RYANNY: He hit you?

ANNIE: Oh no. You think an Englishborn gentleman actor would raise his hand to a lady? Even one with a moustache?

RYANNY: Sorry, I misunderstood.

ANNIE: No no, it was me who kept misunderstanding. I'd look at myself in the mirror and see two great black eyes and ask myself, 'Annie, did you distinguished thespian husband raise his fist to you last night? Why no, he couldn't have. He's the people's darling. I must have walked into a wall.' Come to think of it, I must have walked into two walls, every Saturday night. The feller thought he had a God-given right to take his boots to me, his belt, his dinner plate, his coal-scuttle, his encyclopedia…

She tears the photo into strips. RYANNY takes her hands and holds them still.

RYANNY: Shush. I'm sorry. I'm sorry.

ANNIE: No, I'm the one who's sorry.

RYANNY: I didn't understand.

ANNIE: How could you?

RYANNY: I should have guessed.

ANNIE: No, I should have told you.

RYANNY: Keeping secrets isn't good for you.

ANNIE: I'll…try to bear that in mind.

RYANNY: So. Did you ever hit back?

ANNIE: Once. Not a smart move. So then I came back to the Troupe.

RYANNY tidies up the scraps of photo.

RYANNY: Thank God you did.

ANNIE: You know, you've got this way of becoming necessary before a person hardly realizes it.

Her nerve fails, so she changes the subject.

ANNIE: Imogen, his new wife is called. Good luck to her. Wonder does he still sleep in his boots.

RYANNY: But you said you'd heard!

ANNIE: Yep, Gilbert read me every adjective. You'd think one wedding would have been enough for the feller.

RYANNY: No, not his wedding. In the new issue.

She finds the piece at the back of the magazine.

RYANNY: It's just five lines.

ANNIE: What is?

RYANNY: He died on his honeymoon, Annie. In Leadville, Colorado.

ANNIE: Five lines, you say?

RYANNY points to the opposite page from the one ANNIE's staring at.

RYANNY: Four and a half, really.

ANNIE: That won't please him. He'll have been expecting the full half page.

RYANNY: Ah well. God is good.

ANNIE: Says who?

RYANNY: My mammy. She used to say that when it rained?

ANNIE: Did she still say that when she was dying in the hospital?

RYANNY: I don't know. I wasn't there.

ANNIE: I feel old. The arrows are falling closer.

RYANNY: Don't be talking nonsense. Sure you're in your prime.

ANNIE: Will I tell you a secret?

RYANNY: You probably will.

ANNIE: I'm thinking of quitting.

RYANNY: You're not!

ANNIE: I don't want to spend the rest of my life sitting in draughty dressing-rooms and working for laughs from red-faced strangers.

RYANNY: I thought you loved it up there on stage.

ANNIE: On a good day. I used to love every minute of it, back when it was all new and Tony used to call me the One and Only as if he meant it. But these days it feels like I've sung every one of those stupid songs a million times.

RYANNY: What else could you do?

ANNIE: Anything. Nothing. Rest. Learn to read things for myself. Grow tulips. That's what I built my place in New Jersey for: a bit of ordinary life.

RYANNY: We'd miss you.

ANNIE opens her mouth to ask RYANNY to come with her, but loses her nerve. She addresses the dressmaker's dummy.

ANNIE: What do you say, Miss Dim, will you and me run away to the Jersey Shore? Bet those big hips of yours would float nicely. If I held onto them I'd never drown.

RYANNY: Dimity doesn't listen to loose talk like that.

ANNIE: She can't help it. Got no hands to cover her ears.

RYANNY: She hasn't any ears either.

ANNIE: Aren't you awful quick?

RYANNY: I am not. I'm a harmless girl who minds her own business.

ANNIE: That's just your act.

RYANNY: What am I like, then?

ANNIE: You're the darnedest mixture. I'd take me a lifetime to figure you out.

MUSIC: faint echo of 'The Gentleman Actor'.

ANNIE: Say. Be sure and listen to my song this afternoon –

But RYANNY has exited, and ANNIE is alone again in the dressing-room in 1891.

She digs a long strapping bandage and shirt out of the skip. Music: an echo of 'Could I See My Darling Again' stops her in her tracks. She sings softly.

ANNIE: *I've lost a young maid and I'm really afraid*
I shall never see her no more.
I dote on the girl for she is my pearl,

And a damsel I really adore.
I'd give all I've got, to the West long miles trot,
To a madman myself I would chain.
I'd swallow a sheep, from the Brooklyn Bridge leap,
Could I see my darling again...
Could I see my darling again,
I'd eat hat, necktie, fob watch and cane,
I'd dive into the sea, let a whale swallow me,
Could I see my darling again.

She leaves the shirt and goes into a corner to strap down her breasts.

ELLA, entering, picks up ANNIE's shirt to darn. We are in 1885.

ELLA: This has got to be the coldest, pokiest dressing-room in Montreal. I don't know what Tony Pastor's doing with his millions but he sure ain't spending them down here.

RYANNY: Ella?

ELLA: Mm? Sew that button on real tight. She's always busting it in the final chorus.

RYANNY: Who was that lady you were with yesterday?

ELLA: Which lady?

RYANNY: The one in the corridor.

ELLA: Name's Josie.

RYANNY: That's a nice name.

ELLA: Sure is. You saw me kissing her, didn't you?

RYANNY: I did.

ELLA: You never seen ladies kiss before?

RYANNY: This was different.

ELLA: How?

RYANNY: I'm not a complete gom.

ELLA: Never said you were, whatever it means.

RYANNY: Just because I'm not cracking jokes all the time like the rest of yiz, it doesn't mean I haven't a brain in my head. I do notice things.

ELLA: I've noticed you noticing.

RYANNY: They wouldn't understand that kind of thing, back home.

ELLA: *(Teasing.)* What kind of thing?

ANNIE, picking up her shirt, overhears the rest of the conversation.

RYANNY: Women. Together.

ELLA: They didn't understand it in my home neither.

RYANNY: I never knew such things could happen before.

ELLA: Everything happens in this business.

RYANNY: Don't you care for gentlemen?

ELLA: I care for all sorts of people, but right now it happens to be Josie.

RYANNY: Is it like being married?

ELLA: I wouldn't know. Josie's pretty busy. I only get to see her every now and then.

RYANNY: But don't you want to settle down?

ELLA: Annie tried that, and look where it got her.

RYANNY: She picked wrong.

ELLA: Well, you're more the settling-down type. Have you got a particular feller in mind?

RYANNY: I never found the right gentleman yet.

The dressers exit.

In 1891, ANNIE checks her strapped chest is smooth and puts her shirt on, repeating the end of 'Could I See My Darling Again'.

ANNIE: *I'd dive into the sea, let a whale swallow me,*
Could I see my darling again.

TONY enters on her last line.

TONY: Very nice. Very tuneful.

ANNIE: Well, I won't be opening with that one tonight.

TONY nods respectfully, and turns to leave. Then turns back.

TONY: You will remember to be careful about the words, won't you?

ANNIE: Which words?

TONY: The ones not to say in your patter.

ANNIE: Liar, Devil, Damn –

TONY: Yeah, that's the list.

ANNIE: Any recent additions?

TONY: No, no. Unless…you know about bedbugs?

ANNIE: What should I know about bedbugs?

TONY: They're on the list.

ANNIE: Tony, what could possess me to use the word bedbugs in my patter?

TONY: I never said you would. It's one list for the whole troupe, that's all, no special cases.

ANNIE: I guarantee not to mention insect life of any kind.

TONY: That's the ticket.

ANNIE improvises.

ANNIE: *Home is with the bedbugs,*
The itsy-bitsy mites, the little lice…

TONY laughs as he exits.

ANNIE: *(To herself.)* Homes, weddings and partings, that's what all the songs are about. How can I go out there and sing this stuff like it doesn't matter?

> *MUSIC: music-box echo of 'Could I See My Darling Again'. We are in the dressing-room in 1886. Enter ELLA.*

ELLA: I was listening to your song today.

ANNIE: *(Pretends to be hurt.)* You mean you don't always?

ELLA: You've got it bad for our assistant dresser, don't you?

ANNIE: You reckon?

ELLA: Quit bluffing.

ANNIE: I'd give my right hand for her.

ELLA: *(Suggestive.)* Save it, you might need it some day.

> *They laugh.*

ELLA: I used to think you were just flirting – as you do.

ANNIE: Might as well have been. If a delivery boy so much as smiles at her, I want to smash his head against the wall.

ELLA: I wouldn't give up hope.

ANNIE: We've all heard her say it: Ryanny's going to be married by the age of thirty.

ELLA: That gives you a few years. Think of it like an audience; if the first thing you do falls flat, you just try something else.

ANNIE: I've tried everything. I work harder backstage than on stage. I sing to her, tell her stories, play it happy, play it sad, keep on wisecracking till I think my jaw's gonna fall off.

ELLA: Don't talk so much, then.

ANNIE: What else can I do? I'm a hammy old flirt without the courage of my convictions.

ELLA: Well, what happens when the folks in the stalls won't pay attention?

ANNIE: Ah, there's a couple of old stand-bys no audience can resist.

ELLA: So…

ANNIE: So that's where your comparison's worth diddleysquat! What I have to say is not something Ryanny wants to hear. It's like walking into the spotlight with a song you know is going to make the folks boo and hiss and be sick all over the floor, and –

ELLA: She's not going to be sick all over the floor. She knows about me and Josie.

ANNIE: That's different. She'll be perfectly nice as long as no-one's laying a hand on her.

ELLA: You know she's fond of you.

ANNIE: All the more reason why I shouldn't open my big mouth and make her hate me instead.

ELLA: So you'll have to persuade her not to hate you.

ANNIE: How? Where am I to get the words? There aren't any songs about things like this.

ELLA: Behind that rambunctious exterior, you're the most faint-hearted fool in the world, aren't you?

ANNIE: You only just noticed?

ELLA: You performers! You can change your clothes, you can change your face, but you're too chicken to change your life. What've you got to lose?

ANNIE: The sight of her every morning.

ELLA: Tell you what, though: faint heart never yet won a damn thing.

TONY bawls, offstage.

TONY: Where is she?

He bursts in with a note in his hand, and GILBERT and RYANNY at his heels.

ELLA: I got work to do.

GILBERT: What's going on?

ANNIE: *(Thinking she's the she in question.)* Where was I supposed to be?

TONY: Not you. Ella bloody Wesner!

ELLA: Not now, Tony.

She hurries out.

TONY: Not now? Then when the hell am I –

RYANNY: *(Interrupts.)* Language, Mr Pastor!

TONY: Pardon me, Miss Ryan.

GILBERT: Tell, tell, tell.

TONY: What has the girl done but had the cheek to give notice? She's leaving Grand Rapids in the morning, if you please. Got herself a run as a male impersonator with Koster and Bial's in New York.

ANNIE: She's what?

TONY: There gotta be laws against such a thing.

GILBERT: Well fiddle my dee, she's done it at last.

ANNIE: Did you know about this?

GILBERT: Oh come now, we all knew El had ambitions in the song-and-dance line.

TONY: Nothing a good kick wouldn't cure.

ANNIE: I never knew.

GILBERT: You didn't want to know. I told her she should ask Tony for a spot, but clearly…

TONY looks uncomfortable.

TONY: I'm a busy man.

ANNIE: So she did ask you?

TONY: How was I supposed to know she'd take it so bad? In my book, a dresser's a dresser.

ANNIE: You could have let her try a duet with me or something.

GILBERT: *(To ANNIE.)* She suggested that once, and you giggled.

ANNIE: Did I? I must have thought she was kidding.

TONY: Of all the low-down, upstart little baggages…

RYANNY: Lookit, she'll be getting thirty dollars a week to do what she's always dreamed of. I think we should be glad for her.

GILBERT: It took me decades to get to thirty dollars a week.

TONY: Are we to understand that you knew all about her plans, Miss?

RYANNY: I did.

TONY: Since when?

RYANNY: A while back.

TONY: And in all this while it never occurred to you to –

ANNIE interrupts, stepping between him and RYANNY.

ANNIE: Leave her alone.

TONY: I beg your pardon?

ANNIE: You heard me.

TONY: And since when has she chosen you as her protector?

217

To avoid answering this, ANNIE changes to a soothing approach.

ANNIE: Tony, you won't bring one dresser back by bullying another.

TONY: Miss Ryan knows I have nothing but the warmest regard for her.

RYANNY: Thank you, Mr Pastor.

An awkward pause.

GILBERT: So. Our li'l ol' El hops into the limelight.

ANNIE: Where is she, anyhow?

GILBERT: Bet you a donut I can track her down…

He runs off.

ANNIE: Wonder what her act's going to be like.

TONY: Better concentrate on your own.

ANNIE: What's wrong with it?

TONY: Only one encore last Tuesday…

ANNIE: I've got savings in the bank, you know. I don't have to sit around for another twenty years and listen to this horseshit. Jeez, when I was on twenty shillings a week I got more appreciation than I do now.

TONY: It's not appreciation you need, Miss Internationally-Renowned Hindle, it's management. Swanking around, complaining about the food, treating Miss Ryan like your private dresser…

RYANNY: She doesn't.

ANNIE: Seems to me I've made my fortune by doing the songs I like, the way I like, and if you don't appreciate them like the fans do, then you can hire yourself some mincing nobody like Millie Hylton.

TONY: If you don't shape up by the end of the season, that's exactly what I'll have to do. And you can go earn ten dollars a week at Professor Vladimir's Freak Hall for letting folks throw peanuts at you.

He stomps out.

RYANNY: It's just that he's all fired up about Ella.

ANNIE: It's her we should be bawling out.

RYANNY: Sure anyone might have guessed she's got too much jizz in her to stay cooped up in a dressing-room all her days.

ANNIE: What made you take this job, then?

RYANNY: Half a dollar in my pocket and nowhere else to go.

ANNIE: Are you glad you did?

RYANNY: Glad's not the word for it. I can't imagine who I'd be today if I hadn't.

GILBERT: *(Offstage, to ELLA.)* I always thought a moustache would suit you. What are you going to wear?

ELLA enters with GILBERT.

ELLA: I don't know yet, Gilbert. I've only –

ANNIE: *(Interrupts.)* Weren't you intending to tell me, then? Planning to just slip away into the night?

ELLA: I was gonna take you all out tonight for a steak and explain. I only told Ryanny first because I knew she wouldn't try to stop me.

Through this conversation, ANNIE is tucking in and buttoning up her shirt, fastening her collar, adding a vest and bowtie.

ANNIE: I thought I knew you. Weren't you happy with the Troupe?

ELLA: It's not about happiness.

ANNIE: Impersonation's a ridiculous job. Do you really want to wear false moustaches for a living?

ELLA: What's ridiculous about hard cash and fame and glory? I swear, no one's ever going to say 'Ella Wesner? Who was she?'

ANNIE: Strutting the boards ain't all it's cracked up to be, you know.

ELLA: How would I know? I've never been farther than the wings. All I know is, I'm twenty-nine years old and this is my last chance to change my life.

GILBERT: So what did you sing at the audition?

ELLA: 'A Real Man'.

ANNIE: That's my song.

ELLA: Yeah, but I do it better.

Their staring match ends in laughter.

RYANNY: We haven't even time for a farewell party.

ELLA: It's not farewell.

RYANNY: No, but something to mark the occasion.

ELLA: You'll see more than enough of me in New York.

ANNIE: It won't be the same.

GILBERT: How will we dare to approach the new star of the halls?

ANNIE: The competition, you mean. I'll have to spit at her if we meet on the street.

RYANNY: Oh El, I'm going to miss you. How am I supposed to manage these ragamuffins on my own?

ELLA: Don't get soppy on me now. I'm no different than I've ever been, I've just seen an opportunity and grabbed it.

ANNIE: She's caught sight of a passing star, and hitched her little wagon to it.

ELLA: *(Meaningfully, to ANNIE.)* There's stars passing every day, and none of us is getting any younger.

ANNIE: I hear you.

GILBERT: What's all this?

ELLA: Am I right, Miss Faint Heart?

ANNIE: I said I heard you.

GILBERT: Will somebody kindly tell me what's going on?

ELLA: I wonder if Tony's calmed down enough to talk about back wages. Come with me, Gilbert – you can stand between us. Come on!

She drags him off with her, to leave the other two alone.

ANNIE: That girl. She's staking everything she's got on a song-and-dance.

RYANNY: God looks after the brave.

ANNIE: Does he?

RYANNY: Of course.

ANNIE: Does he give them what they want?

RYANNY: Ah well, that's a different matter.

ANNIE: What if I had something to tell you but I didn't know how?

RYANNY: I like most things you tell me.

ANNIE: Not this. Something I've hidden for much too long.

RYANNY: Why?

ANNIE: Because I didn't think you could bear to hear it.

RYANNY: I'm listening. Tell me.

ANNIE: I can't.

RYANNY turns away. ANNIE screws up her courage and walks up behind her.

ANNIE: Let me show you instead.

She kisses her. RYANNY bursts out laughing.

RYANNY: I wondered how many more years that was going to take you.

ANNIE laughs too, astonished. They kiss again, more passionately.

RYANNY: That's enough now.

ANNIE: It's not half enough.

RYANNY: Leave off.

ANNIE: If you give me one good reason. And don't tell me that it's because I'm a woman.

RYANNY: Any more now would be fornication, Annie. It stains the soul.

ANNIE: Little stain like that would hardly show on a dirty old soul like mine.

RYANNY: It's mine I'm concerned for. You only have to wait until we're married.

ANNIE: That'll be the day.

RYANNY: Name it.

ANNIE: Ho, ho, ho.

RYANNY: It's no joke.

She pushes ANNIE into the traditional kneeling position, and prompts her.

RYANNY: 'My dear Miss Ryan...'

ANNIE: My dear Miss Ryan, would you do me the inexpressible honor of giving me your hand in marriage?

She drops the satirical tone, seeing RYANNY's disappointed face.

ANNIE: What?

RYANNY: Would you ever give over playacting for one minute?

ANNIE: Let me get this clear. I've spent the best years of my life trying to find the courage to kiss you, and now you're proposing marriage?

RYANNY: Wouldn't you want to, then?

ANNIE: Of course I'd want to. Like pigs probably long to fly.

RYANNY: I've been giving the matter a lot of thought.

ANNIE: You have?

RYANNY: What's to stop us getting married for real?

ANNIE: Well, the law, for starters.

RYANNY: Where does it say it?

ANNIE: I don't know where exactly, but it must do. Try convincing a minister it doesn't.

RYANNY: If you kept your suit on, and told him your name was, say, Charles Hindle…

ANNIE: Told who?

RYANNY: The minister!

ANNIE: That is the most outrageous damn-fool plan I ever heard in my life.

RYANNY: But it's the only sensible thing to do.

ANNIE: You wouldn't have it in you.

RYANNY: Lookit, if I could brave the Atlantic Ocean I must have nerve enough for this.

ANNIE: I bet you would, you extraordinary creature. Or we could just skip the ceremony and head straight for the honeymoon…

RYANNY allows her one kiss, but keeps her at arm's length.

RYANNY: We deserve better than that. If a hole-in-the-corner affair is what you want, any chorus girl will do.

ANNIE: You've been all I want for as long as I can remember.

RYANNY: Well then. Doesn't that give us as much right to a wedding as any pair of persons?

ANNIE: It never struck me quite that way before.

RYANNY: I get a lot of time to think while you're up there prancing about in the limelight.

ANNIE: Clearly so.

RYANNY: I'm just an ignorant country girl –

ANNIE: *(Interrupts.)* You are not!

RYANNY: – but there are some things I know more about than you, and I know we should be married.

ANNIE takes the idea seriously for the first time.

ANNIE: It just might work, you know, if the lights were low.

RYANNY: No bother to you!

ANNIE: You'd have an easier life if you picked yourself a regular gentleman for a husband.

RYANNY: You're more of a gentleman than any man I've ever laid eyes on.

ANNIE: Are you sure we need some Holy Joe to join us?

RYANNY: A minister of God, and a witness and a ring, and a certificate to put up on the wall.

ANNIE: Which wall?

RYANNY: The house in New Jersey. You said yourself you didn't want to stay with the Troupe forever.

ANNIE: I suppose…with Ella leaving, and Tony and me fighting like rats…it's time to make a graceful exit.

RYANNY: *(Suddenly doubtful.)* Isn't this what you wanted?

ANNIE: It's much more than I dreamed.

RYANNY: High time you had a proper home, after all these dirty lodgings. Somewhere we can be…private.

ANNIE: I can't imagine anything better than being private with you. I'm still reeling. The most I was hoping for tonight was a kiss.

RYANNY: Weren't you the terrible eejit, not to notice I love you?

ANNIE: But you must be a worser eejit to want to marry one.

> *MUSIC: the introduction to 'Home' calls her on-stage. From the wings, RYANNY watches her perform.*

ANNIE: *If home is where the heart is,*
Then my future is clearly with you.
I'll need no adventures or parties,
If I marry a woman like you.

> *Later that same evening, ANNIE enters the dressing-room cheerfully. TONY, clapping sarcastically, comes in behind her, holding a large chocolate éclair (which he never gets a chance to eat).*

TONY: What was all that about?

ANNIE: Beg your pardon?

TONY: It's down in my show-book, you were meant to do 'Walking on the Balcony'.

ANNIE: Maybe I didn't feel like walking on the balcony.

TONY: But the one you just sang wasn't funny.

ANNIE: Where is it written that I always have to be funny?

TONY: It's only what I pay you enormous sums of money for.

ANNIE: You've been at me for years to clean up my act.

TONY: I meant good wholesome humor, not all this eye-rolling romance. What's got into you?

ANNIE: The crowd loved me.

TONY: Oh, tonight they loved you; it was a novelty. Because Annie Hindle is meant to be funny!

ANNIE: In this business you gotta take risks, don't you, Tony? Aren't you always telling us how you nearly went bankrupt on your first tour?

TONY: That was a calculated risk.

ANNIE: Is that when you want something so much, you calculate it's worth risking everything for?

TONY: No.

GILBERT: *(Shouts, offstage.)* To hell with Tony Pastor and his fancy scenery!

TONY: What?

GILBERT storms in.

GILBERT: I'm halfway through the second verse of 'Shy Suzanne from Gay Paree', when what should begin to descend behind me but a view of the Pyramids. Laugh! They must have wet the floor.

TONY: It was meant to be the new backcloth of the Arc de Triomphe.

GILBERT: Lucky for you I can adlib in couplets. Though I never thought I'd be reduced to rhyming Egypt with fidget.

ANNIE: Didn't you manage to get the Sphinx in there somewhere?

GILBERT: Last line, to rhyme with saucy minx.

RYANNY: That's our boy.

TONY offers his éclair.

TONY: Here, it's the nearest thing I've got to a peace pipe.

GILBERT: You can't soft-soap me with a chocolate éclair.

But he takes it and bites in.

TONY: I gotta get back, the Human Fish must be nearly finished.

As soon as he's gone, ANNIE turns to GILBERT.

ANNIE: Well?

GILBERT: Well what? I can hardly tell which way I'm facing.

ANNIE: I know just how you feel.

GILBERT: Couldn't you two just go about your business nice and quiet like the rest of us do?

ANNIE: Well, the thing is –

RYANNY: No we couldn't.

She is packing her bag throughout this scene.

GILBERT: I've never heard of such an outrageous way of making trouble for yourselves.

ANNIE: So you won't find us a minister, then?

GILBERT: Ten o'clock tonight!

ANNIE: Tonight?

RYANNY: *(Explaining her hurry.)* I thought we should do it right away so Tony can catch Ella before she goes off to New York.

GILBERT: See, if you drop out in a one-horse town like Grand Rapids, and leave the Troupe short of a male impersonator, Tony'll have your balls for breakfast.

He apologizes before RYANNY can object.

GILBERT: Pardon my Swahili.

RYANNY: I'm glad I told you, Gilbert.

GILBERT: You do realize we could all end up in jail?

RYANNY: Of course.

GILBERT: *(To ANNIE.)* You've got yourself a rare bird here, Annie.

ANNIE: One in a zillion.

GILBERT: Why am I shooting myself in the foot by helping the pair of you run off and desert me?

ANNIE: Because you're unutterably wonderful?

GILBERT: That could be it.

RYANNY: So who's this minister you found us?

GILBERT: The Reverend Brooks is a cousin of a friend of my wife's brother-in-law, and all he wants is a donation towards building the first Unitarian chapel in Grand Rapids.

RYANNY: Not a Catholic, then. All well, I'm sure it's as good as. God's not a fusspot.

ANNIE: Does he know what's going on?

RYANNY: God knows everything.

ANNIE: I meant the minister.

GILBERT: Just keep your voice good and deep and you'll do fine.

ANNIE: *(Testing her lowest register.)* And if anyone asks any questions?

GILBERT: Then we say, 'Oops, what a silly mistake', and run for it.

RYANNY: Nothing's going to stop me getting married.

ANNIE: Let's go right now.

GILBERT: There's that little matter of a show to finished.

ANNIE: You know what? I don't give a goddamn.

GILBERT: What do you mean? Annie Hindle never misses a performance. Specially not her last.

ANNIE: How long before I have to go on?

GILBERT: Another ten minutes, I'd say.

ANNIE: Gilbo, if I dry, tonight…

RYANNY: Once you've started a song I've never known you to dry.

ANNIE: No, after. The 'richer for poorer, sickness and health' bit. Will you prompt me?

GILBERT: But if I whisper 'I do', I'll end up married to Ryanny, and then you'll have to shoot me.

ANNIE: That would seem a waste of a pretty face.

GILBERT: Did you write that note to Tony yet?

RYANNY: *(Producing it.)* We thought if we pinned it to Miss Dimity, he'd be sure to find it.

GILBERT: *(Reads it.)* 'Dear Mr Pastor, we are gone to be married and won't be back. We are sorry for the inconvenience.' Well, that just about covers it.

RYANNY pins it to the dummy.

GILBERT: Now I told the Reverend you'd be at the Barnard Hotel by nine forty-five.

ANNIE: That's cutting it a bit tight. What if they encore me?

RYANNY: Say no.

ANNIE: You can't refuse an encore!

RYANNY: No need to snap.

ANNIE: I'm sorry. You know, it's a funny thing, but I can't remember the words to a single song.

GILBERT: 'Jack Spratt and His Fine Top Hat'?

ANNIE: Not a dignified way to end my career.

GILBERT: 'Farewell to All the Scenes of Yore'?

ANNIE: Too gloomy.

RYANNY: God's going to punish me for this.

ANNIE: What?

RYANNY: There's thousands of them out there waiting for you, and there's only one of me.

ANNIE: They're nobody. They're just folks with half a dollar in their pocket and nothing better to do with the evening.

RYANNY: But what right have I to take you away from what you do best?

ANNIE: *(Lewdly.)* Maybe there's other things I do even better.

GILBERT: I presume you've got yourselves a ring?

RYANNY: No!

ANNIE: Yes. Yes we do. My old one. It's in here somewhere...

She rummages in the make-up box until she finds the ring from her first marriage. She gives it a polish on her sleeve.

ANNIE: You don't mind?

RYANNY: It's lovely.

GILBERT: I've got it. Give them 'All Getting Married'.

He helps ANNIE into her jacket as RYANNY dashes off with her bag.

ANNIE: You've got one twisted sense of humor.

GILBERT: It's perfect.

He takes a flower from his dress and puts it her lapel. MUSIC: introduction to 'All Getting Married'. GILBERT sings.

GILBERT: *Behold in this mortal a poor single man,*
Who wanders about all the day.

ANNIE puts on her hat.

ANNIE: *Not a soul in the world cares a jot about me,*
As long as my lodgings I pay.
I always was shy and often did cry,
If any young girl looked at me,
But to tell you the truth all the friends of my youth,
They are all getting married but me.

    ANNIE and GILBERT waltz, singing in harmony.

ANNIE/GILBERT: *The birdsies that fly, the pigs in the sty,*
The fishes and whales, the frogs and the snails,
The mice and the rats, the dogs and the rats,
They are all getting married but me.

    As the music continues, RYANNY runs on in a wedding veil, holding
    a bouquet. ANNIE puts the ring on RYANNY's finger and they kiss.
    They process down the aisle arm in arm, then assume the formal pose
    of a Victorian marriage photograph. RYANNY tosses her bouquet as
    GILBERT throws confetti and the lights fade.

ACT TWO

MUSIC: an offstage echo of 'Fair Irish Girl'. It is later on the night of ANNIE's second comeback, in 1891. She has put her women's clothes back on – except for the wig – and is sitting in the dressing-room with her bag packed, in a state of paralysis. Enter TONY.

TONY: Okey-dokey? Where's your costume?

ANNIE: *(Ironic.)* Which?

TONY: What are you doing in street clothes?

ANNIE: Nothing.

TONY: The others should be in soon. I thought you'd be ready.

ANNIE: I don't know what I'm doing here.

TONY: What?

ANNIE: Look at it this way. I had five years of absolute happiness on the Jersey Shore. Now I'm sitting in a draughty dressing-room again. I don't know what to wear. I don't know what to say. I don't know who to be.

TONY: Spare me the profundities. Wear the bowler hat.

As he leaves, ANNIE calls him back.

ANNIE: Tony. I can't do it.

TONY: You mean you're going?

ANNIE: I don't know.

TONY: Where to, exactly?

ANNIE: I don't know.

TONY: Last I heard, you'd nowhere else to be.

ANNIE: I just don't think I've got it in me anymore.

TONY: What?

ANNIE: It. The maggot. Whatever it is that makes us get dressed up and sing songs that rhyme love with turtle dove.

TONY: You want literature, you go to the library. And I'll tell you what makes you do it: me.

ANNIE: But what's the point? You've put me on as the opener, so you can't think I'm any good anymore. Why don't I just pick up my bag and get out of here? Who's gonna miss me? The audience won't weep if they don't hear 'Frightfully Freddy' tonight.

TONY: Now calm down.

ANNIE bursts into satiric song for a line.

ANNIE: *With a ding, and a dee, and diddley-idle-dee –*
That's hardly going to change their lives, is it?

TONY: I don't care whether you've got 'it' in you or not, but you signed a contract and you're damn well going to do it.

ANNIE: Yes, sir. Just tell me exactly what you're paying for, sir. You want sad? I've been jerking tears since I was five years old.

She puts on a posh English accent and sings.

ANNIE: *Farewell to all the scenes of yore,*
All happiness in life is o'er.

Back to her usual voice.

ANNIE: You want genuine Cockney?

She sings in a Cockney accent and dances.

ANNIE: *My old girl can't fit through the door,*
She's big behind and bigger before.

Back to her usual voice.

ANNIE: You want Eyties, Huns, Polacks, Frogs, dogs, cats? Woof woof! Miaow! You want Punch and Judy?

She mimes punching herself.

ANNIE: 'Who was that woman I saw you with last night?' 'That was no woman, that was my wife!' Boom boom! You want risqué?

She does the can-can.

ANNIE: You want a fart in the face?

She turns her back on him and throws her skirts up.

TONY: I get it. You're trying to provoke Big Bad Tony into kicking you out into the street, so you won't have to make up your own mind. Well, I'm afraid I'm going to be a perfect gentleman and leave you to it.

He exits, leaving ANNIE alone. She seizes her bag, goes to grab the patchwork quilt – but is struck by its associations. MUSIC: a music-box echo of 'The Same Old Game'. ANNIE picks up the tailcoat. Her memory goes back to the cottage on the Jersey Shore in 1889; she turns to find RYANNY coming in from Mass, with an expensive-looking coat and hat on.

ANNIE: Just thought I'd limber up the old vocal cords. You're home early.

RYANNY: That Father Polowski gets through the sermon in ten minutes.

She takes off her hat and coat and starts tidying up, moving the furniture around to suit the cottage. ANNIE puts on the jacket and sings her 'The Same Old Game'.

ANNIE: *Now I've settled down in life,*
And I've got a little wife,
Who is charming, yes, as charming as can be.
Yet I still regret to state,
That I often stay out late,
And won't give up my liquor and latch key.

She does the 'patter', talking between verses.

ANNIE: Shed a tear for a henpecked husband, ladies and gentlemen! I mayn't wear red ties because they don't harmonize with the wallpaper, mustn't smoke except with my head poked out the window…

She sings again.

ANNIE: *But anything that goes amiss,*
I settle with a kiss,
And thus my little tigress I do tame.
For though she can come it strong,
And her nails are very long,
Still I carry on the same old game.

RYANNY: It brings me right back, to hear that song. I could nearly see the chandeliers and smell the orange peel.

ANNIE produces orange peel from her pocket.

ANNIE: No, the orange peel is real.

RYANNY: Every time I have the fruit bowl nicely arranged, you pinch something and topple my bananas.

ANNIE: How have you managed to put up with me for four years, Mrs Hindle?

RYANNY: The Lord only knows. That old jacket stinks of mothballs.

ANNIE: I thought you liked the look of me in tails.

RYANNY: I like the look of you in anything. Or nothing.

She giggles at her own badness.

ANNIE: But you admit I look best in a suit.

RYANNY: The neighbors wouldn't think so.

ANNIE: Hang the neighbors.

She imitates RYANNY before RYANNY can say it.

ANNIE: Language!

RYANNY: You know there'd be terrible talk if you took to wearing trousers.

ANNIE: There must be talk anyhow.

RYANNY: Sure the neighbors don't know we're married. The other day at the cake sale I heard Mrs Bagnall call us 'those Hindle sisters'.

ANNIE: And why didn't you set her straight?

RYANNY: It didn't seem important.

ANNIE: I ended my career for that bit of paper on the wall, and now you say it's not important?

RYANNY: It's very important to us, but not to Mrs Bagnall. I just want a bit of privacy.

ANNIE: Such a fearless kitten you were, that night in Grand Rapids, but now you've lost your nerve.

RYANNY: Well, what would you have said to her, then?

ANNIE: I'd just have stepped right up to her –

RYANNY plays Mrs Bagnall.

RYANNY: Yes, Miss Hindle? Do you wish to purchase a cherry pie?

ANNIE puts on an Irish accent to play RYANNY.

ANNIE: Mrs Big-nose, I'll have you know that I have not, for three years now, been a Miss.

RYANNY: And the lucky gentleman is?

ANNIE: A lady.

RYANNY shrieks.

ANNIE: I mean, me sister here is actually me wife.

RYANNY: Incest! Abomination! Fetch my smelling salts…

She pretends to faint into ANNIE's arms.

ANNIE: Make way! Lady in distress!

RYANNY: Put me down, you bowsie.

She straightens her costume and exits.

MUSIC: an offstage fragment of 'Could I See My Darling Again'. ANNIE, back in 1891, sheds the jacket and opens up her letters box.

RYANNY enters with her darning; it is later in 1889.

RYANNY: Read me one of those old letters.

ANNIE: What's it all add up to, eh?

RYANNY: A heavier box than Harry J. Montague.

ANNIE: I can see them carving it on the headstone now: 'She Had a Heavier Box Than Harry. J. Montague.'

RYANNY: Don't be cynical. It doesn't suit you.

ANNIE: Let's face it, I was never no Bernhardt.

RYANNY: Lookit, you made hundreds of thousands of people laugh and blush and clap and faint in the aisles…

ANNIE: That was mostly the heat from the lamps.

She picks a letter at random from the box and reads it aloud, with only a little difficulty.

ANNIE: 'Dear Miss Hindle, I am sixteen years old this month and I simply…'

Stuck, she shows it to RYANNY.

RYANNY: Swoon.

ANNIE: 'Swoon when you swing your watch on its…chain.'

RYANNY: What's the date on that one?

ANNIE: 1875. She'd be married with six little 'uns by now.

RYANNY: Did you ever get Ella to write back to them?

ANNIE: What was there to say?

RYANNY: What keeps me awake of nights is thinking that I made you give up all that for –

She stops herself from saying 'nothing'.

ANNIE: For all this.

RYANNY: Whenever you got up to New York for the day, I sit here listening out for the last train, thinking to myself, maybe she won't be coming back.

ANNIE: Sweetheart! I just like to stroll around town once in a while, see the sights. I'll always be coming back.

RYANNY: I know. But you must find the time hangs heavy on your hands.

ANNIE: Only once in a while. You think I was never bored rigid standing around waiting for a matinee to start? What I have here, I've never had before: peace. Now what's brought all this on?

RYANNY: Foolishness.

ANNIE: The last thing I want to be is Tony Pastor's whipping boy again, running between the two-a-day halls, trying to remember the words to 'Percy from Pimlico'.

RYANNY: You always did mix up the third verse with 'Bertie Bright from Bond Street'.

ANNIE: There you go. See why I prefer a life of leisure with the daily paper and the prettiest missus on the East Coast?

RYANNY: Give over! I'll be in the pantry, sorting out those pickle jars.

She exits. MUSIC: an offstage fragment of 'Could I See My Darling Again'.

ANNIE, back in 1891, tries to remember when things started going wrong.

RYANNY enters, carrying a towel; it is 1889 again.

ANNIE: What's all this spring cleaning for, in the middle of a heatwave?

RYANNY: I just want to get things shipshape.

ANNIE: You're always exhausted by bedtime.

An awkward moment; RYANNY knows what she's hinting at.

ANNIE: Why don't we get in a maid?

RYANNY: Ah, I'd be ashamed to lord it over some other biddy fresh off the boat.

ANNIE: If I know you, you'd give her the feather duster and do all the scrubbing yourself.

RYANNY: Do you, I wonder?

ANNIE: Do I what?

RYANNY: Know me.

ANNIE: I should think so, by now.

RYANNY: You don't know what's on my conscience.

ANNIE: About us?

RYANNY: No, no. I told a lie.

ANNIE: *(In mock shock.)* No!

RYANNY: A big one.

ANNIE: To me?

RYANNY: To everyone. I denied the Little Sisters.

ANNIE: Whose little sisters?

RYANNY: They said they'd ship me to New York at their own expense, if I joined the Order in Dublin.

ANNIE: The Order? I've married a nun?

RYANNY puts on the towel as a veil.

RYANNY: Sister Peter, at your service.

ANNIE bursts out laughing.

ANNIE: Why didn't you ever say?

RYANNY: It wasn't worth all the mockery I'd get for it in the dressing-room.

ANNIE: But after the wedding. I thought we told each other everything.

RYANNY: Nearly everything.

ANNIE: So why today?

RYANNY: I just need to get it off my chest.

ANNIE: I thought I knew all about you.

RYANNY: Lookit, I wasn't in the convent in New York long enough to take the vows, even. I wasn't good enough.

ANNIE: Says who?

RYANNY: The Mistess of Novices. She told me I was willful because I wouldn't let them give my mother's quilt to the poor; she said it was more than I needed. So I walked out with my bag and quilt and fifty cents in change. When I passed the Dominion Theater, it said on the door, 'Capable Female Required'. So that's how I ended up here.

She exits. MUSIC: offstage introduction to 'Postcard from Gilbert'.
Enter GILBERT, in a nun's habit, writing a postcard.

GILBERT: *Dear Girls, I'm tickled pink*
By Ryanny's past as Sister Pete.
Not even I in full regalia
Could look so sweet.
How this card will find you swell
By morning noon and night,
And that life upon the Jersey Shore
Continues to delight?
The dressers are all clumsy,

And my wife has thrown me out
For a teeny indiscretion –
He turned out to be a lout –
So I'm lodging temporarily
On the Lower East Side.
If you ever come to town,
My little doors will open wide.
Ella swears she'll write, and
I don't know if she will, but
Meanwhile, yours with all
The usual love from Gilbert.

> *He exits. MUSIC: offstage echo of first two lines of 'Could I See My*
> *Darling Again'. Later in 1889, ANNIE sneaks up on RYANNY, who*
> *is asleep in a chair, and sings her gently awake.*

ANNIE: *Could I see my darling again,*
I'd eat hat, necktie, fob watch and cane,
I'd dive into the sea, let a whale swallow me,
Could I see my darling again.

Come down to the water with me, next time, if you're not too tired. The moon was so bright, I nearly pulled this darn dress over my head and ran into the waves. But then I thought I might lose track of which way the shore was, and you'd get mad if I drowned.

> *RYANNY kisses ANNIE's fingers, tasting them.*

RYANNY: Salty.

ANNIE: Amazing to think it's the very same ocean you used to paddle in when you were a girl. Could have been the same drops of water, even, if the tides brought them over a couple at a time.

> *Enter ELLA in a man's suit and hat and huge moustache, carrying*
> *a travelling bag. ANNIE and RYANNY jump apart.*

ANNIE: Who are you and what's your business?

> *ELLA drops her bag, pushes up her hat and laughs.*

241

ANNIE: Ella!

ELLA: I forgot, you've never seen me in this get-up.

RYANNY: She certainly can carry it off, can't she?

ANNIE: What are you doing in New Jersey in your stage clobber?

ELLA: I just find it quicker to travel this way; less nuisance from fellows.

ANNIE: It's the chin. A perfect boy's chin.

ELLA: I don't pass for a boy. You're just jealous because I look so good in a suit.

RYANNY: And doesn't Annie look good in a dress?

ELLA: Pretty as a picture.

ANNIE: You watch yourself, chum.

RYANNY: Tea, anyone?

ELLA: None of that cat-lap stuff.

ANNIE: One large whisky coming up.

ELLA: That's more like it.

RYANNY: Sit down here. You don't look a day older, let alone nearly four years.

ELLA: You do.

RYANNY: I'm fine. Just a bit thinner.

ELLA: No, it suits you. This is quite a home sweet home. So what do you do with yourselves all day?

ANNIE: This and that. I go out fishing with Doctor Murdoch. Gave a speech on tulips to the Horticultural Club last week.

ELLA: Since when are you an expert on tulips?

ANNIE: Ah, retirement has made a new man of me. You know I can read now?

RYANNY: She writes poems too. They're very good.

ELLA: I'll bet.

RYANNY: And I've learned to swim at last.

ANNIE: She wears a natty little striped costume.

RYANNY: Shush. And in the evenings Annie sings to me.

ELLA: Let me guess. 'The Maid of Erin'? 'Wife of My Bosom'? 'O Share My Cottage, Gentle Maid'?

ANNIE: I'd forgotten how fast you talk. You never said much on your postcards.

ELLA: You never came to see me in New York.

RYANNY: Well, we're all three here now, aren't we?

ELLA: Four. I've just remembered, I left her standing on the porch.

She dashes out.

ANNIE: You left someone out on our porch?

ELLA: *(Offstage.)* Come in, come in!

She carries in Miss Dimity, wrapped up in cloth.

ANNIE: The neighbors will really wonder about us now.

ELLA: Miss Dimity here is a very delayed wedding present. She caused quite a stir on the train.

ANNIE: Another woman – how unsuitable!

RYANNY: She brings me right back. Makes me feel I should be running around altering seams.

ELLA: Can't say I miss dresser work.

RYANNY: Who've you got dressing the Troupe nowadays?

ELLA: A ghastly German called Gretel. Makes me stand around for hours in my long johns while she sticks pins in my knees.

RYANNY: Looks like you're thriving on it.

ANNIE: Don't suppose you're on thirty dollars a week anymore.

ELLA: Try multiplying that by ten.

ANNIE whistles, impressed.

ELLA: My favorite sketch is this tipsy dude called Captain Cuff going into a barber shop…

ANNIE: You should get Tony to teach you the one about the bishop.

ELLA: Tell you the truth, I'm not going back to the Troupe.

ANNIE: You're not?

ELLA: Thought I'd do a little European tour. Josie's got friends in Paris.

RYANNY: Josie's going with you?

ELLA: We're meeting in New York tomorrow, at the shop.

ANNIE: Tomorrow? What's Big Jim Fisk going to say about you sloping off with his favorite lady?

ELLA: He's not going to be saying much about anything anymore. Ned Stokes shot him in the stomach this morning, halfway up the stairs of the Grand Central Hotel. I can't hardly believe he's dead yet.

ANNIE: So you're skedaddling to Europe.

ELLA: Josie didn't have nothing to do with the shooting! I just want to get her away from that pack of jackals that call themselves reporters.

ANNIE: I imagine Josie Mansfield is well able to take care of herself.

ELLA: Maybe so. Maybe she's just pretending she needs taking care of, but it feels good anywhichway. After all those years of Aunt Trudi feeding me, you giving me orders for costumes, Tony teaching me routines – finally I'm the one booking the tickets.

RYANNY: We'll miss you.

ELLA: You haven't set eyes on me in four years.

ANNIE: But we always knew you were never more than a train ride away.

ELLA: I'll send cards from Paris.

RYANNY: See you in the morning, Ella.

ANNIE: You off to bed, love?

RYANNY: I'm sorry, I can't seem to keep my eyes open.

ANNIE: Ella can manage another little one.

ELLA: Just a sip.

RYANNY: Goodnight, so.

She carries the dummy off with her.

ELLA: Nighty-night. *(To ANNIE.)* Is she all right?

ANNIE: She's fine, just tired. Well, I got my three wishes, didn't I? Fame, fortune, and the finest pair of arms a body could wake up in.

ELLA: Long may you keep them.

ANNIE: So what are your three?

ELLA: Josie, Josie, and… Josie.

ANNIE: Curvacious kind of girl, ain't she?

ELLA: There's not a straight line about her. Hair's so black it's nearly purple, all coiled up around her little ears.

ANNIE: You still using that contraption you told me about, when you're…doing the agreeable?

ELLA: Can't get enough of it.

ANNIE: I mentioned it to Ryanny once – in case she had a hankering for such like – and you know what she said?

ELLA: What?

ANNIE: *(In RYANNY's Irish accent.)* 'Sure if I'd wanted a great big knob inside me, I could have married one.'

They fall about laughing.

ANNIE: Speaking of which. How's Gilbert these days?

ELLA: Dyeing his hair.

ANNIE: He's not!

ELLA: It looks swell. He's the one who came up with this Europe plan, when I got Josie's telegram this morning.

ANNIE: I hope he stays with Tony. Pastor's Grand Speciality Troupe seems to be dwindling.

ELLA: Tony's the one who always say, 'In this business you gotta keep moving.'

ANNIE: I got sick of moving. I sang in just about every two-a-day hall in America to pay for these walls, and they're built to last.

ELLA: Well. Sweet dreams.

ANNIE: Sweet dreams.

ELLA exits. And ANNIE finds herself alone in 1891 again. She feels the cold; finds the patchwork quilt and wraps it around herself. Unaccompanied, bleakly, she sings a snatch of 'Could I See My Darling Again'.

ANNIE: *Could I see my darling again,*
I'd eat hat, necktie, fob watch and cane...

Enter RYANNY in a nightdress, another night, later in 1890.

RYANNY: Aren't you coming to bed?

ANNIE: In a minute. Didn't want to disturb you.

RYANNY: You never disturb me.

ANNIE: Well. Seems like for a couple months now you're always too tired.

RYANNY: It's the heat.

ANNIE: Nothing else? Sometimes I get crazy thoughts like maybe you just married me for security.

RYANNY: You mean for your money?

ANNIE: The whole package. A ring and a house and someone to talk to.

RYANNY: I had plenty of people to talk to in the Troupe, and I was doing just fine on my own wages. And I'll have you know, I'd refused two good offers from Irishmen in New York.

ANNIE: Which Irishmen?

RYANNY: Never you mind, they weren't important. You haven't two brains to rub together, have you? If I was a regular husband-hunter, how did I come to fall head-over-heels for a woman in a suit?

ANNIE: I know you wanted me back then. But I think you've lost the taste for it now.

RYANNY: Ah it's not that at all.

ANNIE: Do I do the wrong things? Am I greedy? Clumsy?

RYANNY: Never. How could you think that?

ANNIE: What else is there for me to think?

RYANNY: Oh you creature! I've been too wrapped up in my own worries, it never occurred to me... I want you as much as ever I did.

ANNIE: You do?

She moves closer, and starts to unbutton RYANNY's nightdress.

RYANNY: You mustn't.

ANNIE recoils.

ANNIE: All right. I wouldn't ever lay a hand on you without your say-so, you know that.

RYANNY: I didn't mean it like that.

ANNIE: You mustn't force yourself.

RYANNY: You're not to be thinking that. Annie?

ANNIE: What?

RYANNY: What if I had something to tell you but didn't know how?

ANNIE: I like most things you tell me.

RYANNY: Not this. Something I've hidden for much too long.

ANNIE: Why?

RYANNY: Because I didn't think you could bear to hear it.

ANNIE: I'm listening. Tell me.

RYANNY: I can't. Let me show you instead.

Turned away from the audience, she undoes her nightdress enough to show ANNIE her breast.

RYANNY: You see now?

ANNIE: What's made it go like that?

RYANNY buttons herself back up.

RYANNY: I wasn't going to tell you till it starts bleeding.

ANNIE: What does it mean?

RYANNY: It's the same as my mother had. I don't know why it's come now. I ask God at Mass every week, but he's not saying much.

ANNIE: I'm going for Murdoch.

RYANNY: What could a doctor tell me that I don't know already?

ANNIE: There's things they can do nowadays.

RYANNY: It's got a grip on me, love.

ANNIE: There's operations.

RYANNY: I won't go under the knife like my mother did, with chloroform and bandages and strangers chopping me open! Don't ask me to do that.

ANNIE: Sweetheart.

RYANNY: Don't make me go to the hospital.

ANNIE: You don't have to do anything right away.

RYANNY: I won't go. This is my home.

ANNIE: All right.

RYANNY: You swear?

ANNIE picks up the quilt and wraps it around RYANNY.

ANNIE: I swear. You don't have to do anything you don't want to. You're a free woman.

RYANNY: Free as a bird.

ANNIE: How long do you reckon we've got?

RYANNY: I couldn't tell you, love. A while yet.

ANNIE: How bad does it hurt?

RYANNY: Hardly at all.

She cradles ANNIE's head against her other breast.

RYANNY: You're to remember me all smooth and whole, like I used to be, you hear?

ANNIE: What use is remembering?

RYANNY: You must. If you don't remember everything, it'll be like it never happened. Like I never got across the ocean, or we never met, or there was never this house at all, just the bare beach. That's what scares me the most: being forgotten.

MUSIC: sad, offstage echo of 'Fair Irish Girl'.

As RYANNY exits, it is 1891 again, on the night of ANNIE's second comeback. She folds up the quilt. Then takes her bandage and begins to strap her breasts tightly over her dress, talking over the music.

ANNIE: Oh yes indeed, ladies and gentlemen, you just sit tight there on your plush, parasitical behinds and watch me go through my paces. Then you can clap your fat little hands and put your coats on and drive home, feeling kind of peaceful and refreshed, and I'll stay here and live my life over and over and over again…

She forces herself to sing, unaccompanied, 'Fair Irish Girl'.

ANNIE: *They tell me of Spaniards who peep through their curls,*
Saucy Parisians who dance the can-can,
By the banks of the Nile walk the almond-eyed girls,
But what do they matter to this broken man?
My fair Irish girl, dear Irish girl,
How could she equaled be?
Bright Irish girl, dear Irish girl,
One fair Irish girl to me?

Spits her final question at the audience.

ANNIE: Will that do you?

She unwinds the bandage and puts it away. MUSIC: another echo of 'Fair Irish Girl'.

It is the day of RYANNY's wake, at the end of 1890. GILBERT enters in a man's suit, with a bunch of white flowers.

GILBERT: Annie.

ANNIE: Didn't expect you this early. Give a shake.

He shakes her hand.

GILBERT: I'm right on time.

ANNIE: Exactly.

GILBERT: I'm so sorry –

ANNIE interrupts, filling a whisky glass.

ANNIE: Will you join me?

GILBERT: Not just yet.

ANNIE: You look different in street clothes.

GILBERT: I might say the same to you.

ANNIE: What if we snuck off and traded?

GILBERT: I don't think we take the same size in corsets. Listen, I'm so very sorry –

ANNIE interrupts again.

ANNIE: Saw you as the Old Maid in Helter Skelter last year.

GILBERT: That dreadful feathered dress! Why didn't you come behind the scenes?

ANNIE: It's not my place anymore.

GILBERT: It'll always be your place.

ANNIE: So what are you up to these days?

GILBERT: Oh, you know, 'resting' for a while before the next burlesque, then I'm back to tour with Tony.

ANNIE: Sounds swell.

GILBERT: Predictable is what it sounds. I'm aging gracefully into a second-rate, middle-aged dame comedian.

ANNIE: Oh Gilbo, there's nothing second-rate about you.

GILBERT: Correction: I'm first-rate at playing second fiddle.

ANNIE: Bosh. Bunkum.

GILBERT: Twaddle and tosh.

ANNIE: Remember that time in Salt Lake City?

GILBERT: Why are we doing this? Why can't we stop for one single moment?

ANNIE: Stop what?

GILBERT: Performing! I'm standing here with these ghastly flowers that we're both pretending we can't see, and sooner or later I have to put on them on Ryanny's coffin.

ANNIE: It wasn't my idea to have a wake. If it'd been up to me I'd just have towed her out to sea, then drunk every bottle in the house. But she was very firm about it.

GILBERT: Ryanny always did like things to be done proper.

ANNIE: And to hell with little details like laws!

They laugh, then break off as ELLA enters in a black dress, carrying more flowers.

ANNIE: You're in Paris!

ELLA: Yeah, right, I'm a figment of your imagination. I'll have what you're having but in a bigger glass.

ANNIE rushes to pour her a drink.

ANNIE: Gilbert's being a good boy today.

GILBERT: It's wearing off.

ANNIE: This is meant to be an Irish wake, you know, not some poker-assed Presbyterian funeral.

GILBERT: Make mine a double, then, if I must.

ANNIE: So when did you get back States-side, Ella?

ELLA: It's a long and nasty story.

ANNIE: Aren't they all.

TONY enters with an expensive basket of flowers.

TONY: Annie. You have my most, my deepest, my very sincerest sympathies…

ANNIE: *(Interrupts.)* Two fingers or three, Tony?

TONY: Just the one for now.

She pours him a finger-length of whisky.

ANNIE: Never got a chance to apologize for running off that time in Grand Rapids and leaving you without a headliner.

TONY: Ella did just swell.

ANNIE: I'm sure.

TONY: Though I don't mind telling you I was red in the face that night. Why didn't you come to me once you got such a darn-fool nothing into your head?

ANNIE: Because you'd have wasted everybody's time trying to talk us out of it.

TONY: No, I'd just have told Miss Ryanny that she didn't have to let herself be talked into it.

They all stare at him.

GILBERT: The wedding was her idea, Tony.

TONY: A quiet girl like that?

ANNIE: She made me get down on my knees to propose.

TONY, shaken by this information, turns away. He puts his flowers on the piano, and the others do the same.

TONY: Well. Water under the bridge.

ANNIE: Tell me, Tony, how'd you have liked it if you hadn't been let walk your missus down the aisle?

TONY: Point is, not to mince words, most folks would consider a female marriage unnatural.

ANNIE: Since when have I ever given a good god-damn what most folks think?

TONY: You didn't see those letters than came flooding in after your wedding hit the papers.

GILBERT: Flooding?

ELLA: Yeah, I don't remember more than two or three.

TONY: Well, they weren't exactly congratulatory. I'll say no more. No hard feelings, eh?

GILBERT: Kiss and make up now, girls.

No response from ANNIE or TONY. So GILBERT heads for the whisky.

GILBERT: Or maybe a little refresher.

ELLA: We'll be staggering to the station.

GILBERT: Your neighbors will know that all those stories about theater folk are true.

ANNIE: That don't matter, I won't be staying.

GILBERT: No? What are your plans?

ANNIE: Don't have any, yet, but they most definitely don't include bachelor life on the Jersey Shore. Maybe I'll see the world. What's Paris like, El?

ELLA: You'd love it.

ANNIE: Yeah?

ELLA: We ran this sort of salon at the Café Americain.

TONY: That like a saloon bar?

ELLA: Much more high-class, Tony. All sorts dropped by. Writers, countesses…say, you'll never guess who I met on the arm of this rich painter woman.

ANNIE: Who?

ELLA: La Bernhardt herself!

ANNIE: No! I never took the Divine Sarah for one of us.

ELLA: Oh, they're all trying it nowadays. Specially the wives: *très chic.*

TONY: Not on this side of the Atlantic they're not.

ELLA: How would you know, Tony? What do you think goes on at those 'sewing circles' of Mrs Pastor's, anyway?

TONY: I've always said it, you suffer from a diseased imagination.

GILBERT: Dirt's in the eye of the beholder.

TONY: I'm being ganged up on by dissolutes. Where's Miss Ryanny when I need her?

His joke falls painfully flat.

ANNIE: She was a dissolute too.

TONY: She was a good woman.

ANNIE: Till I led her into evil ways?

GILBERT: He didn't mean that.

ELLA: *(To TONY.)* Take it back.

TONY: What? What did I say? I shouldn't drink liquor so early in the day.

GILBERT: *(To ANNIE.)* Tell Gilbo, now, what did you have for breakfast?

ANNIE: Couldn't face it.

GILBERT: Here.

From his jacket pocket he produces a donut wrapped in paper, and ANNIE takes it.

ANNIE: I may chuck it up all over your feet.

GILBERT: But if we don't sober you up you may topple into the grave, and that would be just too Hamlet.

ELLA: Oh Gilbert, you're so reliably shallow.

ANNIE puts the donut down untasted.

ANNIE: How are you getting on with…d'you know, I'm terribly sorry, but I've forgotten your wife's name.

ELLA: He's been known to forget it himself.

GILBERT: Elizabeth and I rub along allright.

ELLA: You two shoulda got hitched, way back.

GILBERT: *(To ANNIE.)* Now why did we never think of that?

ANNIE: We wouldn't have given each other any trouble.

GILBERT: But I'd never have agreed to live in New Jersey.

ANNIE: Snob!

GILBERT: We must be a hundred miles from the nearest good restaurant.

ELLA: There are no good restaurants on this side of the Atlantic.

ANNIE: So what's dragged you back?

ELLA: What drags me anywhere?

ANNIE: How is the lovely Miss Mansfield?

ELLA: None of my business anymore.

GILBERT: Since when?

ELLA: Since she's got hitched again, to her slimy boozer of a lawyer.

ANNIE: Oh, El.

ELLA: I guess the shooting shook Josie up so bad, she wants a bit of respectability. Josephine, she calls herself now.

ANNIE: I should have kept in touch.

ELLA: That's all right.

ANNIE: No, I should have written. I should have told you all that she was sick.

GILBERT: I would have liked to pay a visit.

ANNIE: Ryanny wouldn't have let you. It was the bandages, see; they smelled pretty bad. It got so she wouldn't let anybody in the house but me.

ELLA: Did you write to her folks back in Ireland?

ANNIE: She always claimed they'd moved to another village and she'd lost the address. But yesterday I came across an old letter from her father. Said she wasn't to trouble to write anymore, because any girl who'd run off from a convent was no kin of his. So now they'll never even know if she's alive or –

ELLA: *(Interrupts.)* Serves 'em right, if you ask me.

GILBERT: Folks like that don't deserve the spit out of your mouth.

ANNIE: By the end, I wanted her to die. Can you believe that? She wouldn't eat and she couldn't sleep and she was rotting away from the inside. I never prayed in my life before, but I was praying she wouldn't last much longer.

TONY: Best not to dwell on these things.

ANNIE: And how do you propose I stop?

TONY: Well, I don't know.

ANNIE: It's like a dream where I'm doing some song with an endless number of verses, and my knees are collapsing under me but I can't leave the stage.

GILBERT: Gotta keep your mind on the good times, I suppose.

ANNIE: It hurts even more to remember them.

ELLA: When's the last time you stepped out of this house?

ANNIE: Don't remember.

TONY: Sea air, that's what you need.

ANNIE: Sea air is not what I need.

TONY: We understand.

ANNIE: I doubt you understand the first damn thing!

TONY: All right, so we don't.

In the silence, GILBERT chats to ELLA quietly.

GILBERT: So what've you been up to at the Waverly?

ELLA: Wait till you see my new act: Lightning Quick Change is the future of musical humor.

GILBERT: Not for me it's not. I had a painful experience with a cord-release costume last year in Cincinnati.

ELLA: You gotta be pretty light on your feet. I come on as George Washington, right? Then when the music changes, they pull the little strings backstage and my cloak slips off, and I'm in a washerwoman costume doing a jig. Then one more pull and I'm in a sailor suit with a skipping rope… Hey, it's not *Camille*, but it pays the rent.

TONY: Oh for the good old days when folks came to listen to the music.

GILBERT: Why don't we get Annie to give us a song?

ANNIE: Your timing's way off, Gilbo.

GILBERT: Come on. What's a wake without a song?

ANNIE: Give us one yourself.

GILBERT: I can't sing in a suit! Besides, I asked first.

ELLA finds the tailcoat and brings it to ANNIE.

ELLA: Hey, put this on and you'll feel more like yourself.

TONY: Come along now, curtain's twitching.

ANNIE reluctantly lets ELLA help her into the jacket.

ANNIE: Any reasonable requests considered, ladies and gentlemen.

GILBERT: Give us 'Walking on the Balcony'.

ELLA: No, no. 'Frightfully Freddy'.

ANNIE: I've got it.

> *She sings TONY's trademark number, 'Hold Your Own', hesitantly at first, accompanied by offstage piano.*

ANNIE: *If the world it goes against you*
And you're struggling for a bone,
If the friends that once flocked around you
Have flapped their wings and flown,
If your lady love…

> *She chokes, briefly. The others move closer, and TONY takes up the song.*

TONY: *If your lady love has slipped away*
And left you quite alone –

ANNIE/TONY: *Why that's the time, me laddy buck,*
To grip and hold your own.

> *ANNIE starts into the next verse with verve, her voice magnificent.*

ANNIE: *If luck has turned against you,*
Don't sit around and moan.
If the debt-collectors pay a call,
And take a hateful tone,
Or if you're tossed by fickle Fate,
Let falt'ring ne'er be known,
For that's the time, my laddy buck,
To grip and hold your own!

GILBERT: Yes, yes, yes!

ELLA: Magnifique!

> *TONY slaps ANNIE on the back.*

TONY: You've still got it.

She starts taking off the jacket.

ANNIE: It could do with a brush-down.

TONY: Not the jacket. The knack.

ANNIE: It hasn't been that many years.

As she puts the jacket away, he conspires with the others.

TONY: I've just had a whamdinger of a notion. She should come back to the Troupe.

ANNIE: I'm not a performer anymore.

GILBERT: Ha!

ELLA: Listen to her.

TONY: That's bosh and you know it. I guess you'll need a few weeks to pack things up around here…

ELLA: We could do a duet.

TONY: Two male impersonators, juggling top hats! That'd be one in the eye for Koster and Bial.

ANNIE: I've got a better idea. Why don't you hire some fresh young thing to impersonate me?

TONY: It's not like you to turn down such a generous offer. Who else is going to take you on now you're a little rusty?

ELLA: Seems to me her voice is as good as ever.

ANNIE: Rusty's the wrong word. I'm falling apart here.

TONY: What you need is a twenty-city tour of the two-a-day halls to keep you from brooding.

ANNIE: Maybe what you need is to mind your own business.

TONY: As a mark of friendship, I didn't hear that. Listen, when my first wife passed on, God rest her soul, I worked so hard I got palpitations. But it got me through. So come back to us!

GILBERT: It'd be like old times.

ELLA: Think before you speak, for once.

ANNIE: I haven't missed the business.

TONY: Who'd miss it, if they had Miss Ryanny on hand, night noon and morning? But things are different now.

GILBERT: I don't think she needs reminding.

TONY: What she needs is to be back up on that stage with the lights, the applause, the letters pouring in…

ANNIE: I thought you said they hated me ever since the wedding?

TONY: Ah, the public are like children – real short memories. Anyway, what choice have you got? Who are you going to be now if you're not the one, the only –

ANNIE: Leave it out.

TONY: – the unique, the inimitable –

ANNIE: I said –

TONY: – the irresistible –

GILBERT: Ease off, old boy.

TONY: Miss Annie Hindle!

ANNIE picks up her box of letters and empties it on the floor, howling.

ANNIE: The only good thing about me's going six feet under, and what's left is garbage!

Her guests withdraw and pick up their flowers. ANNIE tidies things away, lifts RYANNY's chair and puts it face to the wall. The guests process off as if to the funeral.

ANNIE is left alone in the dressing-room in 1891. She starts halfheartedly collecting the fallen letters.

ANNIE: I don't have to stay just for them. I never promised. I don't owe anybody anything. I'm free. Free as a bird.

TONY enters tentatively, with his show-book.

TONY: Still a little stage-fraught, are we? Annie, Annie, you've a genius for making things hard for yourself. Look, I want to help you out. I think you could be a star again. All right? Only you're not to give me any more trouble. I'm doing you a favor here. I can't keep handing out chances.

He starts to leave, then can't resist drawing one final moral.

TONY: You know what your problem is?

ANNIE: My problem?

TONY: You're jealous.

ANNIE: Of who?

TONY: Of me. Of what I've got and you don't got.

ANNIE: Tony, I have no wish to see what's in your trousers, but I very much doubt it would inspire me with jealousy.

TONY: But you can never quite forget what you're missing, can you?

ANNIE: All I'm missing is my wife. And you know what your problem is? I'm the one she chose. I'm the one she loved.

TONY: Well, it could hardly have been expected to last.

ANNIE: Beg your pardon?

TONY: You must admit, a woman like that should have got married –

ANNIE: She did.

TONY: – had a family –

ANNIE: We were a family.

TONY: It wasn't a healthy life.

ANNIE: I'll bet she was happier than your wife. We had nearly five years. I'd have given her all the years I had left, only she got a lump in her breast. You telling me that was my punishment from the Man Upstairs?

LADIES AND GENTLEMEN: ACT TWO

TONY shakes his head, and exits.

ANNIE addresses the fallen letters, moving them with her foot.

ANNIE: My dearests, my darlings, my ones and onlys, my old faithfuls. Not always faithful, come to think of it, but always there, always looking my way. Thank you for swallowing up most of the days of my life. And if I can't be with you in person tonight, it's only because I'll be catching the next train to anywhere.

She grabs her bag. She's almost reached the door when she hears ELLA and GILBERT in the corridor, joking as they hurry in.

GILBERT: *(Offstage.)* So I said, 'Stop it, I'm old enough to be your grandfather!'

ELLA: Annie!

GILBERT: Welcome back!

ELLA: Here we all are again.

Assuming ANNIE has only just arrived, ELLA takes ANNIE's bag and starts helping her off with her coat.

GILBERT: You weren't supposed to get here before us. You were meant to rush in late, and I'd leap out at you and shout, 'Surprise!'

He does it, holding out his present for her.

ANNIE: Whose eyebrow is this?

GILBERT: It's a brand-new, ultra elegant moustache.

ANNIE: Listen –

GILBERT: It's for luck.

ELLA starts unfastening ANNIE's skirt, to dress her.

ANNIE: Listen, I can't stay.

ELLA: What?

ANNIE: I was just on my way out when you came in.

GILBERT: You can't go.

ELLA shoves ANNIE's leg to unbalance her and make her step out of her skirt.

ELLA: Baloney. Not after all the work we put into persuading you.

GILBERT: Give us one good reason.

ANNIE: How many would you like?

ELLA: Jeez, Annie, I thought you'd made up your mind.

ANNIE: I do. Every five minutes.

TONY stalks in without making eye contact with anyone.

TONY: Here's the new show bill. Gilbert, you're on third and fifteenth. Ella, eighth and twenty-first.

GILBERT: *(Puzzled.)* Who's opening?

TONY: *(As he exits.)* The Bumblebee Boy.

ELLA: What about Annie? Tony!

He's gone. She turns to ANNIE.

ELLA: That's it? You're gonna leave the stage to a human insect?

ANNIE: Looks like my mind's been made up for me.

GILBERT storms over with ANNIE's suit and hustles her into it.

GILBERT: That's the biggest heap of horseshit I ever heard. Annie Hindle never misses a performance.

ELLA: What would Ryanny think of you?

ANNIE: That's not fair.

ELLA: None of it's fair. But if you walk out on us now, you won't be the woman she married.

ANNIE: You think I want to go? This is all I've got. But what have I got left to give?

ELLA: You're as good a performer as you ever were.

ANNIE: But a comeback has to be better. A comeback takes magic. What if I walk out on stage and nothing happens?

ELLA: Faint heart never yet won an encore.

She brandishes the trousers, holding them for ANNIE to step into.

ANNIE grabs them and pulls them on.

ANNIE: I still maintain Tony Pastor is scum.

ELLA: So what's new?

GILBERT: To be fair to the man, he did come to the wake; at least he's loyal to his old performers.

ELLA: Loyal? Don't flatter yourself. He's always had a weakness for blue-eyed girls.

GILBERT: Not just girls either.

ELLA: Gilbert Saroney!

GILBERT: He made up to me once, when I was new to the business.

ANNIE: You never told me that.

GILBERT: Oh, nothing happened. I moved my thigh away till his hand fell off and went on eating my ice cream.

ELLA: And him with his 'good wholesome family entertainment'.

GILBERT: He'd put his dying grandmother on the trapeze to make a buck. That's why we work for him. The man is vaudeville.

They put the finishing touches to ANNIE's costume as TONY starts his introductory patter. MUSIC: on-stage PIANIST plays the 'Roll Up' theme throughout.

TONY: Ladies and gentlemen! You are always treated to a glittering line-up when Tony Pastor's Grand Speciality Troupe comes to town, but tonight you'll find that all that glitters is indeed gold. Very soon you will be charmed by that Belle of every Ball known as Mr Gilbert Saroney, dazzled by a Dozen Dainty Dutch Clog Dancers, left all-agog by Felix Fin's Elastic Skin, amazed by Lifelife Impressions of the President, rendered speechless by Miss Ella Wesner's Lightning Quick Changes, and utterly overwhelmed by the sight of Salome Shedding Her Veils While Juggling Balls of Fire! But first. A little change in the line-up. Our curtain-raising act tonight will be a truly extra-ordinary young fellow from the Outer Hebrides, fast becoming a legend for his remarkable similarities to one of those furry insects that make honey for your ham.

ANNIE comes to the edge of the stage.

TONY: Let me urge you to put your best hands together for the Bumble –

He breaks off in surprise as he catches sight of her. It could go either way…but he introduces her and steps back.

TONY: Ladies and gentleman, Miss Annie Hindle.

MUSIC: PIANIST plays 'A Real Man'.

ANNIE: *I'm an elegant swell, a flash young spark,*
I take snuff, and I'm partial to rum.
By day a roué, a gay dog in the dark,
I can whistle as easy as hum.
So why do the ladies neglect me?
Shun my advances, be coy?
I wish some kind female would tell me
Why I'm still a bachelor boy.
That feller who sits there beside you, my dear,
What's he got? I declare, it's a swizz.
There's no pleasure that I would deny you, my dear,
My pocket's as heavy as his.
So why must I do without kissing?
I'm as real a real man as they come.

Please tell me, what could I be missing?
As men go, I'm much realer than some.
I've been to the east and I've been to the west,
From Philly right through to San Fran,
Of the fellers I've met, I'm the out-and-out best,
I'm the model of modern man.
So you mustn't forget me, dear madams,
When the last curtain tears us apart –
When each Eve hurries home with her Adam,
Don't deny me a place in your heart.

Curtain.

DON'T DIE WONDERING

Scenes

Don't Die Wondering

A one-act play, first produced at the Dublin Gay Theatre Festival, 2005.

Adapted by Emma Donoghue from her radio play of the same name, produced by BBC Radio 4 (2000).

Dramatis Personae

SAOIRSE ALLEN (pronounced SEER-sha) a chef in
her twenties

BARBARA CONNOLLY a police officer
(Garda, entry level) in her twenties

GER ALLEN Saoirse's mother, a grocer in her fifties

KNEEZER GROGAN a video-rental shop owner,
in his fifties

JOHN DOHENY Saoirse's boss, a bar/restaurant owner,
in his fifties

THE SERGEANT a police officer (one level above Garda),
in his forties

THE REPORTER (can double with the Sergeant)

SALAD

We hear SAOIRSE ALLEN half-singing, half-humming something upbeat. She enters in a stained chef's uniform with a huge bowl of salad, sets it down and adds more ingredients. JOHN DOHENY bursts in and tastes a leaf.

SAOIRSE: Did you wash those hands?

DOHENY: Is that what you call a mixed-salad appetizer?

SAOIRSE: What's wrong with it?

DOHENY: It could be a Special of the Day at twice the price.

SAOIRSE: Fire away.

He starts to leave.

SAOIRSE: The salmon's getting a bit elderly.

DOHENY: It'll have to do.

KNEEZER GROGAN puts his head into the kitchen.

KNEEZER: Mister Doheny.

DOHENY: Kneezer Grogan, how are you tonight?

KNEEZER: Never better.

DOHENY: How's the video rental trade?

SAOIRSE: Must be the last hold-out in Ireland!

KNEEZER: Saoirse Allen. New York was too much for you, was it?

SAOIRSE: Ah, how could it compare to Ballyaigan?

DOHENY: We should get out of the girl's way.

KNEEZER: It was a pint and a short I wanted.

DOHENY: Is Mick not on the bar?

KNEEZER: He's chatting up the lady golfers.

DOHENY rushes out to rebuke his barman.

KNEEZER: So. Saoirse. You've filled out a bit since you were a teenager.

She gives him a withering look.

He sticks his finger into her salad and sucks it.

SAOIRSE: Get out of that!

KNEEZER: Tasty.

SAOIRSE: I'm sure your drinks are ready.

He hangs around, examines her colourful coat, her bag covered in old badges.

KNEEZER: What's that?

SAOIRSE: What?

KNEEZER: 'Don't Die Wondering'. Good one. I think I've heard of them.

SAOIRSE: I doubt it.

KNEEZER: Is it not a band?

SAOIRSE: It's not a band.

KNEEZER: What is it, then?

SAOIRSE: I'm trying to work here.

KNEEZER: Can't you talk and toss salad at the same time? I don't think Doheny would want you being unfriendly to his customers.

SAOIRSE: It's a lesbian thing.

KNEEZER: You what?

SAOIRSE: 'Don't Die Wondering.' It means you never know till you try.

KNEEZER: You haven't tried me yet!

SAOIRSE works on.

KNEEZER: Are you serious? You're a lezzer?

SAOIRSE: Are you the alternative?

NEIGHBOURHOOD WATCH

In the Garda Station, the SERGEANT and BARBARA CONNOLLY are at screens side by side. She is working at speed; he is watching something funny online.

BARBARA: There you go, Sergeant.

SERGEANT: Good work. What's that?

BARBARA: I just cc'd you on my report on burglar alarms for the Neighbourhood Watch.

SERGEANT: Great girl.

BARBARA: It's nineteen pages long and says that having a burglar alarm just might help stop you from getting burgled.

SERGEANT: Have we been failing to stretch you of late, Barbara?

BARBARA: I was wondering when I might get to do some real work.

SERGEANT: The Neighbourhood Watch is a crucial element of community policing.

BARBARA: You mean it keeps the aul biddies off your back. I'm learning nothing.

SERGEANT: You're honing your skills. Tact, patience, euphemism… Besides, it'll help you put down roots in Ballyaigan.

BARBARA: Is that part of the job?

SERGEANT: There's more to life than the job.

BARBARA: I thought maybe I could look into that knifing.

SERGEANT: Fergus is onto it.

He checks the time on his phone, and puts on his coat.

SERGEANT: Safe home now, Barbara.

BARBARA: Night, Sergeant.

She works on till her phone rings. She winces at that particular ringtone, but eventually answers it.

BARBARA: Mum. At work. I'm just finishing up. No I can't just swan off home at five o'clock. Lots of stuff, some of it urgent. Well, for instance, at the moment I'm…liaison officer on a community outreach initiative. No, Neighbourhood Watch is only part of it.

SACKED

DOHENY approaches SAOIRSE in the kitchen.

DOHENY: Saoirse –

SAOIRSE: Try this.

DOHENY: No, listen to me –

SAOIRSE: Try it!

He accepts the spoonful.

SAOIRSE: Fucking fabulous, or what?

DOHENY: Have you got a minute?

SAOIRSE: Do I look like I've got a minute?

DOHENY: There've been complaints.

SAOIRSE: Is it the salmon?

He shakes his head.

She guesses.

SAOIRSE: How many complaints?

DOHENY: What did you say to Kneezer Grogan?

SAOIRSE: Ah not this again.

DOHENY: Is it true? I don't mean, is it true what he says you said to him, because I don't need to know, I couldn't care less what you do in your spare time, I just need to know as a matter of record if you said what he said you said?

SAOIRSE: I suppose that depends what he said I said and whether he was too drunk to hear, remember and pronounce it correctly enough for it to be a matter of record.

DOHENY: Saoirse.

SAOIRSE: But of course you couldn't care less, so hey, what does it matter?

DOHENY: I care about my staff provoking the customers. He claims you made a personal attack on him and on men in general.

SAOIRSE laughs.

SAOIRSE: Kneezer Grogan is the biggest bollix in Ballyaigan.

DOHENY: He's also a regular and so are all his friends.

SAOIRSE: He's a regular arsehole.

DOHENY: Lookit, I'm as liberal as the next man. Didn't I put that condom machine in the jacks years before the other pubs? I've never barred tinkers or asylum seekers. I don't mind who or what anybody may or may not be so long as they don't go rubbing anyone else's noses in it and alienating the clientele.

SAOIRSE: I wouldn't rub Kneezer Grogan's nose for any amount of money.

DOHENY: The thing about an incident like this –

SAOIRSE: *(Interrupts.)* There was no incident! I answered a question.

DOHENY: Well, let's put it behind us.

SAOIRSE: Fine by me.

DOHENY: I just need you to guarantee me there'll be no more scenes.

SAOIRSE: Fine, if you'll guarantee me there'll be no more bollixes.

DOHENY: I'm serious now.

SAOIRSE: So am I.

DOHENY: You've never been serious for five minutes in your life. Listen, all I'm asking you to do is button your lip.

For the first time, she stops cooking.

SAOIRSE: You don't pay me enough for that.

DOHENY produces a thick fold of banknotes and starts to count some out.

DOHENY: Then here's to the end of the week.

SAOIRSE: I don't believe this.

She walks out without the money.

PICKET

Early evening, the next night. SAOIRSE takes her stand outside DOHENY's with a scrawled placard that reads VICTIM OF UNFAIR DISMISSAL.

SAOIRSE: Howarya, Eileen. Mr Duggan. Evening, Father.

DOHENY bursts out the door.

DOHENY: What in Jesus d'you think you're at?

SAOIRSE: What does it look like?

She warns an approaching customer.

SAOIRSE: This is a legitimate picket line – are you sure you want to cross it?

She smiles in satisfaction as the unseen customer veers away from DOHENY's.

SAOIRSE: Good call.

DOHENY: You and what union? You were cash in hand, under the table. Go on home to your mammy and don't be making a show of yourself.

SAOIRSE: I'm not the one who's afraid of bad publicity.

DOHENY: Get away from my door this minute.

SAOIRSE: I've a right to picket. This is a public space.

DOHENY: You can pick your nose out here for all the good it'll do you.

He disappears back inside.

SAOIRSE walks up and down. Begins to flag a little. She sits down crosslegged, leaning her placard against her head.

KNEEZER GROGAN comes out, drunk, mirthful. Uses his beer bottle as a mike.

KNEEZER: Would you look who it is. Ballyaigan's own Martina, striking a blow for sexual freedom. Maybe she's just making the best of things, though. Maybe she hasn't had an offer in so long, she's given up. Somebody should do something, maybe. It'd be a kindness. What d'you say, lassie? Full Cure Guaranteed Or Your Money Back.

He approaches, stagily undoing his flies.

SAOIRSE: Get the fuck away from me or I'll strike a blow to free your bollix from your body.

KNEEZER: Would you listen to Miss Butch!

DOHENY puts his head out in response to the raised voices.

KNEEZER nonchalantly covers his flies with his crossed hands.

DOHENY: Ah now, Kneezer.

KNEEZER: Night, Doheny.

He moves off slowly, waving to SAOIRSE.

DOHENY: How long are you going to keep up this malarky?

SAOIRSE: Believe me, I'd rather be cooking.

Sound of a bottle smashing.

PROTECTION

In the Garda Station, a little later. The SERGEANT is websurfing when SAOIRSE enters.

SERGEANT: Saoirse. How's Ger's hip?

SAOIRSE: Ah…knitting up nicely, thanks.

She places the stump of a beer bottle on his desk.

SERGEANT: Recycling's round the back.

SAOIRSE: No, I want to report… I'm looking for protection.

SERGEANT: Condoms, is it?

SAOIRSE: No! John Doheny sacked me for being gay, so I'm picketing the restaurant, and Kneezer Grogan just threw this at my head.

SERGEANT: Right.

SAOIRSE: He's at home above his shop this minute if you want to arrest him.

SERGEANT: Did you ever hear how Kneezer got his name, Saoirse? Any player got in his way, he'd knee him in the goolies when the ref wasn't looking.

SAOIRSE: And that's relevant…how?

SERGEANT: This is a busy station.

SAOIRSE looks around and snorts with amusement.

BARBARA comes in with two mugs and a packet of biscuits.

SERGEANT: Garda Connolly!

His delighted tone puts her on guard.

Then she does a double take as she recognizes SAOIRSE.

SAOIRSE: Hiya. I thought it was you at Mass.

Confused, BARBARA looks at the SERGEANT for instruction.

SAOIRSE: Seven o'clock tomorrow night outside Doheny's, so.

She walks out before anyone can object.

SERGEANT: That young one is on some class of strike, and wants 'protection' from yobbos.

BARBARA: I knew Saoirse Allen at boarding school.

SERGEANT: Excellent: the two of you can catch up.

BARBARA: She's a complete timewaster.

SERGEANT: So's ninety-nine per cent of the public.

BARBARA: Ninety-nine per cent of the public aren't out picketing pubs.

SERGEANT: Weren't you dying for something to do? You'll be keeping the peace, pouring a bit of oil on the old hot potato.

BARBARA: Have you ever tried pouring oil on a hot potato?

SERGEANT: Herself never lets me in the kitchen. As a favour, Barbara?

BARBARA: I want the next knifing. Even if it's not a knife.

SERGEANT: The next assault with a weapon on the mean streets of Ballyaigan is yours.

THE WORLD AND ITS MOTHER

Tonight SAOIRSE's placard says WHAT'S WRONG WITH MY COOKING?

DOHENY leans out the door and holds up one index finger.

DOHENY: One more full week's wages, and let's hear no more about it.

> *SAOIRSE puts up her middle finger.*

> *BARBARA arrives and takes up her position as far as possible from SAOIRSE.*

SAOIRSE: Babs!

BARBARA: It's Barbara, these days.

SAOIRSE: Good of you to join me.

DOHENY: Garda, I'd like this eejit had up for loitering, or trespass, or breach of the peace, or something.

BARBARA: Can't be done, Mr Doheny.

> *Sound of a phone, inside: he goes back in.*

SAOIRSE: So how's life been treating you? Still got your prefect's badge? Arresting people, that must be a sight more exciting than just getting them expelled.

BARBARA: Look, I don't have to make conversation. All I've been assigned to do is stand here.

SAOIRSE: I suppose it's like guarding the President.

> *GER ALLEN storms down the street towards her daughter.*

GER: I had to hear it from a customer! 'A book of stamps and an apple, please, and is it true your daughter's bringing her case to the European Court of Human Rights?'

SAOIRSE: That'd take way too long.

GER: I was scarlet!

SAOIRSE: It's not like it's news. I told you I was gay the day I got back from America.

GER: You never said you'd be telling the world and its mother about your private business.

SAOIRSE: How's it private business if it gets me sacked?

GER: You're a brilliant cook, Saoirse. You could get another job in the morning.

SAOIRSE: I liked the one I had. You wouldn't understand, you've never…

She trails off as she realizes her mistake.

GER: You wouldn't call it a real job, to raise the five of you and help your father run the greengrocer's on the side?

SAOIRSE: You know what I mean.

GER: What would he think?

SAOIRSE: Dad? I really doubt he's looking down from heaven and fretting over what the neighbours say.

GER: We always loved all our children equally –

SAOIRSE: *(Interrupts.)* Ah don't start.

GER: – and nothing could change that, not if you told me you were selling drugs in kindergartens.

SAOIRSE: Well I hadn't considered that as a career option yet, but you never know!

GER storms off.

BARBARA: I can't figure out why you're doing this. Standing on a cold street whining for your crappy job back.

SAOIRSE: It wasn't that crappy. I take full credit for introducing the citizens of Ballyaigan to quinoa and bok choy.

BARBARA: You're the same old messer, holding up the class with your smartaleckery.

SAOIRSE: I seem to remember it used to make you laugh, the odd time, Babs.

BARBARA: It's Barbara. Seriously, though –

SAOIRSE: *(Interrupts.)* Seriously, straight As in your Leaving Cert and where did they get you? Standing on the same cold street as me!

BARBARA: I'm going to make Inspector by the time I'm forty. I've never told anyone that.

SAOIRSE: I'm touched.

BARBARA squirms, regretting having confided.

SAOIRSE: So your job matters to you, then?

BARBARA: I see where you're going.

SAOIRSE: Would you fight to keep it?

BARBARA: It's hardly the same.

SAOIRSE: What if they sacked you for something stupid?

BARBARA: They wouldn't.

SAOIRSE: The colour of your hair?

BARBARA: They couldn't.

SAOIRSE: Your taste in music?

BARBARA: Jesus, with your attitude I wouldn't hire you to stack shelves.

DOHENY rushes out with a bucket of water.

BARBARA: Put that down, Mr Doheny.

DOHENY: Surely I've a right to clean up the footpath outside my own establishment?

BARBARA: Childishness will get us nowhere.

He puts down the bucket.

DOHENY: How else am I supposed to maintain the right of way to my door?

SAOIRSE: I'm not blocking your door.

DOHENY: You're putting off the clientele.

SAOIRSE: I'd blame the food. Is that chicken and chips I smell? You sad bastard!

ULTIMATUM

The next night, SAOIRSE is going out with a placard that says 'It's Not Me That's Bent, It's the System' when GER bars her way.

GER: Not tonight, love. You're making a laughingstock of yourself.

SAOIRSE: You always said I should make something of myself.

GER: Why didn't you stay in America?

SAOIRSE: I suppose it was too big.

GER: Well, Ballyaigan's too small. What did you come back here for at all if you're only going to cause havoc?

SAOIRSE: I was making a salad, and I answered a question. I didn't pick this fight, but I'm not going to lose it.

She steps forward and GER moves out of the way.

GER: If you go out tonight, you're not coming back in.

SAOIRSE: I hear you.

She goes off in the direction of her room.

GER, misled and relieved, calls after her.

GER: It'll all blow over now, you'll see. Sure you'll find something better. Will you have a cup of tea?

SAOIRSE emerges with a backpack and sleeping bag, and heads out.

SAOIRSE: Bye, Mam.

SLEEPING BAG

Much later, the street is deserted. KNEEZER GROGAN leans over SAOIRSE, who is partly immobilized because she's sitting in her sleeping bag.

KNEEZER: You know what happens to girls like you?

SAOIRSE: We let out one screech and perverts like you get arrested.

He shakes his head, amused.

KNEEZER: You might even find you've a taste for it. Don't die wondering, eh?

BARBARA's torch lights up the two of them.

BARBARA: Step back, Mr Grogan.

SAOIRSE grins, amazed that her bluff proved true.

SAOIRSE: Would you look at that: my security detail.

KNEEZER: This is a private conversation, *Mizz* Connolly.

BARBARA: I'm waiting.

Reluctantly he walks off.

SAOIRSE: 'I'm waiting.' Armed only with a small torch, SuperBabs saves the day!

Pulling her sleeping bag up around her, SAOIRSE unwraps a homemade sandwich and offers to share it.

BARBARA: What are you doing here?

SAOIRSE: Eating my dinner.

She offers the other half.

SAOIRSE: Avocado and rocket on walnut bread?

BARBARA: Doheny's is shut on Mondays.

SAOIRSE: It slipped my mind.

BARBARA: Besides, it's twenty to one.

SAOIRSE: So what are *you* doing here?

BARBARA: I happened to see you out the window of my flat. Just as well, because that could have gone really pear-shaped.

SAOIRSE: Kneezer? Ah, he's all talk.

BARBARA: Says you! So why aren't you at home tonight?

SAOIRSE: Stalled negotiations with my mother. Hey, it's like the Dublin Lockout of 1913!

BARBARA: Yeah, no.

SAOIRSE: Nice and quiet here now. You don't know what you're missing.

She makes a show of enjoying her sandwich.

BARBARA: Goodnight.

BARBARA starts to cross the street.

SAOIRSE: Night-night, Babs.

BARBARA turns back.

BARBARA: Barbara!

SAOIRSE: OK, OK.

BARBARA: Say it.

SAOIRSE: Barbara.

BARBARA: I've a sofabed.

SAOIRSE: You must be very proud.

BARBARA: Just for tonight, mind.

SAOIRSE: But could you guarantee my safety, Officer?

BARBARA: Forget it.

She goes. SAOIRSE stumbles out of her sleeping bag, grabs her possessions and follows.

OOPS

BARBARA is opening a second pair of beers. SAOIRSE examines a sports trophy.

SAOIRSE: I watched you win this one.

BARBARA: Did your mother really lock you out?

SAOIRSE: You haven't a clue. Been a good girl since the day you were born.

BARBARA: Here we go.

SAOIRSE: This picket is the hardest thing I've ever done in my life, and Mam thinks I'm just acting the maggot. Like when I broke her windscreen playing golf in the street.

BARBARA: Or the time you got me stoned in the graveyard.

SAOIRSE laughs, reminiscent.

SAOIRSE: Nobody put a gun to your head.

BARBARA: I thought it was a cigarette! I didn't know how my dad managed forty a day of them.

SAOIRSE: I nearly broke myself when you leapt up on that headstone.

BARBARA: The statues were dancing, I swear.

SAOIRSE: Then you threw up in choir and Sister Breda threatened to bring in the guards.

BARBARA: Jesus.

SAOIRSE: Ah, well. It was a bit of a thrill.

BARBARA: I never meant to get you expelled, you know. When I found you in the sandpit with – what was his name?

SAOIRSE can't remember either.

SAOIRSE: Freckled guy.

BARBARA: I was sure they'd just give out to you, make you wise up in time for the exams.

SAOIRSE: Ah, so that was the plan: rehabilitation of the juvenile delinquent.

BARBARA: Seriously, I'm sorry. I've always been sorry.

SAOIRSE: If you really want to make it up to me…

On impulse she touches BARBARA's hand.

BARBARA recoils.

BARBARA: Must you be so fucking predictable?

SAOIRSE: Oops.

BARBARA: Just because I wear a uniform doesn't mean I'm repressed, all right?

SAOIRSE: All right. Sorry.

BARBARA: I think I'd have noticed by now if I was attracted to women, don't you think?

SAOIRSE: Whatever you say.

BARBARA: Why do you always have to push your luck?

SAOIRSE: I said I'm sorry!

BARBARA heads out of the room.

SAOIRSE starts putting her shoes back on.

BARBARA: You're still welcome to the sofa.

SAOIRSE: I'm grand.

BARBARA: You don't have to go.

SAOIRSE: Well, I sure don't have to stay.

BARBARA: Have you enough on you for a B&B?

SAOIRSE: What do you care?

KEEPING THE PEACE

In the station, the following evening, the SERGEANT puts his phone down.

SERGEANT: They've picked up a lad with an eight-inch blade. Where's Fergus?

BARBARA: Gone home.

SERGEANT: It's your lucky night, so. C'mon.

BARBARA checks the time.

BARBARA: Except that I should be getting along to Doheny's.

SERGEANT: Ah, I think the old Dyke Strike has dragged on too long already.

BARBARA: Still, as long as she's there, there should be a police presence.

SERGEANT: I'll have a word as we drive by, tell her enough is enough and we can't waste any more taxpayers' money.

BARBARA: It was an unjust dismissal, out of sheer bloody smalltown smallmindedness. She has every right to strike.

SERGEANT: Ah, Barbara. Our job's to keep the peace. Justice is another department.

IMAGINATION

A little later, BARBARA stands alone outside Doheny's, fuming.

Sounds of a motorbike coming to a stop.

SAOIRSE strolls up carrying a placard that reads 'A Queer Case of Predjudice' [sic].

SAOIRSE: Hiya, Babs.

She turns to wave goodbye to the unseen biker.

SAOIRSE: Don't wait up!

Sounds of the biker revving and riding away.

SAOIRSE: Well. Is that a truncheon in your belt or are you just pleased to –

BARBARA cuts her off before the end of the old joke.

BARBARA: You're late.

SAOIRSE: I couldn't let Paula do all the washing up.

BARBARA: If you think I'm going to waste another week of my life standing around freezing on a street corner –

SAOIRSE: Off you trot, so. I'm fine on my own.

BARBARA: You're such an embarrassment. You can't even spell prejudice!

SAOIRSE: There's more to activism than spelling.

BARBARA: You and your amateur agro and your slogans-on-a-stick, you're a far cry from Tiananmen Square.

SAOIRSE: Paula says global battles start local.

BARBARA: Well, no offence to your girlfriend but she knows sod all.

SAOIRSE: Paula's not my girlfriend.

BARBARA: Whatever. The point is, one week on, and what have you achieved?

SAOIRSE: I don't have a girlfriend.

BARBARA: The customers don't mind passing you anymore, they think you're a laugh. If you want to scare Doheny into giving you your job back, you'll need way more publicity.

SAOIRSE finds this advice helpful.

SAOIRSE: Like what, a Twitter feed?

BARBARA: I don't know. Chain yourself to the railings like the suffragettes. Use your imagination.

SAOIRSE: I wonder where I could get a helicopter.

BARBARA rolls her eyes, giving up.

LOCAL NEWS

Next day. BARBARA, in her flat, has the radio on as she gets ready for work.

Outside DOHENY's, SAOIRSE has handcuffed herself to the door under a sign that says 'Hungry for Justice'.

REPORTER: This is Micheál MacMachúna, reporting live from John Doheny's Bar-Restaurant in Ballyaigan, where just over a week ago lesbian chef Saoirse Allen began her hunger strike for justice.

BARBARA rushes over to the radio, then to the window to see. She rushes around putting on her uniform.

DOHENY: Hunger strike my hole, I saw her scoffing a panini on this spot yesterday.

SAOIRSE speaks into the mike.

SAOIRSE: He's a liar and a bigot. Homophobia is alive and well and living in Ballyaigan.

GER: Saoirse, would you ever give over this nonsense and come home?

SAOIRSE: No, Mam, you go home!

DOHENY: Give us the keys to the cuffs.

SAOIRSE: Not till I have my rights.

REPORTER: Mr Doheny, how would you respond to the accusation that –

DOHENY: *(Interrupts.)* Gimme the keys this minute.

SAOIRSE: I couldn't even if I wanted to.

GER: Why?

SAOIRSE: I swallowed them.

DOHENY: Ye lying tinker!

He attacks, trying to check SAOIRSE's mouth for the keys. GER defends her daughter. The REPORTER videos the struggle.

GER: If you so much as chip a tooth of hers, you're paying for it.

SAOIRSE bites into DOHENY's finger and won't let go.

REPORTER: Now tempers flare as tradition and liberalism come to blows on the battleground that is Ballyaigan.

BARBARA dashes up and pulls DOHENY off SAOIRSE.

SAOIRSE: Babs! Arrest the bastard.

BARBARA: *(To DOHENY.)* Is that what you want?

DOHENY: I was trying to access my own property and the little bitch bit me!

KNEEZER GROGAN strolls up.

KNEEZER: I don't fucking believe this.

BARBARA: Move along now, folks.

REPORTER: Garda, what's your own view on this struggle for the soul of modern Ireland?

She switches off his mike.

BARBARA: I said move along.

KNEEZER: *(To SAOIRSE.)* I thought I told you to get out of this town.

SAOIRSE: It's my town too.

BARBARA steps between him and SAOIRSE, and gets the punch meant for SAOIRSE. The REPORTER captures the whole thing on video.

GOOD MORNING

Next day, BARBARA is home again, looking at the write-up in the local paper, and talking on the phone.

BARBARA: Well, you can't believe everything you read, Mum. Because it's my job. No, I wouldn't rather be a dental hygienist.

A knock at the door.

BARBARA: Listen, I have to go. All right, later, bye-bye.

She lets SAOIRSE in.

BARBARA: I said stay away from me.

SAOIRSE: And good morning to you too, sunshine. What are you so cross for? You made your collar. 'Assaulting a Police Officer.' You'll probably get promoted.

BARBARA: That's not how it works. And you have such a nerve, claiming you were on hunger strike.

SAOIRSE: You said I needed publicity.

BARBARA: I didn't mean barefaced lies.

SAOIRSE: Well, I was definitely off my food.

BARBARA: Pity about you.

SAOIRSE: My appetite's back now, though. If you've eggs in the fridge I could whip us up an omelette.

BARBARA: I haven't.

SAOIRSE: Guess what. Doheny offered me my job back.

BARBARA: Yeah, the Sergeant said he'd put the squeeze on him.

SAOIRSE: So I told him where he could stuff it.

BARBARA: You what?

SAOIRSE: If that man thinks I'd so much as fillet a fish for him again…